D1051658

Don't miss Diana's new hardcover
Dangerous
coming in June!

Also by Diana Palmer

DIANA PALMER

HEARTLESS

HQN™

HQN™

Recycling programs
for this product may
not exist in your area.

ISBN-13: 978-0-373-77450-0

HEARTLESS

Copyright © 2009 by Diana Palmer

This edition published by arrangement with Harlequin Books S.A.

For questions and comments about the quality of this book
please contact us at Customer_eCare@Harlequin.ca.

www.HQNBooks.com

Printed in U.S.A.

To the Art Department:
your beautiful covers help sell my work.
I value your creativity and dedication so much.
Thank you from the bottom of my heart...
Diana Palmer

HEARTLESS

1

GRACIE MARSH'S CELL PHONE exploded with the theme to the newest science fiction motion picture. She jumped, and dirt from the ground where she was busily cleaning out her flower beds splattered her spotless yellow sweatshirt.

"Oh, darn," she muttered, wiping her hands on her old jeans before she dived into a pocket for the very loud instrument.

"Where's that music coming from?" Mrs. Harcourt, the housekeeper, called from the front porch, where she was setting out pansies in a massive planter.

"It's just my phone, Mrs. Harcourt," Gracie assured her. "It's probably Jason...hello?" she gasped.

There was an amused pause. "Don't tell me," came a deep, drawling, masculine voice. "You're up to your neck in dirt and now your pocket and your cell phone are smeared with it."

She laughed in spite of her frustration. Her stepbrother knew her better than anyone else on earth. "Yes," she admitted.

"I'd be cussing."

"I did say 'darn,'" she replied.

He sighed. "I'll have to take you in hand, Gracie. Sometimes the situation calls for something more elegant and descriptive than 'darn.'"

"You'd know," she retorted, recalling that he cursed eloquently in two languages, "especially when one of your cowboys does something you don't like." She frowned. "Where are you?"

"At the ranch," he said.

The ranch was his property in Comanche Wells, where he ran purebred Santa Gertrudis cattle and a new equally purebred Japanese breed that was the basis for the famous Kobe beef. Jason Pendleton had millions, but he rarely stayed in the family mansion in San Antonio, where Gracie spent most of her time. Jason was only here when business required it, but his heart was on his huge Santa Gertrudis ranch. He lived there most of the year. He could wheel and deal with the international business set, chair board meetings, run huge corporations and throw incredible parties, with Gracie's help as a hostess. But he was most at home in jeans and boots and chaps, working cattle.

"Why are you calling me?" she asked. "Do you need somebody to come help you brand cattle?" she teased, because he'd taught her to do that—and many other things—over the years. She was as much at home on the ranch as he was.

"Wrong season," he replied. "We drop calves in the spring. It's late August. Almost autumn."

She frowned. "Then what are you doing?"

"Rounding up bulls, mostly. But right now I'm getting ready to come up to the auction barn in San Antonio for a sale," he said. "They've got some open Santa Gert heifers I want," he added, referring to the purebred native Texas Santa Gertrudis breed that was founded on the world famous King Ranch near the Texas coast. "Replacement heifers to breed so they'll drop calves next spring."

"Oh." She tried to remember what that meant.

He sighed loudly. "Open heifers are young cows that haven't been bred for the first time," he explained again. "They're replacements for cows I've had to cull from the herd and sell off because they didn't produce calves this year."

"Sorry," she murmured, not wanting to emphasize her memory problems. She forgot things, she plunged down steps, she lost her balance in the most unexpected places. There was a physical reason for those lapses, one which she'd never shared with Jason, not since she and her mother had moved in with him and his father almost twelve years ago. Her mother had been frantic about keeping the past secret, swearing Gracie to silence. Cynthia Marsh had even told everyone that Graciela was her stepdaughter, not her real daughter, to make sure any background checks on Graciela didn't turn up information on her daughter, herself and her late husband that would damage Graciela's place in the Pendleton family. Graciela's father, a widower with a young daughter, had died in the Gulf War, Cynthia emphasized again and again. He was a war hero. It wasn't the truth, of course. The truth was more traumatic.

"One day you'll get the hang of it," he said easily. He was patient with her, as some people in her life hadn't been.

"Why are you calling me, if you don't need an extra ranch hand?" she asked merrily.

"I thought you might like to go to the sale with me," he said comfortably. "I'll buy you lunch after we're through."

She grinned. "I'd love to," she said.

Not only did she enjoy his company, but she loved the atmosphere of the sale barn. It was always crowded, always fun. She liked hearing the auctioneer's incredibly rapid spiel as he prompted buyers to go higher and higher on prices for the various lots of cattle. She liked the other cattlemen who turned up there, many of them from Comanche Wells, as well as Jacobsville, which was only a few miles from Comanche Wells. There was a select group of environmentally staunch ranchers to which Jason belonged. They raised old grasses that were earth-friendly, they improved the land and provided habitat for wild animals, they used modern methods of feed production that were kind to the ecology, and they were fanatics about the good treatment of their purebred cattle. These cattlemen never used growth hormone and they only used the necessary antibiotics, most particularly those that prevented bovine pulmonary disorder. They didn't use dangerous chemicals to control weeds or pests. Cy Parks had introduced the idea of using predator insects to control many pests. The lack of poisonous substances on plants helped grow more colonies of honey bees, which were essential to pollination of grain and feed crops.

None of the environmental group of Jacobs County ranchers ran beef cattle; they were all producers of herd sires and champion young bulls, cows and heifers, which they sold for herd improvement. It got them into trouble sometimes with beef producers who wanted a quicker profit. There had been some notable fistfights at cattle conferences in the past. Jason had been involved in one of them. Gracie had gone to bail him out of jail, bursting into laughter when she saw him, disheveled and bloody and grinning like a Cheshire cat as they led him out of the detention cell. He loved a good fight.

"I said I'll pick you up in about twenty minutes," he repeated, because she hadn't answered him.

"Okay. What should I wear?"

"Jeans and a T-shirt," he said. "If we walk in wearing designer clothes, the price will jump twenty dollars a head before I sit down. I don't want to be recognized."

"Fat chance if we show up in your Jaguar," she drawled.

"I'm driving one of the ranch pickups and wearing working clothes," he drawled back.

"All right. I'll finish cleaning out my flower beds later."

"As if we haven't already got enough damned bulbs poking up in the front yard. You're getting soil ready to put out more this fall, aren't you?" he muttered. "And I'll bet you've got Harcourt refilling those planters on the porch."

He knew her too well. "It's just pansies—they'll last until late autumn. I won't plant bulbs until October. But bulbs are beautiful in the spring, Jason," she defended herself.

"Why do I pay a yard man to do outdoor work?" he grumbled.

"Because he does the heavy work that Harcourt and I can't," she replied saucily. "I'm hanging up now."

"Don't keep me waiting," he said. "We'll barely make it there in time, as it is. I got held up with an accident."

"You weren't hurt?" she exclaimed quickly.

There was a slight pause. "No," he said softly. "Not me. One of my cowboys got stepped on by a bull. Broke his foot, but he'll be all right."

She let out the breath she'd been holding. Jason was

her life. He didn't know how she felt about him. It was impossible anyway. She could never do those things with men that most modern women did. She remembered her mother coming out of the bedroom, the blood staining her nightgown…

She grimaced. "I thought you just hired a new man to go to local sales representing the ranch to buy cattle for you."

"I did. But I've heard some things about him I don't like. He's supposed to be at this auction. I can see for myself."

"He'll recognize you."

"In my working clothes? Fat chance! Besides, he's only seen me once, behind a desk."

"Suit yourself. I'll be ready."

"Better be, or I'll dress you myself," he warned.

"Jason!"

But he'd already hung up.

She got up, putting aside her trowel. "Mrs. Harcourt, we need to tell Manuel to finish clearing these beds for me," she said as she mounted the steps. "Jason's taking me to a sale."

"All right, darlin'," the graying old woman said with a smile. She was tall and amply padded, with black eyes and a lovely smile. She'd come to work for the family before Jason was born and was considered part of it. She and the maid, Dilly, and the chauffeur, John, were all part of the family. There was other staff that worked part-time, but the old retainers were full-time.

Gracie loved living here on the big estate in San Antonio. The staff did go down to the ranch in Comanche Wells occasionally for a few weeks, especially when Jason had company down there. If he did, though, it wasn't the same local society crowd he invited to the San Antonio mansion. It was often world leaders who needed a break from the backbreaking pressure of their daily lives, high government politicians running from scandals, even an occasional billionaire who wanted privacy even for a few days. Jason chose his friends by their character, not their wealth. It was one of many things Gracie loved about him. He had a big heart and he was a soft touch for people down on their luck. He gave heavily to charities. But he didn't seem the sort of man who could be approached.

He was an introvert. It was hard for him to connect to people. Consequently he was intimidating to a lot of guests, who found him hard going in private conversations. Only with Gracie could he relax and be himself. It was, she considered, a matter of trust. He felt safe with her, as she did with him.

What a pity, said her friend Barbara, who ran a café in Jacobsville, that Jason and Gracie were brother and sister, when they had so much in common. Gracie had reminded her that there was no blood relationship there. Jason's father had married Gracie's mother, who was killed only a couple of weeks after the wedding in an automobile accident. Myron Pendleton had kept Gracie, who had no other living relatives, and soon gave her another stepsister, Gloryanne Barnes—now Mrs. Rodrigo Ramirez—when he married Glory's mother, Beverly, months later. Glory and Gracie had more in common than anyone else knew. They were best friends. It was the two of them against the world when they were in school, because both had scars from their childhoods and neither was comfortable with boys. They rarely dated. They were targets of some vicious bullying, which Jason had quietly and efficiently nipped in the bud. Even today, Glory was still the closest thing to a sister Gracie had ever had.

She showered and dried her hair, dressing in jeans with a vine of pink roses embroidered down one leg, with a pink T-shirt. Impulsively she brushed out her long, pale blond hair and braided it into pigtails. She grinned at herself with twinkling gray eyes. She had a soft complexion with radiant smoothness. She wasn't beautiful, but she was pretty, in her shy way. She frowned, wondering if it was appropriate to wear pigtails at her age. Sometimes she did things that seemed odd to other people. That little glitch in her brain did a lot of damage to her ego, from time to time.

Well, it was too late to worry about it now. She put on her fanny pack and pulled on her boots over thick socks. A horn was blowing outside the front door. Jason, impatient as always.

She ran down the staircase, almost stumbling head over heels, remembered that she'd left her cell phone in her room. She hesitated. What the heck, Jason had his. She continued down the stairs and out the front door.

"I'll be out for lunch!" she yelled.

"All right, dear," Mrs. Harcourt called back.

Jason was tapping his fingers on the steering wheel. He glowered as she quickly descended the front steps of the elegant brick mansion and hurried down the paved walkway to the circular driveway where his big black ranch truck was waiting with the door open.

She tumbled in beside him and slammed the door.

"I know, I know, I'm late, but I had to have a shower," she rationalized as she fumbled with her seat belt. "I couldn't go out with dirt on my hair!"

He glanced at her from under the wide brim of his creamy Stetson. He didn't smile, but his black eyes did.

He was wearing jeans, too, with wide leather batwing

chaps, old disreputable brown boots with turned-up toes from too many soakings and stains everywhere. His shirt was chambray and faded. Despite the immaculate cleanness of his beautiful, tanned hands, he looked like a poor, working cowboy.

Heavens, he was sexy, she thought as she gave him a covert appraisal. Tall and broad-shouldered, with that physique rarely seen outside a Hollywood Western film, jet-black hair in a conventional short cut, and a light olive complexion that was a legacy, like his black eyes, from a Spanish grandfather. He wasn't conventionally handsome, but he had a very masculine face, lean and square-jawed, with deep-set eyes and high cheekbones and a mouth that was so sensuous it made Gracie squirm. He'd never kissed her. Well, not in the way a man would kiss a woman, anyway. They didn't have that sort of relationship. Nor was he a womanizer. He had women, certainly, she was sure. But he never brought them home.

"Deep thoughts, tidbit?" he teased, grinning at her with perfect white teeth.

"I was thinking how handsome you are," she blurted out and then flushed and laughed nervously. "Sorry. My mouth and my brain are disconnected."

He didn't smile. His black eyes slid over her face and back to the road. "You aren't bad yourself, kid."

She toyed with her seat belt. "Are any of the Jacobsville crowd coming up for this sale?"

"Cy Parks, J. D. Langley and Leo Hart," he said. "The Harts are after another one of those Japanese bulls grown for Kobe beef. They're moving into new breeding programs."

"Don't tell me Leo's gone off Salers bulls?" she exclaimed.

He laughed. "Not completely. But when you consider how well Japanese beef sells, it's no surprise. It's tender and lean and appeals to shoppers. We're in a consumer-driven market war, grubbing for new methods of production and new marketing techniques to overcome the slump in sales."

"Don't you still chair a committee on marketing with the cattlemen's association?"

"I did. Had to give it up. This damned German business is wearing me ragged."

She recalled that he was haggling for another computer company with a concern in Berlin that produced a new brand of microchip. Negotiations for a merger were going into their third week while the bosses hemmed and hawed about whether or not they wanted to sell for the price Jason was offering. Eventually he was going to have to spend some time overseas working personally on the takeover, because the man he'd delegated that authority to was quitting. His wife was English and he wanted to move to London. Jason would have to replace him, but there was no time for that now. It was too sensitive a negotiation to bring in a new outsider. Jason would have to do the job himself.

"You could send Grange to Germany and let him deal with them for you," she murmured with a mischievous grin, naming his new livestock foreman. Grange had worked for the Ballenger feedlot, but Jason liked him and had hired him on at the ranch for a bigger salary. Grange had proved to be an asset. His military background had made him the perfect foreman. The former army major had no trouble throwing out orders.

He made a face at her. "Grange negotiates like a military man. You know they won't let men fly overseas with guns."

"Grange is big enough to intimidate those businessmen without guns."

He gave her a cool appraisal. He didn't like it when she talked about Grange. He didn't like Grange's interest in her. Not that he made an issue of it. He just made sure Grange was otherwise occupied when Gracie visited the ranch. His black eyes slid over her slender body in the tight jeans and T-shirt. His hand on the steering wheel contracted violently. Gracie didn't notice. She was smiling out the window at a group of children playing in the dirt yard of an old, ragged house beside the road.

THE SALE BARN WAS FULL. Gracie walked behind Jason, pausing when he did to speak to cattlemen they knew along the way. The auctioneer spotted Jason the moment he walked in and they nodded at each other. She didn't see the Jacobsville cattlemen, but there was a huge crowd. They might be on the other side of the arena. The only seats left were against a wall, but he didn't mind that.

He politely addressed a strange cattleman wearing a designer suit and highly polished new boots. The man looked him over with faint distaste, noting the working-cowboy gear, complete with spurred boots, batwing chaps and old chambray shirt.

"Nice day for a sale," Jason said cordially.

The man smirked. "For those of us who can afford to buy something, sure it is. You work for a local ranch?" he added, giving Jason a demeaning look. "They sure must not pay very well." He turned away again.

Gracie noted the exchange and grinned up at Jason, but he didn't return the smile. His black eyes were fiery. They sat down and waited for the noise to subside so that the auction could begin.

She leaned up to Jason's ear. "Who is he?" she whispered, indicating the man a row in front of them.

He didn't answer. Instead he gestured toward the auctioneer at the podium tapping the microphone.

He welcomed the cattlemen, summarized the contents of the sale and began with a lot of purebred Black Angus calves. Jason leaned back, just watching, as bidding opened.

Gracie loved going to these auctions with him. It was one of the more pleasant memories of her early teens, tagging along after him through sale barns and learning the cattle business. It had irritated him at first, and then amused him. Finally he understood that it wasn't the business that attracted her, but the novelty of his company. She was standoffish, even cold, with boys her own age and men of any age, but she adored Jason and it showed. As the years passed, she acquired a nickname— Jason's shadow. He didn't seem to mind. Glory had never cared much for cattle, but Gracie had always been fascinated by them. Even now, he rarely asked anyone except Gracie along when he went to auctions or to look at new equipment or even just for a drive over his property. A loner most of the time, he was supremely comfortable with her.

She studied her program and tapped his hand. He glanced where she was pointing at the program and nodded.

It was the next lot, a consignment of purebred Santa Gertrudis open heifers. Jason kept replacement heifers, as any cattleman did, against necessary culls after breeding season. But these young females were exceptional. They were from a division of the King Ranch, with exquisite bloodlines. Jason wanted to improve his seed stock. This was a bargain at the price.

The auctioneer named the consignment and opened bidding. The fancy rancher in front of them raised his hand to accept the price. There was an increase on the base price of ten dollars a head. Jason scratched his ear. The price jumped by twenty dollars a head.

"I told you they knew I was coming," the cattleman in the row ahead of them said smugly. "Didn't I tell you prices would jump when I started the bidding?"

Jason didn't say a word. But his eyes were coldly amused. The cattleman ahead of him jumped the ante by ten dollars, Jason doubled that bid. The price went up a hundred, five hundred, a thousand, two thousand.

"Who the hell's bidding against me?" the cattleman in front muttered in a whisper to his companion, looking around. "Nobody here looks like they could afford to buy a cattle trailer, much less purebred Santa Gerts!"

"Bid higher," his companion suggested.

"Are you nuts?" the man grumbled. "I'm at my limit. I wish I could get in touch with my boss, but he's not in his office. He won't be happy that I let someone outbid me for these heifers. He was keen to have them."

The bid came again. The cattleman in front sat mute, fuming. Jason scratched his ear.

The bid was called once, twice, three times, and the auctioneer banged his gavel and shouted "Sold!"

He didn't name the buyer, as Jason had already agreed before the sale began. He had Jason's blank check and he knew where to send the consignment, and how. Jason and Gracie got up and walked out of the auction barn into the sunshine. The cattleman who'd been in front of them walked out, too, punching in numbers on his cell phone. He ran into Jason and bumped him.

"Watch the hell where you're walking, will you?" the man snapped at Jason and kept walking.

Jason stared after the man with retribution in his dark gaze. But after a minute he stretched comfortably and glanced down at Gracie. "Hungry?"

"I could eat a cow," she murmured with twinkling eyes. "Even a Santa Gert!"

"Barbarian," he chuckled. "Come on."

He was driving one of his standard ranch pickup trucks. They were nice, but not top-of-the-line. He cut costs where he could. The grumbling cattleman and his companion climbed into a luxury car and roared off. It was a nice car. But it wasn't in the same league as Jason's big Jaguar.

"I hope we don't run into that fancy rancher who was in front of us," she muttered. "He's got a major attitude problem."

"He'll get it fixed soon enough," Jason said easily.

"Nice of him to come over here and show us how real cattlemen dress for a sale," Gracie remarked as she climbed up into the pickup and belted herself in. She gave him a speaking glance. "You're disgracing us, dressing like that for a fancy auction!"

"Speak for yourself," he shot back as he put the truck in gear. "You're not exactly the belle of the ball."

"I'm comfortable," she said. "You said not to dress up."

His dark eyes cut around to hers and he gave her a look that made her feel warm all over. "You'd look good in a flour sack, honey," he told her solemnly. "But I like the pigtails."

She laughed nervously, tugging at one. "They're too young for me, I guess, but I couldn't get my hair up this morning."

"I like it."

He pulled out onto the road and drove to a nearby steak restaurant that he favored, parking on the side. He and Gracie walked up onto the porch just as the luxury car pulled into the front parking lot.

Jason gave her an amused grin. "Well, he does have good taste in food."

"I'll bet somebody had to tell him it was a nice place to eat," she shot back.

The waitress showed them to a table about the time the cattleman and his companion got to the line.

"Look what the cat dragged in," Cy Parks drawled as Jason and Gracie were seated at a booth across from his table.

"Look who's talking, Parks," Jason shot back.

"How's Lisa?" Gracie asked.

Cy's eyebrows levered up and down. "Pregnant," he said with an ear-to-ear grin. "We're over the moon."

"Wow," Gracie said softly. "Congratulations."

"Our son needs a playmate," he explained. He looked up as J. D. Langley and Harley Fowler, who was Cy's foreman, and Leo Hart came walking back to his table with full salad plates. He gave them a snarly look. "Salad! Good God, I never thought I'd see the day when ranchers would sit down to plates of rabbit food!"

"We're joining the green lobby," Leo chuckled. "Hi, Jason. Gracie. Been to the sale?"

"Yes," Jason replied. "We didn't see you there."

"We were on the other side of the barn," J.D. muttered, glancing toward where the grumbly cattleman and his companion were just about to be seated. "Avoiding the plague in designer suits."

"Who is he?" Gracie asked.

Harley Fowler grinned at her. "You ought to know."

"Me?" she exclaimed, fuddled. "I know him?"

"Well, Mr. Pendleton ought to know him, anyway," Harley added.

Jason gave Harley a scowl. "Mr. Pendleton was my father."

Harley flushed a little. "Sorry."

"He's not big on ceremony," Gracie told the younger man, smiling. "We don't play that sort of game."

"The hell we don't," Jason said, and his eyes kindled as the visiting cattleman came toward them. His big body tensed.

"Jason," Gracie warned softly. She didn't fancy a brawl in here, and Jason had a low boiling point. That designer rancher had already made him mad.

"If it isn't the Jacobsville lobby," the visitor said with a sarcastic smile. "The cattle-petting cattlemen, in person."

Jason leaned back in the booth, stretching out his long legs. "Nothing wrong with treating cattle decently," he said deliberately.

The man gave him a faintly contemptuous look. "Excuse me, but I don't remember asking for your opinion. You may work cattle, son, but I'm sure you don't own any. Now why don't you mind your own business and let cattlemen talk cattle?"

Black eyes bored into his face with an expression under them that would have made an impression on a man less thick-skinned.

"You didn't get that lot of Santa Gertrudis heifers you came after, did you?" Cy Parks mused.

The man made a face. "Rub it in. I know you were the high bidder."

"Nope. It wasn't me. I was there for the lot of Santa

Gert calves. I got those." Cy's green eyes narrowed. "Your boss sent you there to get those heifers, I hear."

The man's lip pulled up. "Sent me there with half the amount I needed to bid for them," he said angrily. "And told me not to go higher. Hell of a boss. I'll bet he wouldn't know a heifer from a bull, sitting up there in his office telling real cattlemen how to buy cattle!"

Cy studied him coldly. "That attitude won't get you far in the Pendleton organization."

"Not my fault if the boss doesn't know how to bid for cattle. I'll have to educate him."

There was a collective intake of breath at the table. Beside it, Jason's brow quirked. He was beginning to enjoy himself.

"Do you know who trumped my bid for those heifers?" the man asked curiously.

Everybody at Cy Parks's table pointed to Jason Pendleton. Gracie did, too.

The visiting cattleman turned to the man he'd been putting down for most of the day. Jason took off his Stetson and cold black eyes bored into the man's shocked face.

"You bought those heifers? With what?" the arrogant rancher exclaimed. He glanced at Gracie. "You don't look like a man who could afford a sick calf, and your girlfriend there sure hasn't got money. So who do you work for?"

Jason didn't like the crack about Gracie. His amusement morphed into pure dislike. "I could ask you the same question," he said icily.

"I work for the Pendleton organization," the man said.

Jason glowered at him. "Not anymore."

"And who do you think you are, to tell me that?" the man demanded.

Jason's black eyes glittered at him. "Jason Pendleton."

The fancy rancher stared at the ragged cowboy with patent disbelief. But then, in his mind, he recalled the painting in the Pendleton Corporation CEO's office downtown, over the fireplace. The man in the portrait was a match for the man glaring at him from the booth. "You're Mr….Mr. Pendleton?" he stammered, flushing purple. "I didn't recognize you!"

Jason was toying with his coffee cup. His eyes held the other man's. "Pity," he murmured.

The other rancher seemed to lose his dignity and his arrogant attitude all at once.

"I didn't know…" he stammered.

"Obviously," Jason replied curtly. "I wanted to see how you operated before I turned you loose as my representative. Good thing. You like to put people down, don't you? Well, you won't be doing it on my payroll. Collect your last paycheck at the office. Do I need to say the words?"

The rancher's jaw set. "You can't do this to me! Hell, nobody fires a man for losing a bid…!" he began belligerently.

Jason stood up. He was a head taller than the man and he looked dangerous. The ranchers at the nearby table tensed.

"I said," Jason began in a slow, menacing tone, "collect your last paycheck." His big hands began to curve into fists at his side.

The rancher's companion noticed that and grabbed his friend's arm, almost dragging him away. He knew things about Jason Pendleton's temper that the other rancher obviously didn't.

Gracie tugged at Jason's hand gently. He looked at her and calmed a little as he sat back down again. But he was openly glaring at the man's retreating back. The fancy rancher's companion was talking feverishly and nodding toward Jason Pendleton. The rancher glanced back toward the Jacobsville cattlemen and grimaced. But he wasn't going to a table—he was actually leaving the restaurant.

"Who is he?" she asked.

"He is, rather he *was,*" Jason replied with magnificent disdain, "the man I hired recently to go to sales for me. Barker. The one I told you about, who was throwing his weight around. Good thing I checked him out. He'd have cost us business, with that attitude. I don't like men who judge people on appearances. Wealth is no measure of character."

"So that's why you were bidding so high against him."

Jason nodded. "I had to push him to see how he'd react. The auctioneer knew what I was doing, so I won't have to pay the higher price. I worked out a fair deal before the auction."

Gracie pursed her lips and whistled through them. "Oh, boy."

"I'll bet that's not what Barker's saying right now," Harley Fowler said gleefully. "And that's what you get for taking people at face value. Nothing wrong with wearing comfortable clothes." He gave Jason a grin and turned his attention to Gracie. "I don't guess you go out with ranch managers, Miss Gracie, but if you did, I'd love to take you over to Shea's and show you how nicely I can waltz…"

He stopped because Jason was now glaring at him, and with eyes even colder than he'd shown to the pompous cattleman.

"Uh, sorry, I'd better finish my lunch and get back to work," Harley said with a sheepish grin, averting his attention to his plate.

Gracie was gaping at Jason, only diverted by the arrival of the waitress with their own salads and drinks.

"What was that about?" she asked hesitantly when they were back in the truck.

"Barker?" he asked absently.

"No. Harley."

His jaw tautened. "Harley's a boy."

She was disconcerted. "He's a nice boy," she protested.

He didn't say a word.

She shifted in her seat, frowning. Jason was very strange lately. She didn't understand why there was so much anger smoldering inside him. He was probably still angry with that Barker man, she decided, and left him to his thoughts.

Jason was unusually uncommunicative during the ride home, keeping the radio between them while he drove. His attitude toward Harley puzzled her. It wasn't like him to snap at underlings, especially cowboys, and he'd already made it obvious that he disliked men who put poor people down. He didn't know Harley well, but he'd seemed to like the younger man. Or at least, he had until today. It was almost as if he were jealous of Harley's interest in Gracie. That was silly, of course. He was affectionate toward her, but there was nothing out of the ordinary in his demeanor. It was just wishful thinking. She grimaced, thinking about how she might react if Jason ever really pursued her as a lover would. Love was one thing. Sex…well, that was terrifying. She wasn't sure she could function in that respect. Not even with Jason, and he'd been the only man in her life and her heart for years.

2

TWO DAYS LATER, GRACIE WAS back in her flower beds. This time she'd pruned back some aggressive wandering vines that had exploded with growth after the passage of Hurricane Fay when it made landfall. The rains had been torrential. Now everything was overgrown because of the bountiful rain. After months of drought, it was wonderful to see green things again.

It was Friday and she was hosting an important party for Jason this evening. It was business. He hated parties, but he was wheeling and dealing again, hoping to add a new and imaginative software company from California to his roster of acquisitions. The two owners were in their twenties and crazy about soccer, so Jason had invited members of the Brazilian and American soccer teams to this gathering. It was like him to know the deepest desires of his prey and cater to them, when he wanted something.

She wondered absently if he was single-minded and determined like that with women he wanted. It hurt to think about that.

She didn't dare think of Jason in any sexual way. It would only lead to heartache. Her mother had warned her about it, and she herself had seen the result from the time she was very little. Her father could only achieve satisfaction by hurting his wife, savaging her. The blood on her nightclothes testified again and again to the brutality of ardent men. Gracie's entire childhood had been a nightmare of fear for her mother, and for herself. As a child, she'd prayed that her mother wouldn't die, leaving her at her father's mercy. God alone knew what the man might do to Gracie, although he'd never molested her. It was his temper she feared, especially when he drank. He drank a lot. He was violent when he drank.

She shivered, hearing her mother's sobs as the memories washed over her. She remembered comforting the older woman just before her father's death, helping to bathe away the blood and treat the cuts and bruises. Men would be sweet and attentive and tender until they got you into bed, her mother lectured. Then, behind closed doors, the truth was revealed. What was in movies and on television and in books was all lies. This was the reality—blood and tears. Graciela must remember and never allow herself to be lured into marriage. She must remain chaste and safe.

Gracie heard a car screech its tires on the road nearby and she grimaced as her mind returned to the present. Some poor driver had almost wrecked. She knew how that felt. She wasn't the best driver in the world, either. Jason worried when she got behind the wheel of a car because she'd had so many mishaps. It wasn't really that she was a poor driver. Physical trauma from years ago had caused minor glitches in her brain. She would compensate for the injury, a doctor had assured her gently, because she was highly intelligent. But that wasn't much comfort, when most of the world saw her as a flighty, clumsy airhead. Poor Gracie Pendleton, one woman had commented to a friend, was the dodo bird of local society.

She laughed bitterly, recalling the remark she'd overheard at an afternoon tea only a couple of weeks ago. The comment had obviously been made by someone who didn't know her. She knew that if Jason had been privy to that cruel remark he would have made that woman sorry she'd ever opened her mouth. He was fiercely protective of the people he cared about. Her earliest glimpse into his chivalry occurred shortly after Gracie's mother died. Her strangely ungrieving stepfather, Myron, had rushed into marriage to Beverly Barnes, a woman who had a young daughter in foster care. Jason had rescued Gloryanne Barnes from a dangerous situation, taking a young Gracie along to comfort the other girl, who was four months younger. If it hadn't been for Jason's involvement, she and Gloryanne probably wouldn't have bonded so effortlessly.

Jason, she thought as she struggled to cut back the thick vines, was an enigma. She'd lived with him for twelve years and she still felt as if she knew nothing about him. Myron Pendleton had died the year after Beverly Barnes, his third wife, passed away from a stroke. By then, Gracie and Glory were sixteen. Jason had assumed responsibility for both girls, and took great care of them while they finished high school. In fact, he'd spoiled them rotten. He was still doing it. Gloryanne's Christmas present the year before had been a racing-green Jaguar XK. Gracie's had been a meteorite, a fabulously expensive one sold at public auction from an estate. Gracie was crazy about fossils and meteorites. She had quite a collection. She had no great affection for jewels, and she hated furs. But she loved rocks. Jason indulged her.

He even indulged her mania for Christmas decorations, which she started putting out even before Thanksgiving. Jason had never asked why she was so obsessed with Christmas. She hoped he never would.

Thanksgiving was three months away, but Gracie already had garlands of holly and fir ordered, along with three new Christmas trees and a box of new ornaments. She looked forward to the times when Jason left his beloved ranch and came to San Antonio on business. That was when he lived up to the image of a Fortune 500 tycoon and had Gracie hostess society parties for him, to which they invited Hollywood A-listers and sports stars with whom Jason's prospective colleagues could mingle. It often gave him the advantage, his association with the fabled few. Any number of people in the arts and sports were flattered by Jason's friendship. Not only was he dynamic, but he was rich beyond the dreams of avarice and he wasn't stingy with his wealth. Single women mobbed him.

When he wasn't rubbing elbows with the other Fortune 500, he was wearing jeans and boots, chaps and a big Stetson hat, working cattle with his cowboys. Even there he was generous, looking out for his men if they needed help.

Since he was an introvert who didn't mix well with others, he didn't seem the sort of man who had a big heart or even a kind disposition. But there was much more to this man than anyone imagined. He had a business degree from Harvard, but he didn't advertise it. His annual income could have funded the annual budget for two or three small impoverished nations. He didn't live like a multimillionaire. He left the socializing to Gracie, but she had as little love for it as he did. She spent her time doing charity work and finding projects to help people. Jason didn't know it, but she had a good reason for providing funding for women's shelters and soup kitchens and community charities.

People wondered why a sister and brother spent all their time together, she knew. But she and Jason weren't married, and apparently neither of them would ever be. Gracie wanted nothing to do with any physical relationship. Jason had girlfriends, but he was never serious enough to consider marriage. He didn't bring women home. But then, he was considerate about what he called Gracie's medieval attitude toward modern relationships. She didn't sleep around. She didn't like men—or women—who did. Jason bowed to her prejudices. But she knew that didn't stop him from doing what he liked out of her sphere of influence. He was a man, after all.

She grimaced as she noted a new spot of dirt on her spotless but aging white embroidered sweatshirt. She was wearing disreputable jeans with it, relics from a weekend she'd spent on the ranch with Jason while he taught a foreign dignitary how to ride. Gracie was deputized to teach his wife. He was amused at her patience and her skill on a horse. She also knew he appreciated her lack of vanity. She wore her long, pale blond hair in a perpetual bun or pigtails. Her soft gray eyes dominated her oval face with its exquisite complexion that never needed makeup to enhance it. Her lips were a full, soft bow, naturally pink. She didn't even bother with lipstick unless she and Jason were going to some really posh bash, like the opera or symphony or ballet. They had similar tastes in music and theater, and they agreed even on politics and religion. They had enough in common to make an uncommon match. But she and Jason were like brother and sister, she reminded herself firmly, even if they weren't related.

The rosebush she was pruning looked lopsided, and it dredged on feelings of her own inadequacy. She wondered sometimes why her mother had gone to such pains to make sure Gracie's personal history was kept secret even from her new stepfather and stepbrother. But she hadn't questioned Cynthia's resolve. Perhaps her mother had been afraid of Myron Pendleton's attitude if he knew the truth about the beautiful woman he'd met behind the counter at the men's suit warehouse. It was easier—and safer—to lie and tell him that her husband had died in a forward infantry unit in Operation Desert Storm, and that Graciela Marsh was her stepchild, not her real daughter. This elaborate ruse had been concocted to ensure that Cynthia and her daughter could escape from the grinding poverty in which they lived. But the pretense hadn't carried over to the bedroom. Cynthia had sobbed in Gracie's arms the morning of the day she died, confessing that she hadn't been able to let Myron touch her since their marriage. Myron had been furious and hurt, but Cynthia couldn't get past her own history with marriage. She said she couldn't go on living a lie. And later that day, she'd died in an apparent car accident. Gracie knew it wasn't an accident. But she couldn't say so without explaining why. That wasn't possible.

Gracie swept back a loose strand of blond hair with the back of her hand and only then noticed that it was covered with dirt. She laughed softly as she imagined what she must look like by now.

"For God's sake, don't tell me you're clearing even

more ground to plant more flowers?" came a deep, amused voice from behind her. "I thought you finished this job the day we went to the sale barn."

She turned, looking up into dark eyes under a jutting brow. He wasn't smiling; he rarely did. But his eyes smiled in that lean, tanned, rugged face.

"That was making room to plant bulbs this fall. I'm pruning back these rose bushes right now," she replied jovially.

He looked at the bushes that overlapped in the small space and grimaced. "You planted roses on top of roses, honey. You need to transplant some of them."

She sighed. "Well, I ran out of room and I had leftover bushes this spring. It all sort of grew together and the rain made it worse. I guess I could dig up another plot," she murmured to herself, looking around for new unbroken ground.

"Gracie," he said patiently, "our guests start arriving in two hours."

"Two hours?" She stared at him blankly. "Oh. Right! I hadn't forgotten," she lied.

He sat down on the wide stone balustrade that led down from the front steps. He was wearing dress slacks and boots with a white turtleneck sweater and a blue blazer. He looked expensive and elegant, a far cry from the ragged-looking working cowboy he'd appeared at the cattle auction two days before.

"Yes, you had forgotten," he corrected, shaking his head. He drew in a breath and looked around at the lush, formal landscape. "I hate this place," he muttered.

"You always did," she replied. "It's not the ranch."

"What can I say?" He shrugged. "I like cattle. I hate high society."

"Too bad you were born in the lap of it," she laughed.

He studied her covertly. She was pretty, in a shy sort of way. Gracie wasn't really outgoing, any more than he was. But she could organize a party better than anyone he knew. She was a gracious hostess, a tireless worker for her charities, and she dressed up beautifully. In an emergency, there wasn't anybody with a cooler head. He admired her. And not only for her social skills. His black eyes lingered just a few seconds too long on the swell of her firm breasts under the sweatshirt before he averted them.

"We've had a politically incorrect observation from the state attorney general."

"Simon Hart?" she asked. "What sort?"

"My cousin thinks we spend too much time together," he replied easily. "He says one or the other of us should get married and start producing children."

She stared at him quietly. "I don't want to get married."

He frowned. "Why don't you want to marry?"

She averted her eyes. "I just don't."

"Simon's happily married," he pointed out. "He and Tira have two sons."

Her voice tautened. "More power to them. I just don't want to get married."

"You're twenty-six," he remarked quietly. "You don't date anyone. I can't remember the last time you had a boyfriend. At that, you only had one steady one, for the four years you were in college in Jacobsville getting your history degree. And he turned out to be gay." There was an odd edge to his comment.

Gracie recalled that Jason had been actively hostile to the young man. That was surprising, because he was the most tolerant man she knew on controversial social issues. He was a churchgoer, like Gracie, and he said that the founder of their religion wouldn't have turned his back on anyone, regardless of their social classification. He couldn't be jealous…?

"Billy was comfortable to be with," she replied after a minute.

"Yes, but I assume he wasn't given to torrid make-out sessions on our couch."

She flushed and glared up at him. "I don't have torrid make-out sessions with anyone."

"I noticed," he said curtly. "Simon noticed, too."

"It's none of Simon's business how we live," she said defensively. She hesitated. "Is it?"

"Of course not," he snapped. "But he does have a point, Gracie. Neither of us is getting any younger."

"Especially not you," she teased. "You'll be thirty-five your next birthday."

"Don't remind me."

"You just get better-looking, Jason," she said affectionately. "You'll never be old to me."

He held her eyes for a few seconds and smiled. "Thanks."

She cocked her head at him. "Maybe you should get married," she said, wondering why it hurt to say it. "I mean, who'll inherit all this when you die?"

He drew in a long breath and looked out over the yard. "I've been thinking about that, too."

Her heart skipped a beat. "Have you…thought about anyone? Any prospective brides?" she asked, sitting back on her heels.

He shook his head.

"There was that lawyer you dated, that friend of Glory's," she said.

"She wanted a doctorate in law and I could get her a grant," he said with barely disguised contempt.

"Then there was the politician that Simon introduced you to."

"She wants to run for the senate and I have money," he scoffed.

"Jason, not every woman wants something financial from you," she pointed out. "You're not bad-looking and you have a big heart. It's just that you scare people."

"I don't scare you," he said.

She laughed. "You used to."

"Yes, when you first moved in with us," he recalled affectionately. "I lured you out of your room with Lindt chocolates, one at a time. It took months. You always looked at me as if you expected horns and a tail to start growing out of me."

"It wasn't personal," she chided. "Besides," she added with a wicked grin, "after I got to know you, I got used to the horns."

He made a face at her. But his eyes narrowed thoughtfully. "You didn't go out with a boy at all until I made an issue of it in your senior year of high school. You were asked to the prom, but you didn't want to go. I insisted. I thought you were unnecessarily shy."

"So I went with the first boy who asked me," she reminded him venomously.

He grimaced. "Well, he seemed nice."

"Did he, really?"

His dark eyes glittered. "I understand that his new front teeth look almost natural."

She shivered even with the memory. Violence still upset her. But the boy had been drunk and insistent. He'd left bruises all over her in a futile attempt to disrobe her. Gracie had to call Jason on her cell phone. She'd locked herself in the boy's car and he'd been crashing rocks into the passenger window trying to force her to open the door. Before he could break in, Jason skidded to a stop in front of the car and got out. Even now, so many years later, Gracie could still see the sudden fear on the boy's face when he saw the furious tall man approaching him. Jason was elegant, and usually even-tempered, but he could move like a striking cobra when he was angry. The boy had been tall, too, and muscular—a football star. But he hadn't lasted ten seconds with Jason. Those big fists had put him down in a heartbeat. The confrontation had made Gracie sick. Jason had saved her, though. And it wasn't the only time he'd stepped between Gracie and trouble. There was a saying on the Rocking Spur ranch, that any cowboy who wanted a quick trip to the emergency room only had to say something unsavory about or to Gracie in front of Jason.

After he'd rescued her, that long-ago night, he'd driven her home in a tense silence. But when they got home and he realized how frightened she was, even of him, he calmed down at once and became her affectionate stepbrother.

Now, he was as familiar to her as the flower garden she was working in. But there was still that distance between them. Especially since he'd been spending even less time at the San Antonio mansion. He had a way of looking at her lately that was disturbing. He went broody sometimes, too, as if his life was disappointing him.

While she was thinking, she nipped the last overlapping limb of a rosebush away from the fall chrysanthemums, which were just starting to branch out. She smoothed over them with her hand, smiling, considering how beautiful they would be in a few months, all gold and bright as the cold weather moved in. Her bulbs would need to be dug and separated, but that could wait for cooler weather. She'd planted some new bulbs at the ranch, too, last autumn, but Jason's big German shepherd had dug them up and eaten them. Fuming mad, she'd told Jason that the animal was a squirrel. No self-respecting dog would eat a helpless bulb. He'd almost bent over double laughing at her outrage. But he'd replaced the bulbs and even reluctantly loaned her one of his cowboys to help her replant them; one of his oldest and ugliest cowboys, at that. He went to great lengths to put distance between her and his ranch foreman, Grange.

"What are you thinking?" he asked.

She laughed self-consciously. "About Baker eating my bulbs last fall."

He grinned. "He's developed a taste for them. I had to put a fence around your flower bed."

"A fence?" she wailed.

"A white picket fence," he assured her. "Something aesthetic."

She relaxed. "You're nice."

He lifted an eyebrow. "I am?"

She put down the trowel and stood up, brushing at the dirt on her sweatshirt. It only smeared. "Darn," she muttered. "It will never come out."

"Harcourt can get anything out. She has chemicals hidden in the pantry."

She glanced at him and laughed delightedly. "Yes, but Dilly does the laundry."

"Dilly has chemicals, too."

She looked down at her feet. Her sneakers were caked

in mud. "I'll never get through the house in these," she moaned. She slipped out of them, standing in her stained socks. "Oh, darn!"

"I need to teach you how to cuss," he mused.

"You do it well enough for both of us, and in two languages," she pointed out. His Spanish was elegant and fluent.

He chuckled. "So I do."

"The ground is cold," she said absently.

He stood, moved close and suddenly swung her up into his powerful arms as if she weighed nothing at all.

She gasped at the strength in those powerful arms and clung to his neck, fearful of being dropped. She'd never liked being carried, although it was agonizingly stimulating when Jason did it. She felt shaky all over, being so close to him. This time, her body betrayed its fascination with him. She felt the whisper of his coffee-scented breath on her face as he shifted her. He smelled of faint, expensive cologne and soap, and muscles rippled in his chest. The ache that had begun to consume her became almost painful. Her mind filled with unfamiliar, dangerous thoughts. She should be still, she should pull back. She was thinking it even as she suddenly nestled closer to his warm strength and buried her face in his throat. She thought he shuddered, but that was doubtful. She'd never known a man in better control of himself.

"I know, you don't like being picked up," he said in a husky tone. He laughed softly. "But you can't walk on the white carpet shoeless with dirty socks, pet," he added. He curled her even closer, so that her small, firm breasts were crushed against warm, hard muscle. "Just lie still and think of England."

She frowned as he carried her up the steps and into the house, shifting her weight for an instant to open the front door. He kicked it shut behind them and started for the stairs that led to the second floor of the huge mansion.

"England?" she asked, diverted.

He carried her up the staircase, smiling. "Think about it."

"England." She'd never been to England. Had she?

He stopped at the door to her room. His black eyes pierced into hers. He was much too close. She could feel his clean breath on her face. The feel of his arms under her, his warm strength so close to her, made her feel exhilarated and breathless. She didn't want to move. She wanted him to hold her even closer.

"Those old movies, where women sacrifice themselves for the good of their country?" he prompted, still smiling. But his eyes were taunting, wise, hinting at things that Gracie knew nothing about.

"What old movies?" she asked absently. Her mind was on how fast her heart was beating.

"Never mind," he said heavily. He put her down abruptly, looking frustrated.

"I don't watch old movies, Jason," she said, trying to placate him. "We don't have any."

"I'll buy some old ones," he muttered. "Maybe some documentary ones, too."

"Documentaries? About what?" she asked blankly.

He started to speak, thought better of it and made a thin line of his lips. "Never mind. Don't be too long."

"I won't." She hesitated. "What shall I wear?" she added, wanting to soothe him because he liked it when she asked for his advice, and he seemed angry with her for some reason.

He paused. His eyes swept down her body with a

strange slowness. "Wear the gold gown I brought you from Paris," he said softly. "It suits you."

"Isn't it too dressy for a cocktail party?" she wondered.

He moved back to her. He was so tall, she thought, that her head only came up to his nose. He looked down into her puzzled eyes. "No," he replied. He touched her damaged coiffure. "And let your hair down for once. Wear it long. For me."

He made her feel warm and jittery. That was new. His voice was deep and slow, as soft as velvet. Her lips parted in anticipation as she stared into his eyes.

He lifted her chin with his thumb and forefinger. His thumb moved suddenly, dragging across her mouth in a rough caress that made her breath catch.

His large, black eyes suddenly narrowed, and his jaw clenched as he looked down into Gracie's stunned gray eyes. "Yes," he said quietly, as if she'd said something aloud. He let go of her, very slowly, and went down the staircase.

She watched him go, fascinated. Her fingers lifted to her sensitized mouth and touched it lightly. Her heart was beating so fast that she thought it might try to fly out of her chest. She couldn't quite get her breath. Jason had touched her in a new way, a different way than he'd ever touched her before. She didn't dare think about it too deeply. Not now. She turned quickly and went into her room.

THERE WERE A LOT OF people here tonight, she thought as she came down the long, curving staircase and surveyed the throng of well-dressed guests. It didn't take much imagination to spot the computer company partners; they were wearing suits that didn't quite fit and they looked out of place and uncomfortable.

Gracie, a veteran of social gatherings, understood their confusion. It had taken her a long time to adjust to luxury cars and designer clothing and parties like this. In many ways, she was more comfortable with Jason's cowboys than this elegant mix of professionals and big money. But she was fairly certain that she looked presentable, in the clingy gold gown that covered all of one arm and left the opposite arm and shoulder enticingly bare. It fell to her ankles, but the back drooped in a flow of silky fabric to lie just over the base of her spine, leaving the honey-smooth skin bare. Her pale blond hair swung around her shoulders in soft profusion. With the gown she wore a gold necklace of interlocking rings, with matching earrings. She looked pretty, and much younger than her real age.

She walked up to the skinny, freckle-faced redhead who seemed the dominant partner and smiled. "Do you have everything you need?" she asked him gently.

He looked down at her and flushed. "I, uh, well, I… that is…" he stammered.

His round-faced, dark-skinned partner cleared his throat. "We're sort of out of place here," he began.

Gracie put her arms through theirs and drew them along with her into the ballroom, where a small live band was playing, and guided them to the bar. "Nobody stands on ceremony here," she explained pleasantly. "We're just plain people, like everybody else."

"Plain people with private jets and world-class soccer stars for friends," the redheaded one murmured, looking around.

"Yes, but you'll be in that same society one day yourselves," she replied, smiling. "Jason says you're both geniuses, that you've designed software that revolutionizes the gaming industry."

They both stared at her. "You're his sister," the shorter one guessed.

"Well, his stepsister," she said. "I'm Gracie Marsh."

"I'm Fred Turnbill," the round-faced one said. "He's Jeremy Carswell. We're Shadow Software."

She shook hands with each of them in turn. "I'm very glad to meet you."

"Your…stepbrother," Fred said, nodding toward the tall, elegant man with a champagne flute in one hand, talking to a famous actor. "He's very aggressive. We weren't even interested in being acquired, but he just kept coming. He's offered us creative control and executive positions and even stock bonuses." He laughed nervously. "It's hard to turn down a man like that."

"I know what you mean," she said.

"He seems very much at home here," Fred sighed. "I guess he is, considering his financial status."

She handed them flutes of champagne. "Listen," she said confidentially, "he does what business requires of him. But you might have a different picture of him if you could see him throwing calves during roundup. And especially if you could see him ride." Her gray eyes grew dreamy. "I've never seen anything more beautiful in my life than Jason on a running horse."

They were both looking at her with curious expressions. "On a horse?" Fred murmured.

"Throwing calves?" Jeremy added.

She smiled, still staring at Jason. "He owns a Santa Gertrudis ranch down in Comanche Wells. When he isn't managing acquisitions, he's busy working cattle right alongside his men."

"Well!" Fred exclaimed. "So he's not just some greedy businessman trying to own the world."

"Not on your life," Gracie said softly. "He goes to extremes to be environmentally responsible. He won't even use pesticides on the place."

At that moment, Jason seemed to feel her gaze, because his head turned and black eyes lanced into hers across the width of the ballroom. Even at the distance, Gracie's knees went weak and she seemed to stop breathing. It was the first time he'd ever looked at her like that. As if, she thought absently, he could eat her alive.

She dragged her eyes away from his with a small, nervous laugh. "He isn't what he seems."

Fred pursed his lips and exchanged glances with Jeremy. "That sort of puts a different complexion on things," he said. "A man who gets out and works with his people isn't the image we had of Mr. Pendleton. I guess we're all victims of assumption."

"You never assume anything with Jason," she told them. "When God made him, He broke the mold. There isn't another one like him in the world. When Jason gives his word, he keeps it, and he's the most honest man I've ever known."

Jeremy smiled down at her. "Well, you've sold us. I guess we're about to join the corporation."

"You're about to join the family," she corrected. "Jason believes in holiday bonuses and good benefit packages, and he looks out for his people."

Jeremy lifted his glass. So did Fred. "Here's to a prosperous future."

Gracie raised hers, as well, and toasted them. "I'll drink to that."

She excused herself to go the rounds of the other guests. She noticed a few minutes later that Jason was talking to the two software executives and smiling. She chuckled. It wasn't the first time she'd nudged a deal into completion. She was getting good at it.

Around midnight, she and Jason ended up together at the drinks table. Couples were out on the floor dancing to a lazy, romantic melody.

"Care to dance?" she asked with a grin.

He shook his head.

She wasn't really surprised. He'd danced with several other women during the evening, including an elderly woman who came to the party alone. But he never danced with Gracie these days, no matter how hard she worked at convincing him to.

She frowned. "You dance with other people."

He glanced down at her. "I'm not dancing with you."

She felt unsettled by the refusal. She didn't understand why he was this way. She might be clumsy, but she did all right on the dance floor. She picked up a champagne flute and filled it.

"Don't get your feelings hurt," he said curtly. "I have reasons. Good ones. I just can't discuss them."

She moved her shoulder. "No problem," she said, putting on her party smile.

He turned to face her, his jaw taut. His black eyes were oddly glittery as they met her wounded gray ones. "You look, but you don't see, Gracie," he said curtly.

She stared up at him miserably. "I don't understand."

He sighed. "That's an understatement," he said under his breath.

She sipped champagne. One of his lean, beautiful hands came up and took the flute from her fingers. He lifted it to his mouth, sipping the sparkling amber liquid from the exact spot her lips had touched, and he looked straight into her eyes while he did it.

The act was deliberate, sensual, provocative. Gracie's lips parted on a rush of breath while he held her eyes in a bond she couldn't break. She felt an explosion of sensation so intense that it left her speechless.

"Shocked, Gracie?" he wondered as he handed the flute back to her.

"I...don't know."

His fingers came up and traced a line from her flushed cheek to the corner of her lips. He stared at them intently. "You closed the account."

"What...account?"

"The computer account. They're in, thanks to you. I didn't even have to introduce them to the soccer players." His fingers trailed over her soft mouth. "Amazing, that gift you have for putting people at ease, making them feel as if they belong."

"A gift," she whispered, not really hearing him. What he was doing to her mouth was very erotic. She moved closer.

His head bent, so that what he was saying couldn't be overheard. Her response to him was electrifying. He was on fire.

"Gracie," he whispered, bending closer, "I can hear your heart beating."

"Can...you?" Her eyes were on his firm, sensual mouth.

His lips parted as they hovered just above her own. His tall body corded at the enticement she presented, her hands going to his shirtfront and pressing there. His heart began to race. "What are you going to do if I bend an inch more, and put my mouth right over your lips?" he asked in a rough, sensual tone.

She wasn't hearing him. She couldn't hear anything. She could only see his mouth, filling her mind with images so sensual and sweet that her legs began to wobble under her. Her fingers contracted on his shirt. She felt thick hair and muscle under the crisp, clean fabric.

"I could bend you back over my arm and hold you so close that you couldn't breathe unless I did," he whispered gruffly. "Kiss you so hard that your mouth would be swollen from the intensity of it!"

She was on tiptoe, feeling the muscles clench even through the fine cloth of his dinner jacket as her small breasts pressed hard into his chest. Her mouth was lifted, pleading. She felt tight, hot, achy all over. She was trembling. She knew that he could see, and it didn't matter. Nothing mattered, except that she wanted him to come closer, to kiss her until she felt on fire, until the sharp ache he was arousing was satisfied, until the backbreaking tension stopped racking her slender body…

"Jason," she choked, tightening her grip on his shoulders.

"Hey, Jason," came an exuberant voice from behind him, "could you explain to Ted here how that new computer software works? He wants to get in on our deal with those California techies you're trying to assimilate."

Jason stood erect, looking as if he'd been shot. He had to work, to control himself before he turned abruptly away from Gracie, to the businessman standing behind him, nursing a whiskey highball.

"Let's find the inventors and get them to tell him," Jason said, forcing a smile. "Come on."

He didn't look at Gracie. The businessman did, frowning at her odd expression, but he was feeling the liquor and passed off the little tête-à-tête he'd just witnessed as an aberration brought on by whiskey. Jason wasn't likely to be kissing his stepsister in public, after all!

3

JASON SEEMED AS RELIEVED as Gracie that they weren't thrown together again. He didn't seek her out or even look her way for the rest of the evening. He did say good-night to her after the guests left, but in a curt and perfunctory way, as if the interlude earlier had embarrassed him. It had seemed like a deliberate attempt at seduction earlier, but it was beginning to feel more like an unwanted loss of control. He'd spoken to her in a way that changed their relationship. Perhaps he'd had one highball too many and was now counting his regrets, she thought.

But Jason never drank whiskey. He drank white wines or champagne, and precious little even of that. When he'd been close to her, she didn't recall smelling any liquor on his breath at all. So Gracie didn't know what to think. She was mortified that she'd given away her helpless attraction to him, something she'd never wanted him to see. It would be like making promises she couldn't keep. But it was Jason's behavior that unsettled her.

She went up to her bedroom and actually locked the

door. She was still reeling from the shock Jason had given her before they were interrupted; not from his actions, but from her own response to them.

She had…wanted him. Actually wanted him. It was the first time in her adult life that she'd felt physical desire. She'd thought for a long time that she was simply under-sexed, that she didn't feel desire at all. Now her body was awake and she was in anguish at the things she'd just learned about herself. She wasn't impervious to men. Not anymore. She was vulnerable. And Jason knew it.

Her mother's warnings echoed in her tired mind as she put on a long cotton gown and climbed into her canopied bed, huddling under the spotless white covers and hand-embroidered sheets. She stared at the canopy fabric over her head in the light of her bedside lamp, trembling from the impact of Jason's soft teasing. She knew that she'd never be able to forget that hunger in his eyes, in his touch. He was a stranger in this respect, a man she didn't know at all. Had he meant to go that far? Or had he really lost control of himself? It wasn't like him to be so forward with any woman in public, least of all Gracie.

It was becoming clear why beautiful women hung around him like satellites. It wasn't his money at all. It was the man, the sensuous, tender man, who drew their atten-tion. Gracie was curious about his changed attitude to her. She was also curious about why he'd refused to dance with her. It hadn't been the first time. For over two years, now, he'd avoided any close physical contact with her. What had happened to change that, in the space of a day?

No, she thought. No, it wasn't just today. He'd been different when they went to the cattle auction, too. It was the way he looked at her. It was almost predatory. He was like a big cat straining at the leash. If he broke it, what would he be like? A small part of her ached to find out. But the bigger part was afraid, even of Jason, in that way.

She tossed and turned all night, longing to see Jason again and dreading it at the same time. How could she ever be herself with him again after what had happened?

SHE DRAGGED HERSELF DOWNSTAIRS the next morning without makeup, with her hair in a ponytail, wearing old jeans and a long cotton shirt and sneakers. She wanted to look as little like a siren as possible. Just in case Jason was still prowling.

But it was a wasted camouflage because he wasn't at the breakfast table when she went in and sat down. She noticed as she unfolded her napkin and went to pour coffee in her china cup from the carafe that only one place was set.

Mrs. Harcourt came in with a small platter of meats and eggs.

"Isn't Jason here?" she asked the housekeeper.

"No, dear, he took off like a hurricane this morning, before I got the biscuits in the oven," she said, frowning. "Tense as a pulled rope he was, and out of sorts. Took off in that big car like a posse was on his tail." She whistled. "No wonder they call them Jaguars. It sounded like a wounded wildcat when he went down the driveway."

Translated, that meant he was angry. He tended to take his temper out on the highway, a flaw that had resulted in a good number of traffic citations. He didn't drive recklessly, but he drove too fast.

She ladled eggs onto her plate slowly. She didn't know which was stronger—relief or disappointment. It was really only postponing the reckoning. Certainly they couldn't go back to their old relationship after what had happened between them.

"You're very glum this morning," Mrs. Harcourt said gently, her dark eyes smiling as she moved dishes of food closer to Gracie. "Bad party?"

"What? Oh, no, not really," she replied, sighing. "It was just long and loud." She smiled. "I'm not really a party person."

"Neither is Jason," Mrs. Harcourt said quietly. "He'd rather live on his ranch and just be a cowboy."

"How did he come into that ranch?" Gracie asked suddenly.

Mrs. Harcourt looked oddly unsettled, but her face quickly lost its confused expression. "He bought it from my family," she said surprisingly. "It was my grandfather's place. Not that it was in very good shape," she added. "I was afraid it would go for subdivisions or a shopping mall." She smiled. "I'm so glad it didn't."

Gracie was thoughtful as she sipped coffee. "He bought it the year before his father died," she recalled.

"Yes." Mrs. Harcourt's soft voice had a sudden edge.

"Mr. Pendleton didn't move with the times, did he?" she asked as she put down her coffee cup. "He hated the ranch and Jason working on it. He said it was beneath a Pendleton to do manual labor."

"Oh, he was a stickler for class and position," the older woman said bitterly. "He refused to let Jason's first ranch foreman in the front door. He told him that servants went to the back."

"How ridiculous," Gracie huffed.

"He and Jason had a terrible row about it later. Jason won." The older woman chuckled. "Whatever his faults, and he doesn't have that many, Jason is no snob."

"Did he love his father?" Gracie laughed self-consciously. "What a silly question. Of course he did. The day we went to the reading of his father's will is one I'll never forget. There were grants to Glory and me, but the lawyer went behind closed doors to discuss the rest with Jason. Afterward, he got drunk, remember?" she sighed. "In all the time I've known Jason, I've never even seen him tipsy. He never cried at the old man's funeral, but he went wild after he saw the will. I guess it took a few days to hit him. The loss, I mean. With his mother long dead, his last parent was gone forever... Mrs. Harcourt! Are you all right?"

The elderly woman had toppled the coffeepot, right on her hand. Gracie jumped up, all but dragging the woman into the kitchen to the sink. "You hold that right there," she instructed, putting the burned hand under running cold water. She went to the bathroom and rifled through the medicine cabinet to get what she needed. She walked briskly back to the kitchen and put the supplies down by the sink.

"Miss Gracie, I can do that," she fussed. "It isn't right, you waiting on me."

"Don't you start," Gracie muttered. "We don't do the master-and-servant thing in this house. You and Dilly and John are family," she said firmly. "We all look out for each other."

Tears misted the older woman's eyes. Gracie couldn't tell if emotion or pain caused it, but she smiled gently as she treated the burn. "Honestly, I don't know what in the world we'd do without you."

"That's so kind of you, Miss Gracie."

"Gracie," she corrected. "You don't call Jason 'Mr. Jason,'" she pointed out.

"I do when he's around," the housekeeper corrected.

"And you get fussed at. He doesn't like it when you

treat him like the boss." She hesitated as she fastened the bandage in place. "He's…very strange lately," she said softly. "I don't understand him."

Mrs. Harcourt looked as if she'd smother trying not to speak. Finally she said, "He just has a lot on his mind. There's that computer company in Germany that's bothering him because it competes with his own new line. It could hurt him in the market. He said he hopes he won't have to go over there, but the owners are dragging their feet about selling."

"God help them if he does go over there." Gracie chuckled. "Jason is like a bulldozer when he wants something."

"He is," Mrs. Harcourt agreed. "Thanks for patching me up."

"Oh, I have an ulterior motive," Gracie told her. "I need your help to smuggle in some more Christmas decorations. You have to help me get the boxes into the attic so Jason won't see them if he's around when they arrive."

The older woman hesitated, clearly disturbed.

"He just grumbles," Gracie reminded her. "He doesn't say I can't put up trees and wreaths and holly garlands." She frowned. "Why does he hate Christmas?" she wondered, and not for the first time. But she'd never asked Mrs. Harcourt about it before.

Mrs. Harcourt grimaced. "His father didn't mind a tree, but he never bought presents. He said the holiday was nothing more than an excuse for commerce. He was never here at Christmas, anyway, not once during Jason's whole life," she added bitterly. "I bought little gifts for him, or knitted him caps and scarves or made afghans for his bed," she said softly. "Dilly and John and I tried to make it up to him. He was a lonely child."

"How terrible," Gracie murmured.

"Why do you love it so much?" the older woman asked.

"I was never allowed to celebrate Christmas," she blurted out. "Not even with a tree." Her face flamed. She hadn't meant to give that away.

The older woman was clearly shocked. "But you go to church with Jason. And you decorate everything— even Baker, once, with fake antlers…!"

"My father was…an atheist," she whispered. "He wouldn't let us go to church or celebrate Christmas."

"Oh, my dear." Mrs. Harcourt hugged her close and held her. Gracie sobbed. Except for this warm, matronly woman, Gracie hadn't known real affection since her mother's death. Myron Pendleton had been kind, in an impersonal way, but he wasn't the hugging sort. Really, neither was Jason.

"You won't tell him?" Gracie asked, finally moving away, to dab at her eyes with a tissue Mrs. Harcourt pressed into her hand.

"No. I'm good at keeping secrets," she added with a smile that looked oddly cynical. "But why don't you want him to know?"

"My mother taught me never to talk about my childhood. Especially after we came here."

Mrs. Harcourt sensed that there was a lot this young woman had never shared with anyone. "Come on and finish your breakfast," she coaxed. "I'll make you a lovely chocolate cake later."

Gracie laughed self-consciously. "You spoil me, Mrs. Harcourt. Me and Glory, too. You always did."

"I missed having girls of my own," she said. "My husband was sterile."

"I didn't realize. I'm so sorry."

She smiled sadly. "I loved him, but he was a hard man to live with. He broke horses for Jason. He was kicked in the head by a mustang and died right there in the corral. I had no place else to go, no family, so I stayed here."

"I'm glad you did," Gracie said. "You made this place a home. You still do."

Mrs. Harcourt beamed. "For that, you can have a chocolate cake with buttercream frosting."

"My favorite!"

The older woman chuckled. "I know. Now that I'm patched up, I'll get started on that cake. You finish your breakfast."

"Yes, ma'am."

Gracie went back to the table. Life was hard on everybody. Poor Mrs. Harcourt, a widow without even a child to comfort her in her old age.

IT WAS A SLOW LUNCH day for Barbara's Café. The owner sat at a booth with Gracie, nibbling on a salad. She was twelve years older than Gracie, with thick blond hair and pretty eyes. Everybody knew her locally and loved her. She'd been a widow for a long time, but she did have family. She'd adopted Rick Marquez, the San Antonio homicide detective, when he was in his teens. Now he was the joy of her life.

"Why don't you set your sights on Rick?" Barbara teased. "He's young and single and incredibly handsome, even if I do say so."

"He carries a gun around," Gracie pointed out.

"So does your stepbrother," the older woman replied.

"Yes, when he's on the ranch, but Jason doesn't spend his life around dead bodies," she added.

"Having seen a couple of his cowboys from the Rocking Spur eating lunch over here last week, I could debate that. They said they'd just come in from pulling cattle out of mud, and they looked like death warmed over."

"So does Jason, when he's helping with roundup or rescuing mired cattle," Gracie said.

"A multimillionaire, out working cattle," the older woman sighed, shaking her head.

"It's where he'd rather be all the time, if he could."

Barbara smiled. "I remember when he took over that ranch. He looked as if he'd won the lottery."

"I'll bet he had to pay a lot for it," Gracie mused. "It's huge."

"Actually I heard that he inherited it," Barbara said.

Gracie laughed. "Not likely. It belonged to some of Mrs. Harcourt's family. They sold it to him."

Barbara shrugged. "I must have misunderstood. Speaking of the devil, how is Jason?"

Gracie shifted in her chair. "I don't know."

Something in the tone of her voice made Barbara tense. "Why don't you know?"

"I haven't seen him for days, or even heard from him," she said. "I planned a dinner party for two of our friends who are getting married. He hasn't said if he's coming over for it or not."

Barbara was surprised. "Have you quarreled? But you and Jason never argue, even about those hundreds of Christmas decorations you stick everywhere starting at Thanksgiving that drive him nuts…"

"We just had a misunderstanding." Gracie couldn't bear to talk about what had really happened. "He left without a goodbye when he came down here."

Barbara slid a hand over the other woman's where it

rested on the table. "You should go over to the ranch and talk to him," she said. "He's awkward with people sometimes, like most loners are. Maybe he wants to make up and just doesn't know how."

Gracie brightened a little. "You're perceptive," she said. "Yes, he is awkward with people. He doesn't ever come right out and apologize, but he works it around so that you understand what he means. He holds things inside." She sighed. "My stepsister, Glory, used to say that Jason got his feelings hurt more often than any of us realized, but he never showed it. She said he thought of it as a kind of weakness."

"That was his father's doing," Barbara said coolly. "The old man loved women, plural, but he was never much good at commitment. He only married women he couldn't get into bed any other way—out of desire, never love. He never loved any of them. He taught Jason that love was a weakness. He said women used sex as a weapon to extort money from men."

"Good Lord!" Gracie exclaimed. "How do you know that?"

"One of my cousins used to work for Myron Pendleton. He overheard him talking to Jason about women one day. He was absolutely disgusted. In fact, he quit the job. He said he wasn't working for a man who had no respect for his womenfolk."

Gracie shook her head. "I've lived with him all these years and I didn't know that."

"You've lived under his protection, honey, not under his roof," Barbara said drily. "You and Glory were away at school, but when you came home, Jason lived down here and left the two of you up in San Antonio with Harcourt and the others. Didn't you notice?"

Gracie hadn't. It was only just dawning on her that Jason, while spoiling and protecting them, had kept them apart from him at the same time.

"Don't you really know what's wrong with Jason?" Barbara asked in a peculiar tone.

Gracie gave her a blank look. "What do you mean?"

Barbara let go of her hand and avoided her eyes. "Nothing. I was just thinking out loud. It's probably something to do with business that's got him grumpy, don't you imagine?"

Gracie relaxed. "Yes. I imagine it is." She sipped coffee. "You know, I think I will stop by the ranch on my way home. He can't miss this party."

"That's the spirit." Barbara glanced out the window and winced. "Bad weather coming again. Probably that tropical storm headed our way. Look at those dark clouds!"

"I'd better get moving," Gracie replied. "It's getting dark, too."

"You don't want to be on the roads at night when it's raining," Barbara said worriedly. "The road up to the ranch isn't paved. You'll go into the ditch for sure. It's not safe. There have been some kidnappers around here lately, and you would be a good catch for those horrible criminals."

"I drive a VW," Gracie said with easy confidence. "I'm not sliding into any ditches! As for kidnappers—this is Jacobsville. Nothing happens around here."

THIRTY MINUTES LATER, sitting on the side of the road in the dark with rain pounding on the roof and the car at a drunken angle in a ditch, she ate those words. She called the ranch on her cell phone. Grange, Jason's foreman, answered.

"Grange, can you tell Jason I'm stuck in the ditch on the side road from the ranch?" she asked plaintively. "I lost control of the car."

"Sure I can. Want me to come out with the truck and get you?" he asked.

She hesitated. Once she would have said yes. Now, with Jason acting so strangely, she didn't want to put Grange in any awkward situations. "Better call Jason this time, I guess," she replied.

"No problem," he said gently. "You okay?"

"I'm fine."

"I'll get him. He's out with the boys checking for mired cattle, so it may be a few minutes. Sit tight."

"Sure thing. Thanks." She ended the call. Oh, boy. If Jason was in the middle of something, she was going to catch hell. She'd only wanted to make up with him. Now, things were worse.

Time seemed to drag while she clutched her purse in her lap and tried not to slide into the passenger window of the little car, sitting at an odd angle in the ditch. It had been an impulsive decision to drive out here. She should have waited.

Gracie looked out the windshield at the rushing water that came up to the hood of her little car and hoped that Jason would hurry. Then she felt guilty that he was going to have to come out and rescue her again. She was such a klutz, she moaned silently. Nothing she did ever ended well. She was disaster on two legs. If only she wasn't such a scatterbrain. If only…

She heard the roar of a pickup truck and looked ahead to see one of the big, double-cabbed black ranch trucks speeding toward her. He always drove too fast. The dirt road was muddy and flooded, too, and she had visions of disaster if he braked too hard. She could feel his temper in the way he swung the truck to the side of the road and stopped it. He didn't slide. He was always so much in control of himself, even when he was raging mad.

She drew in a shaky sigh. She would be all right. Jason was always there to save her from herself. Even if he didn't like having to do it.

Another truck, a wrecker, pulled up behind his truck. He slammed out of the driver's seat and spoke to the driver of the wrecker. Then he came toward Gracie with long, angry strides, his wide-brimmed hat pulled low over his eyes, his yellow slicker raincoat flapping over his boots.

The car was lying at an angle. Gracie was sitting at a forty-five-degree angle, sideways. Jason jerked the door open and glared down at her with compressed lips.

"Come on," he said gruffly, holding out both hands.

She hesitated. He couldn't possibly know why she resisted being lifted in a man's arms, even if he was used to her idiosyncracies.

"Come on," he said again, gentler this time. "Gracie, I know you don't like being carried, but there's no other way unless you want us to pull the car out of the ditch with you in it. The damned thing could roll."

She bit her lower lip. That was even more terrifying. "O…okay."

She lifted both her arms, clenching her jaw. Jason caught them and pulled her up, effortlessly, until he could pick her up. He swung her free of the car. She wasn't wearing a raincoat—another stupid oversight—and she was quickly soaked as he carried her toward his truck.

He stuck her in the passenger seat, after sludging

through an inch or more of thick red mud. "Fasten your seat belt," he said curtly and slammed her door.

He spoke to the wrecker man and pointed down the road, toward the highway, not the ranch. Obviously he was showing the man that he wanted her car taken to the house in San Antonio. He didn't want Gracie at the ranch. That hurt.

He got back in beside her, still wet, still mad, still uncommunicative. He fastened his own seat belt, made sure she'd done the same, started the engine and gunned the truck as he pulled back onto the highway and started toward San Antonio.

"The ranch is that way," she said in a small voice, pointing behind them.

"I'm taking you home to San Antonio," he said shortly. "You're not staying down here overnight."

She didn't dare ask why. She averted her eyes to the road and wished things were the way they had been, before he'd said things neither of them would ever forget.

"What the hell were you doing on the ranch road in the rain?" he asked shortly.

She moved her purse in her hands. "Hoping we could make up."

"Oh."

She glanced at his taut profile. He wasn't giving away anything with that expression. He was simply unresponsive. "Okay, I know," she said with a long, wistful sigh. "I screwed up again. I should have waited for a sunny day. Maybe there's a market for women who can't do one single thing right. I might go into theater."

He made a rough, amused sound deep in his throat. "I remember your one time on the stage."

She grimaced. Yes. In tenth grade. She was in a play,

with a minor role. She'd tripped walking to her mark, bounded into another actor and they'd ended up in a tangle on the stage floor. The audience had roared. Sadly the play had been a tragedy, and she had a monologue—left unspoken—about death. She'd left the stage in tears, without speaking her lines, and had been kicked out of the play the same night by a furious director. Jason had gone to see the man, who put Gracie right back in the play and even apologized. She never had the nerve to ask why.

She looked down at her lap. "Maybe I could get work as a mannequin," she suggested. "You know—stand upright in a boutique and wear different things every day."

He glanced at her. "Maybe you could take karate lessons."

"Karate? Me?"

"They teach self-confidence." He smiled faintly. "You could use a little."

"I'd aim a karate chop at somebody, hit a vital spot and end up in federal prison for murder." She sighed.

He glanced at her, but without answering. He turned on the radio. "I want to listen to the market report. Do you mind?"

"Of course not." She did, but she couldn't force him to talk if he didn't want to. So they listened to stock prices until he turned into the driveway of the mansion in San Antonio and pulled up at the steps. He cut off the engine, went around the truck and opened her door. The rain had followed them. It was pouring down, and the driveway was almost underwater.

"I can walk," she said quickly.

He raised an eyebrow and glanced pointedly at the several inches of water pooled on the driveway.

She was wet, but she didn't want to ruin her new shoes. She bit her lip hard.

He gave her a quizzical look. "Some women are aroused by being carried," he said in a worldly way. "You act as if I'm carting you off to a guillotine every time I have to do it."

She swallowed uncomfortably. "It's just…it reminds me of something bad. Most especially when it storms."

"What?"

Her face tightened. "Just…something. A long time ago."

He studied her, while rain bounced off his hat and raincoat, and he realized that he knew absolutely nothing about Gracie's life before her mother married his father. He remembered having to lure Gracie out of her room with chocolates, because she'd been so frightened of him at the age of fourteen. It had taken him months to win her trust. He scowled. His father had never discussed her with Jason, except to tell the young man that Gracie would always need someone to look out for her, to protect her. That hadn't really made much sense at the time.

"You keep secrets, Graciela," he said deeply, using her full name, as he rarely did.

The sound of her name on his lips was sexy. Sweet. It made her hum with sensations she didn't want to feel. She had nothing to give, and he didn't know it. She could never let anything…romantic…develop between them. Never. Even if she wanted to. And she did. Desperately. Especially since he'd whispered those exciting, sensually charged remarks to her at the party.

She managed a smile. "Don't you keep secrets, too?"

He shrugged. "Only about my breeding program," he said drily, mentioning the genetic witchery and technological skills he practiced to produce better and leaner purebred herd bulls.

About women, too, she was about to say, but she didn't dare trespass into his private life.

"Some secrets are better kept," she said.

"Suit yourself." His eyes twinkled. "You work for the CIA, do you?"

It was the first olive branch he'd extended. She laughed with pure delight. "Sure. I have a trenchcoat, a blindfold, a cyanide pill and the telephone number of a Russian KGB agent in my purse." She gasped. "Jason, my car!"

"The wrecker will be right behind us. It's going slower than we were. I told him to tow it up here and bill the ranch. Come on, baby. I've got more work to do before I can call it a night." He sighed. "I was out looking for mired cattle, supervising two new cowboys who don't know a bull from a steer, when a fence went down under a wash in the rain, and cattle scattered to hell and gone. I've got a full crew out trying to round them all back up. But the new hands need watching."

"You hire men to work cattle and then you get out and do it yourself."

He shrugged. "I'm not a desk sort of man."

"I noticed."

He reached in and slid his arms under her knees and her back and swung her out of the truck as if she was light as a feather. "You're such a cat, Gracie," he mused. "All sleek lines and light weight. You don't eat enough."

"I'm never hungry."

"You run it all off." He turned toward the house.

A huge flash of jagged lightning split the rainy, dark sky, startling Gracie, who suddenly clung to him and hid her face in his throat, shivering. "Oh, I hate lightning!" she moaned as the thunder rolled and rumbled around them. Her face moved again, just as his head turned, and her mouth brushed over his with the action. It was so perfectly synchronized that it seemed as if she'd timed the turning of her own head, to produce that sweet little caress to tempt him.

Jason's tall, fit body contracted violently and he stopped in his tracks. He didn't say a word, but Gracie could feel his breathing quicken. The soft contact had flamed through her young body. She wondered if it affected him the same way.

It became quickly apparent that it had. In the light of the wide porch, he looked down at her with pure heat in his black eyes. They narrowed as they fell to her mouth.

The lightning came again, and the thunder, but Gracie didn't see it. She only saw Jason's face as he stared at her with growing intensity. She could feel his broad chest against her breasts, moving roughly, as if he had trouble keeping his breath steady. Her heart ran away. The silken touch of her mouth on his had acted as a spark to dry wood.

"Jason?" she whispered, disconcerted by the harsh look on his face. He seemed angry out of all proportion to what had happened. "I'm sorry! I didn't mean to…"

"Didn't you?" he asked through his teeth as he stared right into her eyes.

His arms, steely and warm, contracted fiercely around her body. His teeth clenched as his gaze fell to her soft mouth. He hesitated, as if he were fighting a battle with his own instincts. But he lost it. Gracie saw with dawning shock the aching hunger in the black eyes that began to narrow and glitter as the storm broke around them.

"What the hell," he muttered as he suddenly bent his

head. "I'm already damned, anyway!" His mouth suddenly ground down into hers, parting her lips, as urgent as the lightning, as frightening as the storm as he gave in to a surge of desire so hot that he couldn't breathe through it. His arms contracted hungrily, grinding Gracie's slight breasts into the firm, muscular wall of his chest. He groaned against her lips and crushed her even closer, his brows drawn together in an agony of visible need as his mouth moved insistently on her lips, parting them.

She couldn't believe it was happening. She loved Jason. She'd always loved him. But this was a side of him that she'd never seen before. The passion and expertise of the kiss were worlds away from her mother's frightening lectures about how it was between men and women. Involuntarily her body reacted to the feel of him; her mouth warmed to the furious need in his kisses. She felt a shock of pleasure beyond anything she'd ever known as his mouth grew more demanding.

But she fought it. This was only how it began, her mother had told her, with fierce need that blinded a woman to the reality of a man's desires. It began like this, but it ended in pain and humiliation and, ultimately, tragedy. *Tragedy.* Gunshots and the metallic taste of blood…

And then, quite suddenly, Jason's hard, warm mouth slid down her neck and right onto the fullness of her breast, pressing so hungrily that she panicked.

Memories from the past surged up in her mind, frightened her. His mouth was insistent on her breast, twisting. In a few seconds, she knew, his teeth would bite into her, and she would look like her mother had, bleeding…!

She pushed at Jason's broad chest, fighting the images in her mind as certainly as she fought this unexpected loss of control in a man whose place in her life had been tempered with iron control. She didn't know Jason like this. His arms were contracting, and his mouth was opening, as she knew it would…! She pushed harder.

Jason realized, belatedly, what he was doing and he lifted his head. A shudder ran through him as he felt her body move frantically against him. But she wasn't trying to get closer. She was fighting to get away from him.

"Jason, no! Put…me down! Please!" she cried, panic in her face, in her choked voice. She pushed harder. "Let me go! Let me go!"

"Damn you! You started it," he ground out, as shocked by his own feverish lack of control as by her rejection of him as a man.

"I know. But I…I didn't mean to! I didn't want…that! I'm sorry!" she sobbed.

He put her back on her feet abruptly and let her go. She looked up at him with shocked, anguished eyes. He stepped back, his jaw clenched. He looked down at her with smoldering black eyes in a face harder than rock. There was violence and barely leashed passion in his expression. He looked at her as if he hated her. A harsh sob burst from her lips. She had started it, even if accidentally, and now he was angry again. It was her fault. He hated her for tempting him…!

Before he could speak, she was gone, into the house, running like a madwoman for the staircase. He stared after her with turbulent emotions, his eyes blazing, his body tense and aching. Desire evaporated slowly out of him, to be replaced with embarrassment at his lapse, with Gracie of all people. He was furious with himself. Then he was furious with her, for the teasing that aroused him and the deliberate touch of her mouth on his that had kindled his passion and made him cross the line. She'd permitted the intimacy at first, and then, when he turned up the heat just a little, she'd pushed him away as if she found him utterly repulsive. He replayed the episode in his mind, and anger grew from the embarrassment, along with rejection and humiliation and wounded pride. He'd betrayed his desire for her, and she'd been…disgusted. He'd seen it in her face.

The pain hit him like a flood. At first he was hurt. And then he was enraged. Damn her! Why tempt him into indiscretion and then behave as if he was totally responsible for it?

He turned on his heel and stalked back out to the truck. At that moment, he didn't care if he ever saw her again as long as he lived. He cursed her every mile of the way back to Comanche Wells, so unsettled that he didn't even see the wrecker pass him on its way to San Antonio. He'd never had anything hurt so much. Gracie didn't want him. She was afraid of him now, running scared. He would never be able to erase this painful episode from both their minds. In a heartbeat, they had become enemies.

He stepped down hard on the accelerator. He didn't care if he got a speeding ticket. Nothing mattered anymore. Not now.

UP IN HER ROOM, Gracie stood in the darkness, shivering. Hateful memories flooded her mind. Screams from the bedroom. Tears. Bruises and fear and blood, staining the bodice of her mother's nightgown. Her mother, crying. Her father scathing, brutal, accusing. Other memories; of the boy who'd brought Gracie home, far too late because of a flat tire. Her father, snatching her up in his arms and throwing her at the wall with all his might. She'd fallen, dazed, bruised and terrified, only to have him come at her with a doubled-up belt. He'd snapped it on the way to her. The sound, loud even above the thunder of the storm outside; the horror of the blows, the blood...

She turned on the light and went to look in her mirror. Her face, like her mother's had been, was covered with tears, flushed, anguished. The boy had never come back. Gracie had been bundled out of the house, bloody and sobbing, by her mother. Her father's threats had followed them as they ran next door for help. Her mother got away. Gracie didn't. She wasn't quick enough to escape her father's pursuing rage. She was lifted, carried forcibly back to her own home while her mother screamed and begged from the yard next door.

Blue lights flashing. Sirens. Men in a van, dressed like soldiers, but all in black. Big guns. Gracie trapped in her father's arms, being dragged to the door, the pistol held at her head, her father laughing. Her mother might leave him, but Gracie would die, and she'd have to live with it. Taunting, refusing to speak with a negotiator. He wanted the news media to know it was the fault of Gracie's faithless, whoring mother. Gracie would die now, in time for the six o'clock news! He yelled it to the policemen who were standing with their weapons drawn in the street. And he started to pull the trigger.

A shot. One shot. A crack like thunder. Wetness on Gracie's face, in her mouth, metallic and thick; a searing pain in her head as she and her father both fell to the wet ground...

She jerked her mind back to the present. Jason had kissed her. His mouth had pressed down hard on her breast. Had he meant to grind his teeth into her flesh, the way her father had done to her poor mother? She'd told

Gracie never to marry, that a man lured a woman in, and then he beat her and tortured her in the bedroom, because it was the only way he felt any pleasure or release. Gracie understood. Sex was only for a man's pleasure, and a woman paid for it with pain. Blood and screams and pain...

Gracie gripped the edge of her dresser and felt sick. She'd run from Jason. He must think she found him disgusting. She wished she could apologize, but that would involve admitting the truth about her father and mother, and she couldn't do that. If she did, Jason would probably throw her out of the house. It would be a terrible scandal if anyone ever found out about Gracie's past. But it had been a long time ago, and people had short memories these days. Nobody would connect the newspaper article about the bloody little girl crying in a policeman's arms beside her father's body outside the dilapidated little house, with the grown woman who lived in a mansion. Especially when her own mother had told everyone that Gracie was only her stepchild. Nobody knew that her last name had been legally changed in the days just after her father's death, to Marsh—her mother's maiden name. She was safe.

She dabbed at her eyes as she stared at the puffy-eyed woman in the mirror. Her mother had been beautiful. Gracie favored her father, whose face had been ordinary. She had a nice mouth and her figure was well-proportioned, if a little small-breasted. Her long hair, twisted into a tight bun, would have been her best feature if she'd let it stay loose. But it was like Gracie, tied up tightly so that it couldn't ever escape. Inside, Gracie was tied up in horrible memories.

Jason would hate her now. Maybe that was best. He

wouldn't be tempted to touch her again, to make her so weak that she wanted to do anything he liked. She felt a sense of profound loss. She would have loved being a normal woman. Jason was a kind, gentle, very masculine sort of man, for whom women held no mystery. He would make a wonderful husband and father.

But Gracie was certain that she could never submit her body to a man's physical dominance. She had men friends—mostly gay ones—but she'd never had what they called a "hot date." Word got around early in the circles she frequented that Gracie was ice-cold. It suited her that people thought that. It saved her the humiliation of refusing any man who saw her as dessert after a nice dinner. It protected her from amorous advances. Especially now. Jason would think she was frigid, that she didn't want him to touch her. It hurt to let him think that. But it was the only way she could escape her mother's fate. Even Jason, in passion, would be the same as her father. Hadn't she felt his mouth grinding into her soft breast? He hadn't used his teeth—but then, she'd pushed him away just in time. Just in time. She turned away from the mirror. She felt dead inside.

4

JASON WALKED THROUGH the sophisticated New York crowd at the cocktail party in a daze. He was racked with torment over what had happened with Gracie. She'd never forgive him, even if it had been her teasing that had precipitated things. He was trying to forget that he'd crossed the line with her long before she went into the ditch in the rain. It had begun at that party, two days after the auction. He'd gone over the line then. He'd almost kissed her. The night in the rain, he hadn't been able to hold back any longer. His anguished desire for her had consumed him in those scant, passionate minutes on the front porch of the mansion in San Antonio. For a few precious seconds, Gracie had clung to him, answering the hunger of his mouth. But then she'd started fighting him, pushing him away. Her rejection had been absolute. Her expression had been horrified. She'd looked at him as if he were the devil himself.

He was working his way through his second whiskey highball of the evening—an anomaly for a man who never drank hard liquor. He'd only been drunk one other time, when the family attorney had given him the sealed letter that was left with his father's will. In it was a revelation that had knocked Jason flat. His father had been a snob, but even Jason had never expected that he could be so cruel and insensitive.

The letter said that he was leaving nothing to the household staff because they were of inferior birth. Especially Mrs. Harcourt, he'd added. Jason recalled the sacrifices Mrs. Harcourt had made for him over the years, being a surrogate mother after his own had died when he was only five years old. She'd been his comfort, his security. She'd taken care of him when he was sick. Hell, she'd taken care of his snobbish father when *he* was sick. And for that, she was left nothing because she was of inferior birth. Jason had been so repulsed that he'd never shared the contents of that letter. He'd just gotten drunk, amazed that his father could be so damned insensitive. Glory and Gracie hadn't been related to him, but he'd left them money. Why had he been so deliberately scathing about Mrs. Harcourt? he'd wondered. Perhaps he was jealous of the attention she gave Jason, or felt it was inappropriate. God only knew the truth.

The pain of the letter was still festering inside him all these years later. Now it joined the agony his desire for Gracie had carved in him. It was a vicious, unrequited desire that threatened to destroy him as a man. For two long years, it had burned like an endless flame inside him, raging for release. All he'd been able to feed it was one long, anguished kiss. It would be the only one. Gracie would never let him touch her again. Her expression had told him that when she ran from him. It had been repellent to her, apparently, being kissed passionately by a man she'd thought of as a brother. But there was no blood between them. They weren't related, even in the tiniest degree. That hadn't mattered. Gracie would never forgive him for what he'd done. Now, alongside the endless hunger for her would be the revulsion in her eyes, when they met again. He groaned under his breath as he tossed down another swallow of his drink.

A beautiful, vivacious redhead moved to join him at the drinks table where he was adding more whiskey and another cube of ice to his glass.

"Hi," she greeted him. "Are you the reclusive millionaire from Texas that everybody's talking about?" she asked, grinning. She had very pale blue eyes in an exquisitely beautiful face. Long red hair billowed down her back almost to her waist, waves undulating like the sea in its silky length.

"I must be," he drawled. "I'm wearing his clothes."

Her eyes brightened. "They say you have a ranch."

He shrugged. "Honey, every man in Texas has a ranch, and a horse and a gun."

"And a worldwide corporation that manufactures computers and cutting-edge software?" she teased.

"Maybe not that," he agreed. He sipped his drink, looking around at the bright, pretty people in this New York City penthouse. He moved to the window, looking out across the multijeweled expanse of Manhattan, all the way to the Hudson River. "It really is something to see," he mused.

"I'll bet Texas is, too," she said. "I've never been to Texas."

"Now that's a shame," he murmured, smiling down at her. "What do you do for a living?"

"I'm a model," she said with a faintly insulted look. "Surely you read the sports magazine's swimsuit issue."

He did, and he recalled seeing her in it—a long-legged

sexy woman with come-hither eyes. She was using them on him now, and he was weakening. His ego was even with his shoes. He needed to be reminded that some women thought of him as an attractive man.

"Who are you here with?" he asked.

She laughed. "Nobody. I broke up with my latest boyfriend a month ago."

"What a shame," he remarked drily.

"Are you married?" she asked in a soft, purring tone.

"God forbid!"

The smile grew bigger.

HE DIDN'T REMEMBER MUCH of the rest of the party. He remembered starting on his third whiskey highball and muttering that Gracie was a cold fish, and then he stumbled a little. The redhead guided him to the door and down into a cab. The last thing he remembered was sinking down onto a huge, soft bed.

But when he woke up, things suddenly became clear. He was lying under the sheets in his black silk boxer shorts. Next to him was a very nude redheaded woman, sound asleep on his arm.

It didn't take a program to know what had happened. Anguish washed over him in waves. He'd had too much to drink. His throbbing head told him that. In his desperation to forget what had happened with Gracie, he'd gone headlong into bed with this strange woman. If he couldn't remember anything, he was at least certain that he'd neglected to use protection, because he didn't carry any with him. This beautiful creature curled up in his arms had obviously found him irresistible and now he faced the prospect of having fathered a child with her because of his lack of control.

He rolled onto his back with a groan. It had been a long time since he'd had a woman. Not since his passion for Gracie had become an obsession. The abstinence had worked like an aphrodisiac, he imagined bitterly. He was rich and this woman obviously coveted his wealth. He'd been an easy mark. Now what did he do?

Nothing would ever be the same at home again. Gracie would blame him for that furious kiss and hate him for it. He would never have her for his own. He was thirty-four years old, facing a lonely future that yawned ahead like an abyss.

He didn't want to go home alone. He didn't want to face Gracie as he was, with his pride in ashes and his ego lacerated from her rejection.

On the other hand, he wasn't anxious to let this woman out of his sight. If they'd had unprotected sex, she might become pregnant from his lack of foresight. He cringed, thinking how suddenly and permanently he'd just excised Gracie from his life with this act of lust. And what if there was a child…

A child. His child. He smiled at the thought. He could have a child, someone of his own, someone to love and be loved by. His head turned and he looked at the sleeping woman. She was pretty, young, pliable. Whether or not he'd slipped up, did it matter? Why not marry her and have a family? She couldn't be any worse than the other dozen gold diggers who'd stalked him over the years. At least this one was beautiful and desirable. She was even famous, after a fashion.

He imagined walking into the mansion in San Antonio with this woman on his arm, and seeing Gracie's shocked face. She didn't want him. This woman obviously did. He wouldn't think ahead. He wouldn't let himself consider the consequences of the impulsive decision. He'd already gone over the line, in a lot of ways. He might as well let fate take him where it liked. He had nothing left of his dreams. He would settle for what he could get. He laid back down and closed his eyes.

IT HAD TAKEN GRACIE several days to recover. She was sorry that she'd messed things up with Jason again. When she'd gone to the ranch, she had hoped that they could at least get back on a friendly footing. Instead she'd only managed to push them further apart.

It was Mrs. Harcourt's birthday. Gracie had organized a caterer as a treat, sparing Mrs. Harcourt the fuss of having to prepare her own dinner. At least, she thought, even if Jason didn't come over for the celebration like he usually did, Glory and her husband, Rodrigo, would. But at the last minute, Glory called and canceled. Rodrigo had to go to Washington, D.C., on an urgent matter, and she was going with him. She couldn't let him go alone, she'd explained to Gracie. They'd been married almost a year, but she couldn't bear to be apart from him. He was working out of the San Antonio DEA office now, and Glory was an assistant prosecutor in the office of Jacobsville's District Attorney, Blake Kemp. They lived in Jacobsville, but they often visited the Pendleton mansion. Glory had sent Mrs. Harcourt a lovely and expensive handbag and a card, apologizing for having to bow out of the celebration. As the dinner hour approached, Gracie winced at the expression on Mrs. Harcourt's face. The elderly woman was very fond of Jason; and no wonder, she'd been with him all his life. It would hurt her if Jason opted out because of what had happened.

Mrs. Harcourt was worried. "Jason hasn't left a

message on the answering machine while we were out of the room?" she asked.

Gracie shook her head. She felt guilty and hoped it didn't show. "Grange said he was in New York at some business conference. He's been there for over a week. He didn't say when he'd be back."

The older woman looked at the beautifully set table. "Everything's ready in the kitchen," she said miserably. "All that food…"

"We'll give what's left to one of the soup kitchens," she said gently.

Mrs. Harcourt smiled. "That's nice."

"Yes, it is. I…" She paused. A car was driving up out front. Maybe, she hoped, it was Jason!

"You think he came after all?" Mrs. Harcourt asked hopefully.

"I'll go see."

Gracie almost ran to the front door. He'd forgiven her! They were going to make up after all. Everything would be okay.

She opened the door with a beaming smile on her face and suddenly became as still as a stone statue. Because Jason wasn't alone.

He was smiling. He had a beautiful redheaded woman with him. She was hanging on to his hand and looking up at him as if she'd won the lottery. When he glanced toward the front door and saw Gracie, the smile left his face.

"Hello, Gracie," he said coolly. "We came for Mrs. Harcourt's birthday party."

Gracie looked as shocked and hurt as he'd hoped she might. Was that disappointment, too? But too late. Far too late.

She worked at regaining her lost composure. She put

on her party smile. "Hello," she said to the redhead. "I'm Gracie Marsh…"

"Yes, the stepsister," the woman said in an amused, condescending tone. "I couldn't believe it when Jason told me. Imagine, a woman your age still living at home!"

Gracie stepped back as they entered. The balmy breeze kissed her face before she closed the door behind her. It was the biggest shock she'd had in her adult life, and the pain was ricocheting inside her.

"Mrs. Harcourt, come out here, please," Jason called to the woman standing beside the dining-room table, wearing a nice dress, hose and flat shoes.

She came into the room, exchanging glances with Gracie, who was feeling decimated.

"I'd like you both to meet Kittie Sartain," he said softly. "My fiancée."

Gracie didn't pass out. She felt as if she might for one horrible moment, but Mrs. Harcourt stepped in quickly to divert the two newcomers.

"I'm Mrs. Harcourt, the housekeeper," she said.

"What a pretty dining room," Kittie said, ignoring the older woman. She walked around her. "Lovely china," she said. "I'm starved!"

"We'll be eating momentarily," Mrs. Harcourt stammered. She didn't look at Jason.

"Sounds great," Jason said pleasantly. "We've had a rough trip. The planes were grounded for a false alert. We sat on the runway for an hour."

"I hate commercial flights," Kittie said dismissively. "My last boyfriend owned a Learjet. You should get one, Jason, it cuts down on aggravation."

"I'll think about it," he said with a cool smile. "Where's Glory and her husband?" he added.

"Rodrigo had to fly to D.C. on business. Glory went with him," Gracie said in a subdued tone.

"I see."

"What in the world is with all these Christmas decorations?" Kittie burst out, gaping as she surveyed two boxes of wreaths that were sitting outside in the hall—they'd just arrived and Gracie hadn't had time to get them upstairs. She hadn't really expected Jason to show up.

"Gracie likes to decorate for the holidays," Mrs. Harcourt began.

"Red and green, how trite," the newcomer muttered as she glanced in the boxes. She was wearing a silky white pantsuit that was obviously very expensive. It showed off her pretty figure to its best advantage. "Nobody in my circle even celebrates Christmas anymore—it's so retro!"

Gracie didn't know what to say. She'd never had anyone speak to her in such a way. She glanced at Jason, but he was looking at the redhead with pure delight.

"I made a chocolate cake," Mrs. Harcourt began.

"None for me, thanks, I'm dieting. I hope you don't cook with butter and grease," Kittie continued. "I never eat saturated fats!"

"We'll make changes," Jason said comfortably. He sat down at the head of the table. "Happy birthday," he added in a gentler tone. He pushed a jewelry box toward the older woman.

Mrs. Harcourt was obviously fuddled, but she managed to get the box open. She touched the pretty decorative pin with adoring fingers. "Pearls and rubies. My favorites! Thank you, Jason. I'll wear it on my suit for church Sunday."

"Church." Kittie rolled her eyes.

Mrs. Harcourt looked hunted. Jason glanced at Kittie and frowned.

She saw his expression and immediately sat up straighter. "I helped Jason pick out the pin," she said brightly. "I'm glad you like it."

"It's very nice," the older woman stammered.

"Can you bring out the food now?" Jason asked. "We didn't get anything on the plane."

"Sure thing. The caterers fixed the meal, and it's all ready for us," Mrs. Harcourt said.

As she spoke, John and Dilly came into the room. John was tall and silver-haired. He'd been the family chauffeur for years and years. He was wearing casual clothes, as Gracie had told him to. So was Dilly, who did the heavy lifting and scrubbing; she was a large girl a few years older than Gracie, with big bones and a plain face. She was wearing slacks and a sweater.

"This is John, our chauffeur," Gracie introduced. "And Dilly, who helps Mrs. Harcourt with the housework."

Kittie stared at them. "Are they going to help serve dinner?"

Gracie's gray eyes widened. "They're family. They always eat with us on special occasions."

Kittie gave Jason a speaking look. He ignored it.

"I don't mind helping to serve," Dilly said, embarrassed.

"I just came in to tell you that I couldn't stay. My brother's in town and wants to see me," John lied, thinking quickly. "I have my cell phone, if you need me. Happy birthday, Mrs. Harcourt."

"Thank you, John," the elderly woman said, wincing at his expression.

Dilly looked at him piteously, as if she wanted to run for the hills, too, but was stuck.

"John, Dilly, this is Kittie, my fiancée," Jason introduced the redhead. "She's one of the top models in the country. You've probably seen her face on magazine covers."

If not at the post office, Gracie thought wickedly, but didn't say anything.

"Yes, I stay very busy," Kittie said in a haughty tone. "In fact, I'm booked up for the next three months. I'll be doing shoots all over the world. You'll have to manage to live without me, darling," she teased Jason.

He smiled back at her, but only with his mouth. His eyes were empty.

"Congratulations," John told him. "I hope you'll be happy."

"Thanks."

John paused for a moment and then turned and left the room. Gracie's heart was breaking. Their family, their loyal friends and workers were being made to feel like somebody's unwanted houseguests. That horrible redhead didn't even care, and Jason was so cold that Gracie didn't even recognize him. He'd only been gone a couple of weeks, for heaven's sake, how could he have managed to get engaged so quickly and not even tell anybody!

"Are we ever going to eat?" the redhead asked Jason, smoothing her hand seductively over his on the table. "I . . . ungry, Jason."

Gracie pushed back her chair and got to her feet. "I'll help," she told Mrs. Harcourt and Dilly, and went ahead of them into the kitchen.

"Imagine asking the hired help to eat at the table with you," Kittie complained. "And letting your stepsister live with you, at her age?" she exclaimed. "What in the world must people think?"

Gracie dragged the other two women into the kitchen and closed the door, leaning back against it with her eyes closed. She'd walked into a nightmare.

"Who is she?" Dilly exclaimed, horrified.

Gracie took a steadying breath. "You heard. She's Jason's fiancée," she said in a voice so choked with pain that it was barely audible. "He's going to marry her."

Dilly looked sick. So did Mrs. Harcourt, who seemed to be taking it harder than anyone.

There was a tap on the door and Jason pushed it open, accidentally propelling Gracie farther into the room. The three women looked at him with expressions that ranged from shock to despair. What had seemed like a good idea in New York was rebounding with a fury down here in Texas. He felt guilty, and he hid it in bad temper.

"You'll get used to her," he said tersely. "She's not as bad as she seems. She just doesn't know you."

Nobody said a word.

Jason's black eyes narrowed. "Regardless of how you feel, I expect all of you to treat her with respect and make her feel welcome."

"Of course, Jason," Gracie said without looking directly at him. "It's your house, after all."

"Yes," he replied flatly. "It is my house." He went back out.

"If I were us," Dilly told Mrs. Harcourt sadly, "I'd be looking around for another job, just in case."

Gracie was in agreement. Except that she'd never had a job and wasn't sure of her ability, due to her mental glitches, to even hold one down. But one thing was for certain. She could not live under the same roof with that woman, once she and Jason were married.

"This is going to be some birthday, Mrs. Harcourt," Dilly said heavily as she went to look for an apron.

Gracie agreed silently. She looked at poor Mrs. Harcourt, whose eyes were already full of tears. She wanted to hug the older woman and reassure her, but nothing was going to help now. Nothing at all.

IT WAS ONE OF THE worst days of Gracie's life. Kittie complained about everything, nibbled at salad, sipped black coffee and muttered at the quality of the food. After the meal she and Jason retired to the living room, where she curled up on his lap and spent the evening kissing him.

Mrs. Harcourt got a room ready for her, although the women had speculated bitterly that she'd probably move in with Jason. He'd nipped that suggestion in the bud with more force than a surprised Kittie had anticipated.

"Aren't you the old-fashioned one," she taunted. "Especially after how things were in New York," she added insinuatingly.

Gracie was sick all the way to her soul. Jason had removed any doubts that he was interested in Gracie romantically. If he had been, this engagement wouldn't be happening. She'd read too much into a kiss. She was a woman, he was a man, and she'd started it, as he accused. He was only taking advantage of an offer, as any man would. But she'd hoped they could make up, that things would go back to the way they were. Now she realized how impossible that hope was.

Kittie was short with her and with everyone else in the house. She was wearing a huge diamond on her ring finger, and she was never six inches away from Jason except at night. They stayed for a week, during which

Gracie and the other members of the household found reasons not to interact with the visitors. Jason took his fiancée to any number of cultural events, including the ballet and the symphony. It puzzled Gracie that Jason hadn't taken Kittie down to the ranch, until she overheard the woman holding forth on her views about smelly cattle and spending time in a glorified shack with dirty cowboys milling around.

Kittie didn't lose an opportunity to tell the women of the house that changes were going to be made when she came back to spend Thanksgiving. For one thing, they needed a better caterer, and for another, the house was absolutely Gothic in its decor. It needed remodeling badly. Gracie's room, she added with menace, was like a child's room, all lace and pink and white, and needed updating. Of course, she said for the umpteenth time, it was really bighearted of Jason to let his stepsister live with him, but wasn't Gracie old enough to support herself by now? She alluded to Mrs. Harcourt's age and muttered that she was beyond ancient, like the chauffeur. And that Dilly was an absolute embarrassment! She looked far too country to work in a mansion.

Not that Kittie made those remarks in front of Jason. When he was around, she praised everybody, even Gracie. That way, if anybody complained about her to Jason, he'd know they were lying.

Jason tolerated Kittie's advances, but if Gracie had been watching, she might have noticed that all the overtures were hers. He seemed to be playing a waiting game with regard to the lovely model.

He didn't spend five minutes alone with Gracie, which was a relief to her. She was still shell-shocked by his sudden engagement. She'd always thought that he'd marry one day, but she'd expected it to be a woman he knew, someone who shared his background. This model was like someone from another planet. Yes, she was beautiful and cultured and worldly. But she was joyless. She liked the house, but only for its possessions. Sentiment had no place in her life. She liked cold, hard cash and men. Gracie overheard her talking to someone on the phone, bragging about her sexual exploits with a variety of men. She was engaged to a man who was dynamite in bed, she told the listener, so as long as he could satisfy her, she'd stay with him. But there was a Middle-Eastern prince who also coveted her, and he was much richer than Jason. Relationships were such a bother, she sighed. Men only wanted sex, but when they were rich, it was no hardship for her. She could fake pleasure as long as the gifts she got in return were expensive.

Gracie, who'd never known even one man intimately, was shocked by the woman's attitude. Was that really the meaning of life, to have sex with as many people as possible so that you fit in the status quo? It seemed a particularly empty life to Gracie, who was happy with the simplest things and wanted no part of orgies. It must be in the upbringing, she decided. Then she remembered hers and shuddered.

SHE DROVE DOWN TO Jacobsville several days after Mrs. Harcourt's birthday in desperation to escape the constant sight of Kittie plastered to Jason. There was an endless influx of visitors to the mansion, as well, mostly rich and famous people whom Jason knew that Kittie wanted to become acquainted with. That was after the shopping spree at Neiman Marcus, from which the redhead came home with numerous boxes of expensive clothing, shoes, perfume and jewelry.

"Yes, we know about your new houseguest," Barbara said sympathetically. She could read the misery in Gracie's face. "Is he really going to marry her?"

"How do you know about her?" Gracie asked.

"He was showing her off at the ballet. Rick went along as an off-duty bodyguard for Keely Welsh when she went there with Clark Sinclair."

Gracie sighed. "Well, she's beautiful."

"Rick wasn't impressed. She snubbed him. He wasn't rich, you see."

"I thought she'd probably be like that," she replied. "Jason seems to be very happy with her."

"I'm sorry."

She moved a shoulder. "It was inevitable that he'd get married someday. But I can't live with her." She sighed miserably. "I have to get a job and go to work. I have to find a place to live."

"Gracie, don't jump the gun," Barbara said gently. "It's a long way from an engagement to the altar."

"She says they'll marry at Christmas," she moaned.

Barbara winced. "Maybe…"

"Maybe not." She swallowed. "I could teach, you know. I have a degree in history. Maybe there's a night job as an adjunct at the community college. I could teach that without a master's degree."

Barbara hesitated. Then she sighed. "Okay, I know the president of the college. I'll call him tonight."

Gracie smiled. "Thanks. I'll have to find a place to live…"

"No, you won't. You can stay with me."

"Oh, I couldn't impose," she began.

"I'll enjoy having the company. Rick's almost never home lately. I'd love to just have somebody to talk to."

"As if you don't talk to people every day," Gracie teased.

"It isn't the same as talking to a friend. When do you want to start?" She hesitated. "May I make a suggestion? Wait until spring semester. That starts in January. By then, you may not want or need a job."

"Or I may need one desperately," Gracie replied. "I need to find something for Mrs. Harcourt and Dilly and John, too. Kittie will boot them out before she boots me out."

"Jason won't let that happen."

"You don't know this woman," Gracie insisted. "She'll force them to leave and tell Jason it was their own decision and she couldn't talk them out of it. She's a master at manipulation." She looked worried. "Can I bring Mumbles?"

"Your cat?"

She nodded. "He's been at the vet's for the past three weeks, while they get him over a kidney infection. He's old, you know, and he won't last many more years, but I can't leave him behind."

"I love cats. Bring him along."

She brightened. "You're the nicest friend I've got."

"Well, I could return that compliment," Barbara replied. "Now stop thinking doom and gloom and let's have some pie!"

5

As it was, Jason did speak to Gracie just before he and Kittie were driven to the airport by a somber John. Gracie had brought old Mumbles home from the vet, his kidney infection cured. He was a huge feline with big blue eyes and orange tips on his ears and tail. His fur was long and luxurious, and Gracie kept it brushed. With his rhinestone collar, Mumbles was the very picture of a pampered pet. But his beauty made no impression on Kittie, who no sooner walked into the living room where the big cat was occupying a cushy armchair, than she started sneezing her head off. Gracie had removed him to her room with apologies, but Kittie hadn't even answered her. She'd given Gracie a look that promised retribution.

And here it was. Jason looked down at her with smoldering eyes in a taciturn face. "You'll have to do something about Mumbles before we come back for Thanksgiving, Gracie," he told her quietly. "Kittie's allergic to cats."

How ironic, she thought, but didn't say it. "What

would you like me to do with him, Jason?" she asked worriedly.

"He can't be in the house with Kittie," he said, averting his gaze. This stupid engagement was carrying a high price tag already.

"He's twelve years old and he's never been outside in his life," she said miserably. "I can't put him out in the yard."

"Kittie's allergic to cats," he repeated tersely. "She was only sneezing yesterday, but she usually breaks out in hives when she gets around them."

Gracie didn't let him see her eyes. She mustn't cry.

"Oh, for God's sake, he's only an old cat—not a child!" he shouted, angered out of all proportion by the possibility of tears. It was killing him to hurt her like this! He'd given her the damned cat. It had been a revelation, the way she reacted to the gift. He'd wondered if she'd ever had a present in her whole young life. And now the cat was the cause of a major argument with Kittie, who wouldn't compromise and Jason was caught in the crossfire between a fiancée he didn't want and the woman he ached to have who didn't want him. He was furious at his own feeling of helplessness.

The whip of his voice caused Gracie to actually back away from him. Her face was paper-white. It had been years since he'd snapped at her like that, since he'd looked so harsh. It was the end of everything. Kittie hated her and was searching for ways to make her move out of the house. The staff was miserable and resigned to being pushed out, as well. She was sorry about Kittie's allergies, but poor Mumbles was old and sick and had no place to go. Now Jason seemed to be leading up to the possibility of euthanasia!

"He's old, Gracie," he said harshly. "He doesn't have

much time left, anyway. It might be a mercy to just put him down."

"I am not having him put down!" she burst out. Her lower lip trembled. She couldn't remember ever standing up to Jason before. But she was fighting for Mumbles, now, for his very life. Her fists clenched at her side. "If you want us both to leave, just say so."

"And what would you do?" he asked hotly. "Get a job? What are you qualified to do except give teas and hostess parties, Gracie?" he added coldly.

She reacted to the words as if he'd slapped her, and he could have bitten his tongue for the slip.

"I am not an idiot, Jason," Gracie replied tightly. "And maybe I can do a lot of things you don't think I can do!"

He didn't say a word. He just looked at her.

That was the last straw. So that was what he really thought of her, out in the open. He'd never demeaned her like that before. Hurt and furious, she turned on her heel and ran up the staircase to her room as if the hounds of hell were on her heels. Once she was safely inside, she locked the door and sat by the window, shaking all over. This was the only real home she'd ever known. She'd felt secure in this house. She and the staff had loved each other, nurtured each other. Mumbles had been part of the joy she felt in living here for over twelve years, ever since Jason had given him to her as a Christmas present. And now, in the blink of an eye, everything changed. Once that vicious redhead had walked in the door, it was all over. She was going to lose everything she loved. Her family, her home, even her cat. And especially Jason!

There was a loud rap on the door. "Gracie!" Jason called urgently.

She didn't answer him. Her heart was breaking.

He tried the door. It wouldn't open.

There was another pause. "Gracie," he called again, less angrily.

He muttered something. A minute later, she heard his footsteps fading away. Gracie knew then that she was going to be gone before he and his fiancée came back at Thanksgiving.

"Isn't your stepsister even going to say goodbye to us?" Kittie asked in her soft, husky voice as they climbed into the limousine.

His face hardened. "She's upset about the cat."

"It's just a cat," she said breezily. "She can get another one when she has a house of her own."

He frowned. "What do you mean—a house of her own?"

"Well, darling, you don't expect her to live with us?" she exclaimed, horrified. "I mean, what would people think? Besides, I'm not sharing you with other people. Especially not a grasping, greedy woman like that."

"Gracie isn't greedy," he said curtly.

"She isn't making any effort to support herself, now, is she?" she asked. "All these years, living off you, letting you pay for everything she owns—even her clothes. It isn't right. I'm sure people must gossip about the two of you."

He was feeling royally sick to his stomach. His little game of payback had destroyed his family. He got a glimpse of John's pale, set face in the rearview mirror. He'd have to make sure he spoke to the man—and to Dilly—when he came back, to reassure them about their place with him. And especially Mrs. Harcourt, he thought miserably. She'd been so happy that he'd remembered her birthday, only to have Kittie treat her like a servant. He closed his eyes on a wave of pain. She'd had so little in her life. All her sacrifices, and his father hadn't left her a dime. Jason had tried to make sure she was appreciated ever since. He should have said something when Kittie insulted her. And Gracie… She was heartsick about her poor old cat and he'd made matters worse by unleashing his anger on her moments ago.

Kittie saw an opportunity and took it. "You know," she said in a confidential tone, easing closer to him and toying with his shirt collar, "she's in her midtwenties and unmarried. Doesn't that suggest to you that she doesn't want to rock the boat?"

"Excuse me?"

"Well, if she marries, she loses everything…doesn't she? You're not likely to keep supporting her in such an extravagant manner. She can't afford to marry, can she?"

The terrible suggestion unnerved him. He'd never looked at it in that light. Was Gracie so attached to her lifestyle that she stayed single not because she'd never found a man she could love, but because she wouldn't be coddled by Jason anymore? Surely not! He knew she wasn't a selfish woman. Still…

"Are you all right, darling?" Kittie asked, concerned. "You don't look well."

He swallowed the pride he was choking on. "I'm working on a buyout of a German computer company," he said tersely. "It's been frustrating."

She moved close to him and curled up at his side. "I can take care of frustration," she purred. "You just wait and see."

It would be a long wait, he thought miserably. His body had absolutely no interest in her, despite her fabled, sultry beauty. He was unable to make love to her, a fact he'd managed to camouflage with excuses. Her long trip overseas would give him breathing space. But he didn't hold out much hope that he was going to be able to honor the halfhearted commitment he'd made to her. His wounded pride over Gracie's rejection had served him up on a platter to Kittie. As for his thought that he might have gotten her pregnant, that was a laugh. He'd seen her little container of birth-control pills, which she kept on the bedside table.

She'd been amused about their so-called encounter the night he was drunk, when he'd gone fishing in conversation for the chances of her becoming pregnant. Children, she'd scoffed, that wasn't for her. She was a maniac about birth control. Her career was the most important thing in her life. She had no desire to change diapers and give bottles and lose her figure. Besides, she laughed, Jason hadn't even been capable. He'd passed out on the bed and left her to undress him. Later, when he was through all the stress produced by his merger, she said in a world-wise tone, he could make this enforced abstinence up to her. She knew it was business pressure that had made him temporarily incapable. It happened to men sometimes, she said wisely. In fact, her last boyfriend had been similarly afflicted from time to time. So had her other lovers.

Jason felt a skirl of distaste when she bragged about her conquests. He'd heard younger men boasting about how many women they'd had, and it had disgusted him. It reminded him of his father, who'd never been faithful to any of his wives. Jason had never wanted to be like him.

Kittie kept trying to seduce him, but she seemed to realize that he wasn't attracted to her and, worse, she seemed to feel that Gracie was to blame for it. It had made for some catty and insulting remarks that he'd ignored, but he wouldn't be able to ignore them indefinitely. When she was through with her overseas shoots, he was going to have to find some way to break off the engagement. Perhaps with something very expensive that she craved. He knew already that it was his wealth that kept her at his side. She'd insinuated that Gracie stayed around for the same reason. He didn't want to believe that. But what did he really know about the background of the woman he'd shared his home with for so long? Her past was mysterious. His eyes narrowed. He was going to have to do some digging, he decided. He didn't like secrets.

He managed a word alone with John at the airport, but the other man was quiet and unresponsive, refusing to meet his eyes.

"We'll work all this out by Christmas," Jason told his chauffeur firmly.

John's thin shoulders rose and fell. "Nothing to work out, Mr. Pendleton," he said politely. "We're all too old to still be doing these jobs anyway, like your fiancée said. Have a good trip."

"John!"

But the chauffeur was already in the car, driving away.

Jason cursed roundly. He barely heard Kittie calling him from the entrance to the terminal.

He phoned the house while Kittie was in the restroom. Mrs. Harcourt answered.

"Don't let John walk out," he said tersely. "That goes double for you and Dilly. We'll talk when I come home. I'm going to be in Europe for trade talks, but I'll be back here in a week or two. After that, I'll probably have to go to Germany to sort out that mess, but we'll discuss some things at the house first."

Mrs. Harcourt hesitated. "All right, Mr. Jason."

He winced. "Don't call me that!"

"I just work for you," she said quietly. "That's all. You need servants who fit in with Miss Kittie's sort of folks," she said gently. "We'll just be an embarrassment to you. Maybe we already are. Mr. Myron would never have let us stay if he'd lived."

"I'm not my father!"

She swallowed hard. "Still, we can find something else…"

"No!"

She didn't say anything.

"We'll talk about it when I get home. Kittie opens her mouth and words fall out. She doesn't consider other people's feelings. It's the company she keeps." He hated apologizing for the woman. He drew in a long breath. "How's Gracie?"

She didn't say anything then, either.

"Mrs. Harcourt?"

"She's locked in her room, crying," she said heavily.

His eyes closed. "Dear God," he groaned. "I never meant to upset her like that. Tell her we'll do something about the damned cat, if I have to build on another room for him to live in! Besides, you're all making assumptions that may have no substance at all by Christmas."

"I'll tell her," she said.

"I'm sorry I spoiled your birthday," he said gently. "I hope you have fifty more, all better than this one."

"Thank you," she said, and her voice softened. "You be careful, over there in those dangerous places. Come home safe."

"I will. Look after Gracie," he said gruffly. "You know

how she is, when she's upset. I yelled at her. I never meant to hurt her like that."

"I know."

"Don't let her give the cat away."

"All right," Mrs. Harcourt said.

"I'll phone you from Europe."

"Take care."

"You, too," he replied.

She hung up. He flipped his phone shut and stared out over the terminal with dead eyes. His life was so messed up that he wondered if things would ever be the same again. And through it all, the nagging ache he felt when he thought of Gracie tortured him.

WEEKS DRAGGED BY. Then Kittie called and suddenly there was no more time. Gracie moved her things into Barbara's small house and was immensely grateful that she'd meant it about Mumbles being invited to live with them, too. She'd offered to consider euthanasia, in tears.

"Maybe Jason was right. He is old and he gets sick a lot. He'll throw up everywhere," Gracie sobbed, "and he still claws furniture."

"We'll manage," Barbara said firmly. "Gracie, you can't put down a pet who's like a member of your family just because some addlepated model doesn't like animals. It's not even her house!"

"It will be," Gracie said heavily. "Kittie phoned from some Scandinavian country last night to ask if I'd got rid of Mumbles yet. She mentioned that Jason was furious that I argued about getting rid of him." She hesitated, grimacing. "She actually said Jason wanted to ask me to leave years ago, but he felt sorry for me. And then Kittie insinuated that it was like I was a paid companion or something."

Barbara gathered her close and rocked her. "You take things so much to heart, Gracie. Besides, if Jason felt that way, he'd tell you to your face. He wouldn't need to ask someone else to do his dirty work."

Gracie wiped her wet eyes. "Maybe you're right. But there's some truth in it. I've never tried to stand on my own two feet. I've lived under his wing for so long, let him be responsible for me so long, that I forgot I was a grown woman." She pulled away, her expression calming. "Everybody laughs at me. They think I'm air-headed and clumsy and incapable of doing anything really important. Even Jason finally admitted that he didn't think I could do anything except hostess parties. I've let my…my affliction convince me that it was true. But it's not. I can make a living for myself. I can be independent. I'm going to be." Her soft gray eyes took on the glitter of silver metal. "No way am I living with that woman!"

Barbara liked that new resolution in her friend's face. "Listen to you," she teased. "You don't even sound like Gracie."

"Maybe I can be something more in life," she replied, drying her eyes. "Maybe I can teach, buy a car, be a whole person, without Jason standing behind me to prop me up."

"You've got a car already," Barbara argued.

Gracie set her teeth together, hard. "Not anymore. Kittie said Jason gave her permission to use the VW, since he paid for it."

"What?"

She drew in a shaky breath. "She's letting me use Jason's old Thunderbird to go back and forth until I get my stuff down here."

"Generous of her," Barbara scoffed.

"It doesn't matter. I can take care of myself. I'm going to."

"You can, indeed," Barbara reassured her. "A whole new life, Gracie."

"A whole new life." It made her sound like a bright penny, newly minted and full of promise. Now if only she could forget Jason and that interloper who was taking him away from her. It didn't help to think that if she'd put her arms around Jason and kissed him back passionately, she might not be in this predicament in the first place. But by bringing home his new fiancée, he'd made it clear that he wasn't interested in Gracie. He'd only been angry that she'd kissed him, accidentally or not, and tempted him into indiscretion. So maybe it was for the best. Considering her past, she could hardly expect a rosy future with a man, even if the man was Jason.

"Now bring Mumbles into the house and I'll look out for him while you go back to San Antonio and pack up the rest of your things," the other woman added.

"I told Kittie I'd bring Mumbles down here today, before she got to the house. That's when she said she'd be using my car and I'd have to borrow Jason's old Thunderbird," she said miserably. "He took the keys to the Mercedes with him, so I guess that meant he didn't want me driving it."

"Maybe he just forgot, too," Barbara said. "You said he's got a lot on his mind lately with business matters."

"I guess so."

"Listen, try not to drive around at night," Barbara added worriedly. "You know one of Jason's vice presidents was kidnapped last year, and there are new cases every week of people being snatched in the area and held for ransom. It even happened to Glory's husband,

Rodrigo, last year. It's well-known that Jason is wealthy."
She nibbled on her lip nervously. "Rick says that one of
the Fuentes brothers is now an underling to some deposed
South American dictator who's using the kidnappings to
fund a future coup to regain his position. You'd be lovely
bait. Jason would pay anything to get you back. They'd
know that. They have intelligence gatherers everywhere."

"Don't you get paranoid," Gracie chided. "Nobody's
going to look twice at that old Thunderbird, even if it is
a renovated classic automobile."

"I imagine the kidnappers would know every car he
owns and the tag numbers," Barbara added doggedly.
"They're making millions by bartering human lives."

"Mostly it's people from across the border, wealthy
Latinos, at that."

"Jason's vice president wasn't a wealthy Latino.
Neither was your brother-in-law, Rodrigo Ramirez, when
they kidnapped him for ransom," she reminded Gracie.

The younger woman grimaced. "Okay, point made.
But so far they haven't snatched anybody locally this
year. Until they do, I refuse to worry."

"Fine. Hide your head in the sand."

Gracie grinned. "Good advice. I'm going to take it,
too. Anyway, I have to get moved quickly. That nice
college president is going to give me a job, thanks to you,
and a friend of mine at the local elementary school has
invited me to do guest lectures on ethnic history," she
added with a beaming smile. "I'll get paid. First thing,
after I pay you rent, I'll have to go see Turkey Sanders
about buying a car of my own."

"No!" Barbara wailed. "Not Turkey! He'll sell you a
chassis and tell you the engine's extra!"

"I can handle Turkey," she replied calmly. "Wait and

see. I'll bring some clothes from the house, but I'm not packing evening gowns and fancy stuff," she added. "I'll have no use for them here." She laughed bitterly. "Kittie's my size. I expect she'll enjoy the Paris gowns."

"You should bring them along. There are all sorts of gala events up in San Antonio starting this month— symphony concerts, the opera, the Cattle Baron's Ball…"

"All in the past now. I'm no longer a socialite with money to invest in charities. And I wouldn't have a way to get up to San Antonio to attend the balls. Which reminds me," she added heavily, "I've got some pearls and diamonds that were in Mama's jewelry box that Myron gave me. I'm going to pawn them. That will buy me a car and help me pay you rent."

"I don't want rent," Barbara groaned. "You're my friend."

"You're mine, too," Gracie replied. "But I'm not letting you support me any more than I'm letting Jason do it in the future." She swallowed a lump in her throat. "I'm ashamed that I've sponged off him so long without even considering how wrong it was."

Barbara winced. She wished she could say something helpful, but she could see that Gracie was lost in misery and fear of the future.

And she was right. Despite her optimism, Gracie knew it was going to be a rough road to financial independence. She was used to buying anything she liked without considering the cost, to eating in the best restaurants and driving expensive cars. She would have to learn to economize and live at a much lower level. She could do it. But it would take time. She only hoped she had the stuff in her to prove Jason wrong about her opportunities. She was going to change her life, no matter how hard it was.

MRS. HARCOURT HAD ARGUED against the move, and she had a fit when Gracie started packing her last suitcase and left her best things in the closet. "But Mr. Jason said for you not to leave, that he'd do something about the cat," she protested.

"That venomous redhead will have somebody take Mumbles off to the vet and put him down the first time I turn my back," Gracie said coldly. "She's not killing my cat. And I'm not living here with Jason and his woman."

"But your mother's furniture, those antique Christmas ornaments, your clothes and keepsakes!" she fussed.

"I had John help me put the ornaments and the furniture in the attic, along with what few keepsakes I had left," Gracie replied. "I don't think Kittie will want to climb up there to throw them out. It's dusty. Not her type of place at all. If she does, though, it won't be the end of the world. I won't have any place to put that stuff now." She sighed wistfully. "Besides, Jason hates my Christmas ornaments and decorations. He won't mind having them tossed."

Mrs. Harcourt glanced regretfully at the beautiful gowns Gracie was leaving in the closet. "I don't understand why he got engaged to her," Mrs. Harcourt said heavily. "She's not his type at all. She's so shallow, Gracie. She doesn't care about anybody, not even about him, really, she just likes what he buys her."

"I don't imagine it's her emotional makeup that keeps him with her," Gracie said through clenched teeth. "I expect she's dynamite in bed. That's what she tells her friends when she calls them. She says Jason is, too."

Mrs. Harcourt sat down on the bed where Gracie was folding clothes. "He's confused," she said. "I think you are, too. He's not your brother, you know."

Gracie flushed. "Yes, I know," she said tightly, and her expression was revealing.

"So that's it," the older woman said thoughtfully. "Something happened. He frightened you and you ran, and he thought…"

"Don't read minds, it's not nice," Gracie muttered.

"It doesn't take mind-reading to see through people you love," the housekeeper said with a gentle smile. "She's his revenge, isn't she? Because you ran away and hurt his pride."

Gracie's eyes widened. She'd never considered that as a possibility. She looked down into her suitcase. "I don't think it's like that, really. It was flooding out front, and he was carrying me to the porch here after I ran in the ditch at his ranch. He turned his head to say something and I turned mine at the same time and we sort of…well, I kissed him. He was shocked, but then he kissed me back. But when I pushed him away, he was furious." She ground her teeth together. "He said it was my fault for teasing him like that. I was upset and confused. Of course I ran. I would have apologized, but he was long gone the next morning."

"He was standing very close to you at the party, before that," Mrs. Harcourt reminded her. "People talked about it. He seemed unusually interested in you."

Gracie shook her head. "I don't understand any of this."

"He doesn't know about your past, Gracie," she said after a minute. "You should have told him years ago."

She looked at the older woman in shock. "You don't know," she said worriedly. She heard a faint movement and stared toward the hall, but there was nothing there. She turned back to Mrs. Harcourt. "You can't possibly know about my past."

"Your mother confided in me," Mrs. Harcourt told her. "She knew something about me that isn't common knowledge. We traded sad stories during those two weeks she lived here." She squeezed Gracie's shoulder when the younger woman's face paled. "Gracie, all men aren't like your father was. You've lived in the past, afraid to move forward. It's destroying your life, and you're letting it."

"The alternative is to tell Jason the whole story, and if I do, he'll…" She swallowed. "He'll never look at me the same way again. I've lived in fear all my life that it would come out, that he'd be shamed along with me if people knew the truth." Her eyes closed. "It was a nightmare. And we were so poor, Mrs. Harcourt. Some days I couldn't go to school because I didn't want people to see me wearing the same clothes every single day of my life…!"

Mrs. Harcourt hugged her, rocked her in her arms while she cried. "You have to learn not to care what people think. Jason doesn't. And he won't look down on you if he finds out the truth. It wasn't your fault, honey. How can you imagine it was?"

"Daddy was so mad at me. If I'd gotten home on time, he'd still be alive. He died because of me." Tears ran down her cheeks.

"People die when it's time for them to die," the older woman said quietly. "That's God's business, not ours. Gracie, if he hadn't gone out of his mind on liquor and threatened you in the first place, or if he hadn't been so brutal to your mother… He wouldn't even let her work for fear that she'd run around on him. He was paranoid about her, and she never cheated on him. That poor woman. Good Lord, what a nightmare she lived all those years, brutally assaulted and afraid to leave because of what he might do to you." She shook her head. "I can't imagine how you think Jason would blame you."

"He thinks I came from good people, that my father died a war hero, that we were middle class and respectable." She laughed coldly. "It's a lie. All of it. My real mother made up a story that she was my stepmom to throw anyone off the track if they investigated our background. The police shot my father down like a dog to keep him from killing me. He would have, too. He was laughing. He said he'd teach Mama to try and leave him."

"Tell Jason," Mrs. Harcourt said firmly. "Get it out in the open."

"Right. Tell him and lose even his respect." Gracie shook her head. "What a field day the press would have with that story."

"Yes, wouldn't they?" a lilting voice commented wryly from the doorway.

Both women looked up. Kittie Sartain was standing there in a pretty blue pantsuit, with her red hair piled up in wild curls around her smiling face.

"So now I won't have to find ways to make you leave, will I? All I'll have to do is tell Jason what I've just overheard!"

Gracie pulled away from Mrs. Harcourt. "I'm already leaving. I've got a place to go. I'll just need to keep the Thunderbird for a couple of weeks, until I get settled and buy my own car," she said in a hollow tone. Her pride was lacerated. Kittie couldn't have picked a better time to just walk in unannounced. "I've already taken my cat away."

"That saved his life. I was going to take him to the vet for you and have him euthanized. I did say you can borrow that old Thunderbird," Kittie said coldly. "But you'll have to bring it back before Jason notices it missing. He's still mad, you know. He was furious about that cat."

"That isn't what he told me," Mrs. Harcourt replied curtly, glaring at the newcomer.

"Oh, who cares what he told you?" the redhead muttered. "You're just a relic of the past, kept on for sentiment. You'll go, too," she added with a cold smile.

"I won't," Mrs. Harcourt said quietly. "Mr. Jason told me to stay. He won't like it if Gracie leaves."

"He won't like it if she stays," the redhead said spitefully. "If she does, Jason's going to get an earful about his sweet stepsister."

Gracie paled. It was blackmail of the worst sort. But she was sick to her soul at the thought that Jason would know the truth about her.

She held up a hand when it seemed Mrs. Harcourt was about to argue. "Don't, Mrs. Harcourt. It's all right. I'll get the rest of my things and leave right now. But you and the others don't have to go."

Kittie waited in the hall until Mrs. Harcourt came out. She pulled the door shut and smiled haughtily at the housekeeper.

"You think you can stay?" Kittie asked. "I noticed something about you and Jason that his little stepsister never has. And one of my acquaintances in San Antonio knew a private detective who did a little digging for me." She smiled. "I wonder if Jason knows the whole truth about his own past, Mrs. Harcourt?"

For a shot in the dark, it worked like a charm. Mrs. Harcourt's face paled.

"That's right…you think about what sort of story I could give the tabloids, about Gracie and about you. Is it worth it?"

"No, it isn't. I'll go," Mrs. Harcourt said heavily. "Will you let Dilly and John stay?"

"Fat chance! I don't want to run a charity home. I've already told them they're on notice. That John character wanted to argue about it, but I know things about him that he'd like kept quiet. Do you want to argue about it?" she added with a vicious smile.

Mrs. Harcourt did. But she had a secret that she'd rather have died than let Jason know. "I'm sure that none of us want to live in the same house with you."

"That's mutual," Kittie said icily. "You've all got two days to find someplace to go." She held up a set of keys. "Jason gave me permission to remodel the house, and I'm doing it. I've already hired new staff, young people with energy and creative minds, who'll fit in nicely when Jason and I get married. Out with the old, in with the new," she said with a dismissive smile.

She turned on her heel and walked off, pressing numbers into her cell phone.

Gracie came out into the hall with her suitcase, and she and Mrs. Harcourt exchanged miserable glances. "Maybe if I asked, she'd let you stay, at least until Jason gets back," she said hopefully.

The older woman was terrified. She'd known no other home for thirty-five years. But she didn't dare stay. "No," she replied, without explaining. "I'm going to Jacobsville with you. Barbara always needs a good cook. I'll apply there. We'll take Dilly and John, too. We'll find something for them, as well. And you," she added firmly, "are going to show Jason that you're more competent than he gives you credit for. It won't hurt that young man to have his beliefs challenged. Especially now that he's destroyed his life by linking up with that redheaded shark downstairs."

Gracie actually smiled. She'd never heard the easy-going housekeeper talk like that about Jason. She'd always been his champion, never accepting any criticism of him from anyone. Perhaps they'd both grow into better people with the challenges ahead. She didn't let herself think about what life without Jason was going to be like. She didn't dare.

"Don't you worry about your past, Miss Gracie," Mrs. Harcourt said gently. "She won't tell him. He'd throw her out."

Gracie grimaced. "Do you think so? I don't. Come on. Let's talk to the others."

They talked to Dilly, but John had already packed his things and gone. He hadn't told Dilly where he meant to go. He'd looked frightened, too, she said. Gracie hoped they could find him later, but for the moment, she had to get the other two women out of the house. Herself, as well. If she stayed around Kittie any longer, she was going to punch her!

GRACIE WENT TO WORK as a special lecturer for the Jacobs County school system. Her first day was scary, but when she got up in front of the fifth-graders and began to tell them little-known facts about the battle of the Alamo, everybody sat up straight and paid attention. She brought the history of the battle alive, passing out Xerox copies of paintings and documents that emphasized the details she was providing. She got a standing ovation when she finished.

Her self-confidence grew after that. Despite a few disruptive students from time to time, she became known among the students and teachers alike. Before long, she was invited to give her lectures at the ninth-grade academy and the high school. She found her feet as a teacher. She was looking forward to the spring semester in January, when she could begin teaching adult history classes in the evenings at the local college.

She also looked for a car. Turkey Sanders was a charlatan, but he felt sorry for her and said he had just the thing for her—a little old vehicle that was about ten years older than the one she'd had that Kittie was now driving. It was good on gas at least. But the price was beyond her meager reserves.

"I'll have to come back next week, after I get paid," she told him sadly. "If it's still here then, I may try to work out a deal with you."

"You could get your stepbrother to just give it to you," he suggested.

Her expression closed up. "I don't have a stepbrother anymore. I have no family at all. There's just me."

He cleared his throat. "Sorry. Bad idea. You come back in a week, Miss Marsh," he added quietly. "I think that car will still be here."

She managed a wan smile. "Thanks, Mr. Sanders."

"You can call me Turkey," he chuckled. "Everybody does."

She wondered why, but she really didn't want to ask.

THE NEXT WEEK, she pawned her mother's few jewels at the local pawn shop. The owner was horrified and didn't want to take them, but she replied proudly that she had no money and had to have enough to get a car so she could get to and from her job. He stopped arguing. He also gave her the best price he could manage and promised her that he wouldn't sell her treasures for any price.

Gracie had only one real close call, when she started

to buy a coat that caught her eye and suddenly realized that she couldn't even afford it on layaway. She dashed out of the shop red-faced. She'd have to get a credit card in her own name, she decided, one that wasn't backed by Jason's wallet. But first, she had to have the evening teaching position. She wasn't going to go into debt.

She and Barbara got along well together. They were company for each other, especially on weekends, because Rick was working a difficult murder case in San Antonio and was hardly ever home lately. Mumbles settled in and became as much Barbara's cat as Gracie's.

When she had her first paycheck, which she received with enormous pride, she took the money she'd gotten from her mother's jewels and part of her small check and went to see Turkey Sanders. She bought the little VW. Turkey even threw in a couple of mats for the floorboard. She felt independent for the first time in her life. Then Kittie phoned and said she had to return Jason's car pronto.

She phoned the San Antonio mansion and told the man who answered the phone that she was coming up that evening to return the Thunderbird if someone could drive her back to Jacobsville. The man sounded amused and indignant. They weren't a limousine service, he said haughtily. Fine, Gracie muttered, she'd get a cab! She hung up, furious. She wondered where poor old John had gone. She hadn't been able to track him down. Mrs. Harcourt was cooking for Barbara, and Dilly was waiting tables. They were staying in Mrs. Brown's boardinghouse. But John hadn't contacted any of them.

Gracie phoned Barbara and said she was going to San Antonio to return Jason's car and would get a cab home, but Barbara refused to let her. She'd drive up and get her at the mansion. It would be a few minutes, she said, because she had to finish closing up the café for the night. Gracie agreed. She'd go on ahead, she said. Barbara could pick her up on the front steps of the mansion, because she wasn't going inside with Kittie!

She got into the classic Thunderbird, started the engine and headed for San Antonio. She'd barely reached the city limits sign outside Jacobsville when two cars ran up alongside her. One pulled in front of her, blocking her, the other screeched to a halt just behind her. Three men, all masked, jerked her out of the car, pulled a black mask over her head and threw her into the back seat of an automobile. Seconds later, her hands were tied and she was given a quick injection. She lost consciousness before the car was out of Jacobs County.

6

JASON SPENT WEEKS on the road, trying to troubleshoot problems in the corporation that resulted from the country's economic crisis. It was the same all over the world, one market's decline fed into another's. It took guts, gambling, and some speculation to manage a financial empire in times like these. He hated the necessity of so much travel, especially with his personal life in the same sort of shambles the economy seemed to be in. He'd come home briefly just before Halloween to sort out problems on the ranch in Comanche Wells.

He hadn't gone to San Antonio to see Gracie, wary of more unrest in the domestic situation there. He knew she didn't like Kittie. Hell, *he* didn't like Kittie very much, either, but he was sick at heart over Gracie's rejection and trying desperately to find some way to cope with it. Kittie had seemed like a good idea in the beginning, but she'd done nothing except make a bad situation worse. He'd been glad when modeling jobs took her to Europe. He had, to his credit, phoned Gracie while he was in the country, but he never seemed to reach her. He'd given up, in the end, without trying to see her and gone back overseas to deal with his global interests.

It was November when, weary and out of sorts from all the traveling and business meetings, he was finally able to come home to Texas. It had been hard work, trying to convince stubborn corporate boards that his acquisitions would ultimately benefit them, even if corporate stock prices were more depressed just at first. Jason's acquisitions, notably the new software company in California, were risky investments in these tough economic times. He had to be aggressive in his explanations, he had to make promises that he only hoped he could keep. The software the two computer geniuses had created would revolutionize the video game industry, which was one of the fastest moving sectors of the high-tech economy. It would allow actual tactile contact with characters and objects in the games, through a new technology that he had to struggle himself to understand, despite his excellent college education. He wasn't a gamer himself.

Then there was the computer company in Germany that he was trying to buy out. His new laptop computer offered innovative modules that plugged in to interface with all sorts of multimedia, and it was at the top of the market for the next generation of mobile technology. But the German company had improved on his design and added a new computer chip, and was undercutting his prices. It was absorb them or lose to the competition and watch his market advantage drop like a rock. The owners of that German concern were now saying that their stockholders wouldn't approve the deal. Jason was resigned to a hostile takeover, which was now in the initial stages.

He'd seen Kittie once or twice while he was away.

He'd been in London on a layover and he dropped by the photo shoot at Dover to see how she was doing. She was going to finish sooner than she'd expected, she told him, because they'd canceled the Russian shoot. She was going home. She'd asked if she could stay in the San Antonio mansion and do a little remodeling. Nothing drastic, she promised, teasing him. She just wanted to update his curtains and décor, and she had a friend in interior design in San Antonio who would love to help her. Just a little project, she coaxed. Wouldn't he like to change things around, just a little?

He'd agreed absently, his mind still on the German deal, making her promise not to upset Gracie anymore, or the staff. Why, of course, she'd promised, they were going to be family, after all, weren't they? He hadn't replied. He was already sick of the engagement. The photographer who was shooting the layout for a prominent fashion magazine seemed to be very intimate with Kittie, touching her at every opportunity. She almost purred when he slid his hand right over her bottom. Jason wasn't surprised to find that it didn't disturb him at all. He might be engaged, but he felt nothing for this woman. He was more determined than ever to break the engagement. It might be easier, if she was already in San Antonio when he got home. They'd have time to talk. He didn't want to think how Gracie was going to take the woman's sudden arrival, but he was certain that she'd find her stride. She was polite, no matter how angry she might be.

He'd tried to phone her a couple of times on his way back to Texas, but she hadn't answered her cell phone. Probably, he thought miserably, she'd recognized his number on the caller ID and was ignoring him. He regretted the way he'd behaved. He was going to have to make it up to her somehow. If he couldn't have her the way he wanted her, perhaps they could at least go back to a time when they'd been friends and not enemies. He was desperate to have her back in his life, in any capacity. The weeks apart from her had been agonizing. His eyes ached to see her.

JASON HAD PARKED HIS big Jaguar at the airport in a secure long-term area before he flew overseas the second time. He'd planned to drive on down to Comanche Wells and check on his ranch, but he gave way to an impulse to stop at the San Antonio mansion first. He wanted to see Gracie and make sure that Kittie hadn't upset her or Mrs. Harcourt. He also wanted to make sure that Kittie hadn't gone overboard with changes. He was already sorry he'd agreed to allow her to do any remodeling. That was just going to upset Gracie more.

He'd meant to phone the women from London and tell them that Kittie was coming, but he'd gotten busy and forgot. He was sorry, but it was too late now. He only hoped Kittie was being diplomatic. But judging by the past, that wasn't really likely. He was resigned to playing peacemaker.

The first thing he noticed when he walked up onto the porch was the absence of the planters where Mrs. Harcourt had put out pansies. Frowning, he noted that Gracie's flower beds were covered over with mulch and odd modern statues. With apprehension, he unlocked the door with his key and walked in.

He wasn't sure that he was in the right house. The vestibule had been redone, with a black-and-white tiled floor pattern that he hated on sight. It was covering the oak flooring that had been installed by the original owner. Jason had been partial to it. Other shocks followed in short order. The living room's cushy, comfortable furniture had been replaced by ultramodern modular pieces with no armrests. A glass coffee table adorned with a single orchid was in the spot where the beautiful antique cherry coffee table had once rested. The curtains weren't hung, they were draped over a pole and were knobby and the color of oatmeal. Above the mantel, where his father's portrait had hung, was a still life with fruit in a bowl.

A tall young man in a suit came into the living room. "And who might you be?" he asked with faint hauteur. "How did you get in?"

Jason turned, black eyes flashing. "With my key. Who the hell are you?"

"I'm the chauffeur."

"Like hell you are! Where's John?"

"If you mean that old man who used to work here, he's gone…"

"Where's Mrs. Harcourt? Is she in the kitchen?" he asked abruptly.

The younger man shifted uncomfortably. "You must mean Miss Gibbons—she's the cook."

"Dilly?" he persisted.

"Miss Sartain fired her," he said. "She let them all go…she said they were too old…"

Jason moved a step closer and the young man shut up, flushing. "I don't care who you are. This is my house and I didn't hire you. Get out. Find the other new hires and take them with you." He slid back his cuff and checked his Rolex. "You've got thirty minutes to vacate the premises, or I'll have you taken out in handcuffs and charged with criminal trespass!"

"We…we were hired!"

"Not by me," Jason said in a cold, threatening tone.

The man backed away, disconcerted. "You should talk to Miss Sartain," he began.

"Where is she?"

There was a commotion on the staircase and Kittie came tripping down it, wearing a pretty silk pantsuit in oyster-white. "Darling!" she exclaimed, and threw herself into his arms.

He jerked away. His eyes were glittering with bad temper. "Where are my employees?" he asked curtly.

She cleared her throat. "Well, I let them go. Jason, they were old, and that Dilly, honestly, she was just so frumpy…!"

"You had no damned authority to hire and fire here!" he raged. "I said you could do some minor redecorating, not upend my whole damned life!"

She moved back a step. "It needed modernizing," she began.

"It's my house, Kittie," he said coldly. "Mine! You don't make decisions for me!"

She glared at him. "We're getting married…"

"The hell we are!"

She hesitated. Her eyes blinked as if she couldn't quite understand what was happening. "You bought me a ring," she said.

"Keep it, along with the clothes," he snapped. "But get the hell out of my house. Right now."

She laughed nervously. "Jason, you're just upset. Okay, I went a little too far. I can call those old people and ask them to come back…"

He had a sudden, uneasy thought. "Where's Gracie?"

Kittie was really nervous now. "She and I had a long

talk," she said slowly. "She agreed that she needed to support herself…"

"Where?" he demanded.

"I don't know! She borrowed your old Thunderbird and drove down to Jacobsville with that stupid cat and some things out of her room. I told her to bring the car back, but for some reason she hasn't returned it yet. But I'm sure it's all right," Kittie added hastily. However, she actually found it disturbing, because Gracie knew how he treasured that old car. So why hadn't Gracie returned it when she'd asked?!

Her room. Gracie's room. Jason had a cold feeling. He turned, taking the steps two at a time on his way up the curving staircase. He got to Gracie's room and opened it. The sight that met his eyes revolted him. Gracie's beautiful Victorian room was a nightmare of red and black. It looked like a bordello. The furniture, all she had left of her family, was gone, as well. He opened the closet. None of her clothes were there, even the beautiful gold evening gown he'd brought her from Paris. Nothing of Gracie remained. He stared in disbelief at the wreck before him.

"This room was a disgrace," Kittie huffed from behind him. "Rose and white! What sort of woman wants a color scheme like that anymore? It's right out of the 1800s…!"

Jason turned and stared at her with eyes so cold she felt a chill. "Where are her clothes, her furniture?" he asked in a low, threatening tone.

She folded her arms over her chest and pouted. "Well, she took some of her clothes," she faltered. "I gave the rest away."

His fists clenched by his side. He was almost vibrating with rage.

"She was in my way!" she exploded. Her blue eyes sparked at him. "You were obsessed with her! All you ever talked about was Gracie, Gracie, Gracie! You couldn't even kiss me! And here she was, living with you, spending your money, coddling those old people who couldn't even do the job properly. Yes, I threw her out! She didn't argue. She said she was glad to go!" She didn't add that she'd used blackmail to accomplish Gracie's eviction.

He didn't trust himself to speak.

Kittie noticed it, but she didn't care. "If it hadn't been for her, you'd have married me. I'd have been set for life," she blurted out. "I'm sick of modeling. I wanted to come home and mix with the right people, have money to spend, buy what I wanted without having to look at price tags, always have the latest, best cars. I wanted to be rich! And all you wanted was to sit and moon over Gracie." Her eyes flashed. "Well, all right, if you want to ditch me, go ahead. Like I want to live with a man who can't bring himself to touch me because he's lusting after his own stepsister!"

"Watch your mouth," he said in a low, dangerous tone.

"Oh, whatever! I'll get my things. You can call a cab to take me to the airport, and you can buy me a ticket to New York," she said spitefully.

"You're damned lucky I don't press charges," he said in a voice teeming with fury. "You had no authority to destroy my house and fire my staff."

She smoothed back her hair. "Press charges," she said haughtily. "And I'll tell the tabloids your shameful family secret!" she raged without thinking.

"What do you mean?" he asked, frowning. "What family secret?" He took a step toward her. The look in his black eyes was dangerous.

She backed down. "That's for me to know and you to find out," she tossed back.

She turned and ran back upstairs. Jason stared after her with a hollow sensation in the pit of his stomach. He looked around at the ruins of his once tasteful and immaculate home and cursed himself for his own stupidity.

TWO HOURS LATER, Kittie and her newly hired staff were all on the way off the property. Kittie was en route to the airport. She informed Jason that she'd had a spending spree at Neiman Marcus, which was sending him the bill, and she wasn't giving anything back. He told her to keep it all and good riddance. She hurled herself into the limo Jason had ordered to carry her to catch her flight without another word.

The so-called staff were headed back to San Antonio in their own cars and the unemployment line. Jason had a headache the likes of which he'd never known.

He waited until the unwelcome guests had gone before he phoned Barbara. He needed a cool head to deal with Gracie. Barbara would know where Gracie was. He didn't know how to start making amends for what Kittie had done. There was also the anguish of trying to track down Mrs. Harcourt, that sweet and loving woman who'd been tossed out like an old shoe, not to mention John and Dilly. The only good thing was that Kittie hadn't had access to the ranch, or he might be replacing cowboys, as well.

The phone rang at Barbara's Café again and again. He'd almost given up hope of an answer when Barbara's strained voice came on the line.

"Where's Gracie?" he asked curtly.

"I'm not the person to ask," she said miserably. "I don't know where she is, Jason. Neither does anybody else."

"What do you mean?" he asked, with fear spiraling through him.

"That idiot fiancée of yours phoned and said she wanted your Thunderbird returned tonight because you were coming home and she didn't want to get in trouble for lending it to Gracie. I was going to drive up to San Antonio and give her a ride back. So Gracie started that way, but she never arrived."

His heart froze in his chest. "What?"

Barbara sighed miserably. "I found the Thunderbird on the side of the road with her purse and cell phone still in it, just about an hour ago, when I closed the restaurant and drove toward San Antonio to get her." She hesitated. "I called in law enforcement. Sheriff Hayes thinks she's been kidnapped."

He sat down. "Kidnapped?"

"Yes. You've been out of the country so maybe you're out of the loop. Anyway, there have been a lot of kidnappings around here lately. There's a South American dictator hiding out in Mexico, just across the border. Hayes thinks he may be in with the Fuentes drug bunch, but he's not pushing drugs. He's using kidnappings to help fund a future coup to depose his rival and get his country back. So far he hasn't actually killed anybody, but he did leave a pretty young Mexican socialite in a…well…in a damaged way."

"Dear God!" Jason groaned, running a hand through his hair. He'd known about the kidnappings while he'd been overseas, but had been too preoccupied with business to focus on current events back home. Still, he should have kept his guard up. After all, he'd had a vice president who'd been kidnapped in Mexico last year and returned barely alive. "Are they at least looking for

Gracie? If it hasn't been twenty-four hours, they won't file a missing person report."

"Hayes Carson did," Barbara replied curtly. "He put out a BOLO on the cars. One of Cy Parks's cowboys spotted a truck and a car speeding down the road before he knew what had happened. He stopped when he saw me standing beside the Thunderbird."

"Thank God! Maybe they can catch them before they get over the border." He let out a harsh breath. "Why didn't you call me?" he asked angrily.

"I called the house, but that butler or whatever he was said you weren't there and he didn't know how to reach you. I didn't have your cell phone number. Where are you? Are you still overseas?" she asked.

"I got in a short while ago," he said tersely. "I had a whole new staff that I didn't hire, not to mention a wrecked house. It looked as if some bordello owner remade it for business purposes," he added. "Gracie was gone. So was everybody else. Kittie said she'd asked them to leave." His voice was ice-cold. "I threw her crew out and broke off the engagement. I want my people back, but I don't know where to look."

"I've got two of them working for me," Barbara said. "I don't know where John is. Mrs. Harcourt couldn't get in touch with him."

"What a hell of a mess!" he raged.

"Yes, Jason, dear, and whose fault is that?" Barbara added with pure malice in her voice.

"Mine," he said in a subdued tone. "I've ruined every-thing."

Barbara relented. He did sound as if a house had landed on him. "Most disasters yield some opportunities."

"Not around here, they don't." He drew in a long

breath. "I'll phone some people I know. We'll wait for a ransom call. I imagine it will come here, if she was snatched because of who she is."

"You don't know who she is, really," Barbara replied quietly. "You never wanted to know."

"Kittie was mumbling about some family secret. She threatened to make it public."

"I'm not surprised. Gracie wouldn't tell me what it was, but she was terrified because of the threat."

"What's going on, Barbara?"

"That's for Gracie to say. It's her business." There was a pause. "Hayes Carson just walked in. He says they lost the trail at the border."

He cursed. "Let me talk to him."

Barbara handed him the phone, mouthing, "Jason Pendleton."

"Hi, Jason," Sheriff Hayes said quietly. "Sorry to be the bearer of bad news. They got Gracie. I'm sure there will be a ransom demand. I've called in Garon Grier and Jon Blackhawk over at the San Antonio FBI field office. They're on their way down here to investigate. Well, Garon is. Jon said he's going to come to your house with a team and set up surveillance and wiretaps."

"Tell him to come ahead," he replied. "I'll have the gates open. God, what a shock!"

"She should never have been on that road alone in a car that was known to belong to you, with kidnappers running around locally," Hayes said shortly. "She had no defenses at all. She wouldn't even own a handgun. She was an easy mark. Why couldn't you send someone to pick up the car?"

"I was out of the country," he said curtly. "My ex-fiancée asked Gracie to bring it back before I got home, so I wouldn't know she let Gracie borrow it."

"Sweet girl."

He drew in a harsh breath. "I could wring her neck! But it's all my fault. Gracie walked out because of all the changes. So did the rest of my staff. I'm sitting up here all by myself, just off an international flight with a ruined house and I'm half-starved. I don't even know where to find the coffeepot or the coffee."

"Jon will find them. He can cook," Hayes said. "He'll feed you and make coffee." He paused. "Maybe I should send his half brother up. He's a Fed, too, even if he's working undercover down here as a Jacobsville cop."

"I won't let Kilraven in the front door, so save your breath," Jason said curtly. "I know him too well. He's headstrong and he won't follow orders. I don't want Gracie killed." The word hit him right in the heart. Gracie could be tortured or raped or murdered, and he sat here without the means to save her. He felt a wave of utter helplessness that filled him with fury. "Could you talk to Cy Parks and see if he and Eb Scott could get a team together for me, just in case? Money's no object. You don't need to tell the Bureau about it, either."

"I'll do that," Hayes said quietly. "I have great respect for the FBI, but sometimes they move more slowly than I like. Gracie will be taken to one of the roughest areas across the border. A sheltered, gentle girl like her…it doesn't bear thinking about."

"I know." The words were like spikes, digging into his heart. "We have to get her out quickly."

"I'll talk to Parks and get back to you."

"I'll have the cell with me constantly. Here's the number." He paused for the sheriff to write it down. "I don't care what time you call."

"I know that. I'll be in touch." He hung up.

Jason dropped into the ultramodern armchair that was as uncomfortable as hell, even without armrests, and cursed himself for his lack of foresight. He'd been so wrapped up in business and revenge that he hadn't given a thought to Gracie's well-being. She was his life, and he'd put her at risk. His eyes closed. All he could do right now was pray. And he did.

JON BLACKHAWK WAS AS tall as his older half brother, Kilraven. They shared the same pale silver eyes and jet-black hair, except that Jon wore his in a long ponytail down his back. He was dressed in a vested gray suit and he looked as elegant as a duke. Rumor had it that the half brothers, between them, owned half a county back in Oklahoma.

He lifted a black eyebrow when Jason answered the door himself. "A house this size, and you open doors?"

"I just fired the staff," Jason muttered. "Come on in."

Jon looked around and winced. "Good God!"

"That's what I said when I saw it. My ex-fiancée took it upon herself to remodel the whole damned place. I'm looking at a small fortune to put everything back the way it was." He led the way to the kitchen. "I learned to cook in the army, but mostly it was snake or lizard or various bugs, and I'm too tired to go hunting any," he added facetiously. "Hayes Carson says you can cook. I haven't eaten since breakfast, and that was in Amsterdam where I was attending an economic conference."

Blackhawk laughed amusedly. He took off his jacket and vest and looked for an apron. He whipped one of Mrs. Harcourt's around his elegant, lithe body and proceeded to search out food, coffee and equipment. He pulled out a frying pan. "I do a mean omelet. Coffee?"

"Please," Jason said heavily. "I'd rather get drunk, but it really wouldn't help."

"No, it wouldn't," Blackhawk agreed. "Problems only get bigger when you try to avoid them. If it's any consolation, this man, Emilio Machado, has great respect for women. One of his men raped a hostage. Machado had him shot dead on the spot."

Jason relaxed, just a little. "That's something, I guess. Gracie is…well, she's no party girl. She's been sheltered and is rather naive."

"My kind of girl," Blackhawk said gently. "I hate these brassy, pushy modern women who think nothing of propositioning a man minutes after they meet him."

"Throwback," Jason mused.

"Count on it," the younger man agreed curtly. "Actually I come from a unique moral culture."

"Do tell," Jason said, intrigued.

"My father was full-blooded Lakota Sioux. He inherited a fortune in oil shares from his father, who owned land in Oklahoma. My mother, however, is Cherokee mixed with Irish." He shook his head. "Part of me would love to drink. The other part reminds me constantly that I could become an alcoholic with almost no trouble at all."

"Warring inner cultures."

"Yes, like my half brother."

"And his mother?"

"His mother was white. She's dead now," he added quietly and in a tone that didn't invite speculation.

"You shared a father?" Jason asked, confused.

"Yes. Our father was an FBI agent who worked out of San Antonio. Kilraven's mother had married the FBI agent first and had Kilraven. He's two years older than I am. Then his father married my mother. We're both technically Blackhawks, but Kilraven took his mother's last name when he started doing undercover work. We're only half brothers, but we look alike."

"Yes, you do."

The doorbell rang just as Jon was getting eggs out of the refrigerator. Jason answered the door. Three men in suits stood there. One was all too familiar.

"Kilraven…" Jason began curtly.

Kilraven held up a big hand. "Your brother-in-law, Ramirez, has already read me the riot act about not following orders," he interrupted. "He plays chess with my boss. I can't really afford to antagonize him."

Jason groaned. "Rodrigo and Glory. I haven't called them."

"No need. Ramirez already knows. He said to keep them posted." He lifted his head and sniffed. "Omelets?" He looked hungry. "I haven't had any supper. They—" he pointed at the two somber, older agents beside him "—wouldn't stop by a fast food joint on the way here."

"We were told to hurry," the oldest said.

Jason chuckled. "All right, come on in. Your brother's cooking," he told Kilraven.

"This will be a feast," Kilraven commented. "He actually took a cordon bleu cooking course. My mouth is already watering."

"There's plenty, if one of you can cook bacon."

Kilraven raised his hand. "I know how to cook it over a campfire. I'll improvise," he added, brushing past Jason. "Who can do cinnamon toast?"

Jason let the other agents in and closed the door. They all headed for the kitchen. "I can, if your brother can find the bread and butter and cinnamon. The house was wrecked while I was away."

Kilraven made a face as they passed the living room. "Something that ugly could get you arrested for maintaining an eyesore."

"Tell me about it," Jason returned. "Come on in. Jon, can we feed three more?"

Jon looked up and grinned. "Sure. I'll add more eggs." He glanced at his brother and chuckled. "Did I hear you offering to cook the bacon?"

Kilraven rolled up his sleeves. "You bet. Where is it?"

"We need bread, butter and cinnamon, too. And plates."

"And forks," one of the other agents suggested.

"And I thought omelets were finger food," Kilraven scoffed.

"While we're working in here, you two get things set up in the living room," Jon told the older agents. "We're expecting a call pretty soon."

They nodded. One of them was carrying what looked like a suitcase full of electronic equipment. They went to the living room and started unpacking.

The other three men worked companionably in the kitchen and served up a filling meal. They were just finishing second cups of coffee when the phone suddenly rang.

THEY HURRIED TOWARD THE living room. Two of Jon's fellow agents sat down at a table loaded with high-tech equipment. Jon nodded to the agent who was monitoring the second line he'd placed there on his arrival and motioned to Jason to pick up the receiver.

"Pendleton," Jason said curtly.

"We have your sister," an accented voice replied. "We will call you back in a few days to negotiate the ransom. Do not involve the FBI. We will be watching. If they interfere, she will die and we will not call back." He hung up.

Jon was watching Jason's face. "Don't believe everything you hear," he said quietly. "We know what we're doing."

So did he. He knew that if they didn't retrieve Gracie within twenty-four hours, it was likely that they wouldn't retrieve her at all. The kidnappers had said it would be days before they called back. He was worried out of his mind. He hoped that Cy Parks could put together a team and go after her. This high-tech equipment was very good, but the kidnappers were in no hurry and what they needed was fast action, before Gracie became a statistic.

GRACIE CAME TO IN a shack, to the sound of a guitar playing some soulful melody nearby. It was beautiful, like a one-instrument symphony of harmony and poignant reverie. She wondered who was playing it.

She sat up. She was handcuffed, with her hands behind her, but she was no longer hooded. She felt very groggy. She recalled, vaguely, a needle being pressed into her arm when she was run off the road and snatched out of Jason's car by two short, stocky men. Nearby, a small boy in ragged clothing was sitting at the door, watching her. He had huge, soulful brown eyes.

"*¿Como se llama?*" she asked softly.

He stared at her, blinking. It was a surprise to see the lack of comprehension in his eyes. He didn't understand Spanish. She wondered if he was Mayan. And then she wondered where she was. The Mayan people lived in the Yucatan. Was that where she was?

"¡Honee bot may!" she greeted phonetically, using the little bit of Mayan dialect she'd picked up from one of Barbara's acquaintances. There were many dialects of Mayan. In this one, the phrase meant hello. Assuming that she wasn't murdering the pronunciation.

The boy suddenly grinned from ear to ear. *"Honee bot may,"* he replied shyly. He said something else, but she didn't understand. He darted out the door. Seconds later, the guitar went silent. The cloth flap that served as a door was pushed aside and a tall, large, man in jeans and a blue silk shirt came inside, smiling at her.

He was very handsome. He had large, deep-set brown eyes in a square face, with an unruly mop of curling black hair on his head. He had a straight nose and high cheekbones, a square chin, and a very wide, sensuous mouth. He was broad-shouldered and husky, more like a wrestler than a horseman. His complexion was light olive-brown. He had a regal bearing.

He smiled as he studied her. "So, you are awake. And Angel says you speak Mayan."

"Only one word," she replied, her tone hesitant. "But I'm literate in Spanish."

"So am I. My name is Machado. You may have heard of me?" he added, when she seemed to recognize it.

"Yes. We heard that you were with the Fuentes brothers. And that you were the dictator of a country in South America, but you were deposed and sent into exile."

He shrugged. "An approximation of the truth, but close enough. However," he added, and his dark eyes twinkled, "soon enough my nemesis will be fighting to keep his position. I must raise enough money to hire the type of talent I need to regain my former office."

"You kidnapped me."

"Yes, I did," he said in an apologetic tone. "I am desperate for money and I find this a more…tasteful way of obtaining it than selling drugs to young boys who have to steal to afford to become addicted to them," he added in a cold tone.

"You partnered with the Fuentes brothers," she said icily. "They kill policemen and even journalists."

"Insects," he said haughtily. "They are no partners of mine. I permit them to occupy territory here without slitting their throats. That is all."

She cocked her head, curious. "Here? Where is here?" she asked, looking around. "The boy spoke Mayan. Are we in the Yucatan?"

"No, no," he replied. "Only in northern Sonora, just across your Texas border, in fact. Convenient to the best targets for appropriation—rich Americanos," he added with a wicked smile.

She glared at him. "Kidnapping is a federal offense in the United States. A capital crime."

He held up a hand. "Please do not quote the law to me. It is so depressing to be bound by the moral ideals of imperialists"

She caught her breath. "We are not imperialists!"

He made a rough sound in his throat. She shifted uncomfortably and his mouth pulled up at one side. He knelt beside her and produced a key to unlock her handcuffs. "Barbarians, trussing you up like this," he said. "I apologize. I told them you were to be handled gently. A woman of quality should not be treated so roughly."

She laughed shortly. "Woman of quality? I grew up in the slums of El Paso," she said, feeling such a kinship with this stranger that she could tell him things she'd rather have died than share with Jason. "With no money, a brutal father who drank and beat my mother and me, and who was finally killed by a sniper's bullet when he held a pistol to my head and promised to pull the trigger because my mother tried to leave him. Does that sound like a quality upbringing to you?" she added.

He was surprised. "But you are a Pendleton."

"I am a Marsh," she corrected. "My foster brother is a Pendleton. He has the money. I've left his house. I work for a living now and I live frugally. I don't have any money. So if you're hoping to ransom me, you'd have better luck for profit by marketing the eggs those scrawny chickens lay," she added, indicating some free range hens who were scratching in the dirt near the adobe houses.

"He is your stepbrother. Surely he loves you and will pay to get you back," he insisted.

She drew in a miserable breath. "He's more likely to tell you to do your worst and be damned," she said heavily. "His fiancée hates me. She got rid of me by threatening to tell him a family secret that he doesn't know," she added. "She overheard me talking about my past and Jason has no idea where I really came from. You see this spiteful woman uses blackmail to get what she wants. Although I'm sure she'll eventually tell him all about my shameful upbringing, just for fun." Her eyes met his. "I know some of the hostages taken have been killed," she said without flinching.

He glared at her. "I do not kill women," he spat. "As for that hostage, one of Fuentes's men decided he wanted her and forced her in the night. When I learned of it, I had him shot. I do not tolerate such behavior. Not even when I was *El General* in my own country."

She felt less threatened.

"This stepbrother, he would not want you if he knew of your true background? You are certain of this?"

"Very certain," she sighed. She gave him a sad smile. "So, *El General,* do you know the expression about buying a pig in a poke? Because that's what you've just done. Figuratively speaking!"

7

EL GENERAL EMILIO MACHADO, advised that contact had been made with Jason Pendleton, spent a few days deciding how to proceed. Finally he sent his ransom demands to Jason through an intermediary, a minor official in the Mexican government in Sonora Province. Gracie heard him dictate it. She wondered if Kittie would oppose Jason paying any ransom for her rival, and decided that she probably would. Kittie was one of the most malicious women Gracie had ever met. But Jason was loyal to people in his life, even if he didn't like them. He would most likely get together the ransom, for old times' sake. He and Gracie had argued and parted badly, but he still considered her family. He wouldn't desert her. She hoped.

But even so, there was a chance that he might hesitate. If, for instance, Kittie told him the truth about his stepsister. In which case, Jason might not feel obliged to do anything. She didn't know how her captor might react if that happened. Despite his pleasant attitude, he had to have a ruthless side to have conquered an entire nation. The kind man who loved children was probably deadly behind an automatic weapon and wouldn't hesitate to kill if the situation called for it.

She worried about Barbara, not to mention Mrs. Harcourt and Dilly. They would be concerned and fearful for her. She wished she had some way to reassure them that she was at least safe for the moment. How long that would last, she didn't really know.

IF SHE EXPECTED QUICK results, she was disappointed. One day passed, then two, then three, then a week without any word from across the border. Gracie reasoned that the wheels of bureaucracy turned slowly and a number of agencies might be involved in working for her release. The FBI, surely. Or would they be? It was an international kidnapping. Would they send the CIA or the Department of Defense or the NSA? Well, she thought, she could be forgiven for her ignorance on the issue. She'd never been kidnapped before.

Her fears that Machado would harm her slowly dissipated. He treated her with Old-World courtesy and respect. And oddly, he gave her the run of the camp. This caused some argument between him and the Fuentes bunch, particularly a stocky, mean-looking young man who argued with him. This was the same man who often gave Gracie looks that made her skin crawl. Despite Machado's kindness, this was a camp of criminals. These men had killed and would do so again given the slightest provocation.

At first, she'd entertained the prospect of escape, but not for long. Men with automatic weapons patrolled the outskirts of the village, which was surrounded by acres and acres of barren, dry land full of cacti, mostly saguaro, snakes and scorpions. Even a combat veteran with survival skills would be challenged out there, much less sheltered Gracie. For the first time, she was aware of the cocoon she'd been living in, protected from life, insulated from harmful elements of society, kept apart from the day-to-day suffering of the poor. Her charity work was idealistic, and she did know firsthand about poverty, but the intervening years had softened her and made her less aware of how hard it was to make a living without education and opportunity.

She resolved, if she survived this experience, to learn from it and become more involved in the world outside her safety net. She was already getting a taste of it in her new life, where she mixed with ordinary working people. She could see the results of poverty. She was beginning to understand what her life would have been like if her mother hadn't married Myron Pendleton.

She did feel regret that she and Jason would never be close again, in any respect. Kittie had secret knowledge that could destroy Gracie. She wouldn't hesitate to use it, either. Gracie could try to explain her past to Jason, but she doubted he'd even listen. He thought Kittie was the moon in the sky. How painful that thought was. Kittie had already gotten rid of everyone that Gracie cared about, and she'd stolen Jason. Gracie had a new life. It was hard and lonely, despite having Barbara's friendship and support. Kittie would live in her house with Jason, entertain her friends, go to concerts and ballets with Jason. Gracie would live in the shadows of his life and never share afternoons at the sale barn or rides on the ranch with him in close companionship ever again. He hated her for the physical rejection she couldn't help. He didn't even know why she'd pushed him away. She, who loved him more than her own life.

She grieved for what was lost, but her immediate situation took precedence. Would they kill her if the ransom demand wasn't met? Would they kill her if it was? The danger kept her sleepless and killed her appetite. Machado saw that and came to visit her in the small adobe house where she lived with a woman and a child who apparently belonged to the Fuentes organization.

"You think we mean to kill you whether or not we obtain the ransom," he guessed, watching her eyelids flicker. "I can assure you that this will not happen."

"My stepbrother helped Fuentes lose a huge cocaine shipment and was instrumental in the death of one brother and the imprisonment of another," she said sadly. "They want revenge."

His dark eyes flashed. "This is so. But the power here is in my hands, not theirs," he replied. "You see those men, *señorita?*" he asked, and gestured toward a group of soldiers in desert camouflage carrying big automatic weapons. "They do not belong to Fuentes, and would kill him or any of his men were I to order it."

She relaxed a little. "I see."

"You do not," he replied with faint humor. "He has his priorities, I have mine. It was convenient to make a truce here on the border. But he has fewer men than I do, and mine are trained career soldiers. Does that make it clearer?"

She drew in a breath and smiled. "Yes. Thank you."

He shrugged. "They want you back alive and unharmed, and that is how you will be returned to them. I give you my word as an officer and a gentleman," he added with sincerity. "In my country, this means something."

"In mine, too," she replied.

He nodded and looked around as a small woman with black hair braided down to her waist came in with the young boy, Angel. She bowed her head, smiling shyly. *"¿Con permiso?"* she asked hesitantly before she entered.

"A su servicio, señora," he said, and bowed to her, which made her face color.

The General winked at Gracie and left them alone.

GRACIE MADE FRIENDS WITH little Angel's mother and was soon chattering away to the woman, who spoke Spanish, as well as Mayan. These people with Machado were not descendants of the Aztecs who settled around what became Mexico City, but immigrants from Central America. Their ancestry was Mayan, which came as a pleasant surprise for Gracie, who was fascinated with their culture.

Camp life for these women consisted of grinding corn and making tortillas and cooking; and, of course, caring for the children. Gracie helped with the corn grinding, setting to work cheerfully while she and Josita, Angel's mother, talked about children and the hard times in Mexico and the dangers of the border.

The children gathered around her, fascinated with her blond hair. She laughed and told them stories about Kukulcãn, the famed feathered serpent of legend, as well as tales of Mayan conquest and the history of the advanced culture that was gifted in astronomy and making precise calendars. Day by day, as she grew comfortable with her captors, she attracted more young people, also anxious to hear the stories.

Still, she longed for Jason and was homesick for Jacobsville.

One evening, around the central campfire in the adobe house, the General himself sprawled on a colorful woven serape and propped on one elbow to hear her tell about the famed ball games that meant life or death for opposing teams.

When the children were finally shooed off to bed in their hammocks, slung each night inside the dirt-floored adobe houses, the General remained.

"They are truly fascinating, these tales of yours," he said. "Your Spanish is elegant. If badly accented," he teased.

She laughed. "I was taught it by a French professor, so it's not my fault."

He nodded. "I agree." He cocked his leonine head and studied her. "You are not afraid of me."

She shook her head as she smoothed over the sand where she'd been drawing Mayan glyphs for the children, the handful she'd committed to memory. "I see the way you are with the children," she said simply. "They love you. It's hard to fool a child."

He smiled. "I would have enjoyed a family, a big family, with many sons and daughters. Alas, I have spent my life fighting battles. There was no time for a woman. Not a permanent one, that is."

She understood the insinuation. He did look like a man who knew women intimately. He had a way of looking at her that was more flattering than intimidating, despite her lack of experience. He seemed to sense how naive she was, and to be pleased by it.

"You have a youthful appearance, but I think you are at least in your midtwenties," he said surprisingly. "Have you not had the opportunity to marry?"

"Not really," she replied. "I don't…mix well with men."

"Because of your father."

"Because of the way he treated my mother. She said all men were animals once a woman was alone with them."

"I can understand why you might believe this," he replied in a voice deep and soft as velvet. "But it is not true. Some men are animals, yes. Not all."

"She thought my father wasn't. She was fooled."

"A betrayal that had sad consequences not only for her, but for her child, as well. Is she still alive?"

"No. Shortly after marrying Jason's father, she ran her car into a tree and died instantly. They thought it was an accident, that she just lost control. I knew better. But I never spoke of it." Her soft gray eyes met his dark ones across the campfire. "It's so odd, that I can talk to you about this, when I've never breathed a word of it to Jason."

"My opinion is not as essential to your happiness as his would be."

She laughed softly. "You're very perceptive."

"You love him," he said gently. "And not as a step-brother."

Her face closed up like a lotus blossom at night. "For all the good it does me," she told him. "He doesn't feel that way about me."

"A truly blind man," he remarked. "Sad for him. You have qualities that are admirable, not the least of which is your tolerance for different ways of living. I have not heard you say once that it is a pity the people have to live like this, in such squalor."

"It's not squalor!" she protested. "They're happy here. They may not have much in the way of material things, but they love their children and value their families. They aren't obsessed with owning things. They live with nature, they don't try to control it. One day," she said philosophically, "if our technological system should ever crash and burn, it will be people like these who lead us out of the darkness and teach us how to survive in a world that isn't run by computers."

He laughed delightfully. "You speak of the legend of the rainbow warrior."

She brightened. "Yes! You know it?"

"Every indigenous culture has a story about it."

He cocked his leonine head and smiled at her. "You love history."

"Indeed," she confessed with a shy smile. "I have a degree in it and hope to teach one day."

"You certainly have a knack for it." He smiled. "I am amazed at the fascination with which the children here listen to you," he said. "It gives them pride in who they are—something sadly lacking in the dominant societies in which they now live."

"Pride and self-esteem are the keys to success in life," she said. "So many cultures have been debased and then destroyed by conquerors…"

"Ah, now you speak of your own imperialist culture," he teased.

She made a face at him. "You call it imperialism—we call it protecting other democracies. Truth is subjective."

He threw back his head and laughed. "Yes. This is true."

Nearby, the guitarist had changed songs and was now playing a tender love song in Spanish. To Gracie's surprise, Machado started to sing it, his deep voice seductive and alluring in the darkness. Gracie sat up, listening, her pleasure in his talent apparent. The song was about a man who worshipped a girl from afar, without the money to win her. He lost her to a rich ranchero and mourned her every time he heard the rain, like tears, on his roof.

"You sing beautifully," she said when the song ended. "If you hadn't been a dictator, you could have been a famous singing star."

He chuckled. "I sing for my own pleasure. But compared to running a country, *niña,* it is a poor second. I have an addiction to power."

"A failing common to men, I have noticed." She sighed, her thoughts returning to her current predicament.

She hesitated. "Have you heard from Jason yet?" she asked worriedly. She'd asked the same question every day this week, and he'd given her nebulous answers. Her nerves were beginning to wear thin.

He checked the wide watch on his wrist. "We were promised a reply tonight. My man should have made contact by now. I expect that we will be hearing something from your stepbrother very soon. You must be anxious to go home."

"Sort of," she said with a wan smile. "Jason's fiancée will be scathing about the money it costs him to ransom me, if he does, and I don't know how he's going to react. Other than my closest female friends back home, I imagine the only people who will be glad to see me will be the federal agents who oversee the ransom payment. It will be a feather in their caps that they retrieved me alive and in one piece."

"Indeed," he replied. "This fiancée—does he love her, you think?"

She sighed. "I don't know. He seemed to. He certainly took her side against me and the household staff." She moved restlessly. "That's not like Jason. Especially with Mrs. Harcourt. She's been with him since he was born."

He shook his head. "A seductive woman can make a fool of a man, even an older one. But the passion burns bright and then extinguishes itself," he added comfortingly. "Give it time. He will see the light."

She laughed hollowly. "I won't hold my breath."

"Pessimist," he accused. "You have to expect miracles, *niña*, or you will never see one."

"I see them all the time. It's just my relationship with Jason that isn't working."

"Things change. You will see."

"El General!" a deep voice called. "There is a man on the telephone for you!"

"Don't you have a cell phone?" Gracie asked him, surprised.

"Five," he replied, grinning. "So that they cannot be traced. Too many to carry on me, you see. I have workers to do that for me." He got up. *"Con permiso,"* he said with respect, and moved away.

MAYBE IT WAS JASON, Gracie thought hopefully. She wasn't being treated badly here, but she was nervous about the intentions of her captors. One of them, the stocky one who belonged to the Fuentes bunch, watched her constantly. He had arms filled with tattoos. He was muscular and brutish, and she was frankly afraid of him. She wanted to go home.

She rubbed her arms against the faint chill of the evening air. Where she was sitting, at the end of the porch in a rickety little homemade chair, there wasn't a lot of light outside the small adobe house where she was being kept. The children who had been listening to her stories had all gone home and she was more or less alone while Machado spoke to his caller in the main house nearby.

"So you are alone, huh?" a cold, drawling voice muttered from behind her. "I have waited for this moment."

She turned, her face paling as she saw the very man she'd been thinking about moving toward her from behind the adobe house.

THE FBI WAS NEGOTIATING for all it was worth, but the kidnapper kept insisting that he needed more money than was being offered. He also was wary of traps. He wanted assurances, guarantees of safe conduct and no watching eyes or homing devices.

Jon Blackhawk actually threw his cell phone across the room after one harrowing negotiating round. He also cursed. Loudly.

"You can't throw government equipment around like that, not when we're operating in a deficit," Kilraven said, shaking a finger at him.

"It's just so damned frustrating!" Jon snapped.

"I'd like to punch a few people myself," Jason said roughly. He got up and paced. "What the hell do they mean, changing the figure with every phone call?"

"It's just stonewalling," Jon said heavily. "I hate it, too. I know you're worried. I don't like the time it's taking, either. But it's the only avenue we have right now."

Kilraven pursed his lips and glanced at Jason with an odd expression. "Is it?"

Jon stopped dead in front of his half brother and glared at him. "What do you know? Is something going on that you haven't told me?"

Kilraven managed to look innocent. "Me? I'm only

here on loan from my own agency," he said. "I'm not allowed to interfere," he added with an angelic smile.

"Like you didn't interfere when Rodrigo was snatched by the Fuentes gang?"

"That was a special situation," Kilraven protested. "They'd have killed him for revenge. This group doesn't have anything against Gracie."

Jon relaxed a little. "That's true. Hammock, see if I broke the phone, will you?" he called to one of his men. "I didn't mean to field it like that."

Hammock picked it up, punched a button and put it to his ear. He chuckled. "They must have had you in mind when they made this one, boss." He handed it back to Jon. It wasn't even dented. "Nice toss, though."

As the two brothers continued to trade good-natured barbs, Jason moved to the patio and walked outside, lifting his face to the cool night air. For days now, he'd tried to be optimistic, to believe that they'd get Gracie back. Hope was failing. He'd never stop blaming himself for it. He'd pushed Gracie right into the line of fire by putting Kittie in a position to throw her out of her own home. It wasn't like Gracie to let that happen. He wondered how Kittie had really accomplished it? Surely Gracie would have phoned him, asked him if it was what he wanted. Remembering the argument over her cat, however, he wasn't so sure.

His little act of payback had boomeranged tragically, and Gracie was going to pay the price for his wounded ego. What if the kidnappers were just stalling, hoping to get the money and keep her? Worse, what if they'd already killed her? They said that if people weren't ransomed in the first twenty-four hours, chances of getting them back alive plummeted. He felt panic rise in his throat. If Gracie died, he had no reason to stay alive. He had nothing left. He had…!

A big hand came down on his shoulder, hard. "Stop it," Kilraven said firmly. "Torturing yourself won't help."

"Nothing seems to be helping, anyway," Jason replied heavily. "Damn it!"

Kilraven leaned close to his ear while Jon was discussing plans with his two cohorts inside. "They're getting ready to move right now," he said quietly. "They can't know," he added, jerking his head toward the others. "It isn't a sanctioned action. But the way the kidnappers are stalling, Gracie could be dead by the time they arrive at a mutually agreeable figure. We had to act."

Jason's eyes were anguished. "Tell me they won't let her get in the line of fire. Promise me!"

"Eb Scott sent the best he has. I worked with them when Rodrigo was captured. She won't get in the line of fire. And they'll bring her home."

Jason relaxed, just a little. "I hate bureaucracy."

"So does Jon," Kilraven said. "But he's strictly by-the-book, just like our father was. My stepmother goes nuts trying to set him up with women. He's such a prude."

Jason turned and looked the man in the eye. "You don't drink or sleep around or gamble, and you think your brother's a prude?"

Kilraven scowled. "I am not a prude," he said, loudly enough for the men in the room to hear.

"Yes, he is," Jon said from the doorway.

"I smoke cigars!" Kilraven informed him.

"One cigar a year isn't smoking, and you're still a prude." Jon chuckled, enjoying his brother's discomfort.

"We're going to take a break," Jon told Jason. "Maybe he'll call back in an hour or so and we can wrangle for another two hours. I'm sorry about this. Negotiations are hell. Most of us would prefer to rush in shooting," he added with a meaningful glance at his brother, "but this is the safest way."

"Of course it is," Kilraven agreed at once. "Notice that I'm here, instead of out in some run-down border village dressed in desert camo, carrying an automatic weapon."

"I did notice," Jon said irritably. "That doesn't mean you aren't playing advisor to someone who is."

Kilraven just grinned.

THE STOCKY MAN CAME UP onto the porch from the corner of the house, laughing coldly as Gracie stood up and tried to decide if she had a chance to make the door before he got her.

That hope was gone instantly as he reached out a pudgy hand and caught her by the upper arm. He was muscular, as if he worked out with weights all the time. Gracie had no way of knowing that his bulging biceps and tattoos were visible proof of his prison time. She only knew that he was stronger than she was, and that this was going to end badly. She had no martial arts training, except for what she'd learned from Marquez when he was home on weekends at his mother, Barbara's, house. That wasn't much.

She did, however, remember one move. As the stocky man jerked her toward him, she suddenly made her hands into fists with her thumbs sticking out and poked him on either side of his rib cage as hard as she could.

He let go of her, cursing and doubling over. It worked! Relief flooded through her and then she realized that she'd only made a bad situation worse as he grabbed for her.

"Big mistake," he grunted, one grimy hand going to

her breast, the other gripping her buttocks as his mouth aimed at hers.

"Help!" she screamed, struggling.

Angel's mother heard and came to the door, peering out fearfully.

"¡Vaya!" the man ordered, and her head retreated at once.

Gracie heard the door close and knew that she was lost.

While the ruffian was manhandling her, she tried to remember the other moves Marquez had taught her. If she could just get…her…hands…free!

Yes! She cupped them and slammed them against the stocky man's ears. He exploded in pain and rage. She twisted out of his loosened grasp and ran, her long legs carrying her off the porch and out toward the middle of the little pueblo.

"Help!" she yelled. "Help!"

Probably the Fuentes bunch would just look on and grin while the stocky drug dealer had his way with her, she thought in panic, but maybe those armed men in camo would take pity on her and come to help. Or not. Her heart was beating wildly, her breath jerking as she gasped to fill her lungs with air. She'd never felt more frightened during this whole ordeal. If only Jason were here to protect her, she thought wildly. If she'd given in when he'd kissed her, if she hadn't fought him…she wouldn't be in this awful predicament. Now her life was on the line and the violent ravishment of her body by this grimy thug. She would literally rather be dead. She tried to run faster, but she heard the quick thud of footsteps closing in on her. She wouldn't stop running. But she knew she'd lost the battle. There wasn't another human being in sight. There was no help.

The stocky man had recovered his sense, if not his hearing, and overtook her just as she reached a small, closed grocery store.

He jerked her around and bruisingly pinned her to the ground.

"Now," he growled, "you will pay for fighting me!"

8

GRACIE TRIED TO KICK HIM, but he was too powerful. She was out of breath and weak with fear. She was trapped. There was no hope left. But as she lay helpless, at the mercy of yet one more bullying male throwing her around, something rose in her like a fury. She was so tired of being a victim. Well, this criminal might kill her, but she was going to go out fighting. Her mother had been right. Some men were definitely animals. But this one was going to pay a price for what he was trying to do.

Seething with indignation, she turned her head suddenly and bit him on the cheek as hard as she could. She tasted blood in her mouth as he jerked up his head. He yelled, pressing his fingers against his cheek. He felt the blood. He cursed her and drew back a fist.

"Go ahead, coward," she spat at him. "Beat up a woman! Show the world what a brave man you are!"

The taunt rolled right off him. The man, still furious, lifted his fist to hit her again. She gritted her teeth, waiting for the blow, but she didn't close her eyes. She dared him to do it again. If he put his face close enough, she'd bite his nose off next time!

Before the man had a chance to strike her, there was an odd flash of light from somewhere nearby. A crack, like the pop of a firecracker. The man on top of her stiffened. His open eyes stared for an instant before they went blank and he fell on her completely.

She felt something wet on her chest, something with a metallic smell. She was too stunned to move. Past the man's body, a tall man was coming closer. He held a smoking pistol. It was the General himself, grim-faced and unsmiling, moving rapidly toward them.

Gracie shivered with relief, even as she relived the past when another man was killed next to her. Horrible memories intruded. She pushed at the unconscious stocky man, who was heavy on her, but she couldn't budge him. The General caught him by the collar and tossed him away as contemptuously as if he were a dirty rag. He knelt beside Gracie.

"*Niña*, are you all right?" he asked softly. "I am so sorry."

She'd been so brave while it was happening. Now, suddenly, she couldn't stop crying. The big man scooped her up against his chest and cuddled her. *"No llores,"* he whispered. "Don't cry. You are safe. I will never let anything or anyone hurt you. Never, as long as there is a breath in my body."

She caught her arms around his neck and held on for dear life. She felt safe. She wasn't afraid anymore.

The big man shuddered, at her ready acceptance of his protection. He had women in his life, but never one who made him feel so much a man, so necessary. She had almost been ravaged by that little tick lying so still nearby. She must have been terrified, a gentle woman like her. But she accepted Machado's comforting arms without hesitation, as if she felt at home there. His eyes closed on a wave of possession. If only he could keep her, he thought insanely, refuse the ransom and take her home with him, to stay forever.

But this was crazy thinking. She would never fit into the violence of his world, even if he could coax her into loving him. That would be unkind. She was not suited to revolution and assassination attempts. He smiled sadly as he stroked her disheveled hair. But dreams were sweet, and he had this little time with her, until she was returned home. He would savor it.

JASON THREW HIS OWN cell phone across the room, cursing so formidably that the agent, Hammock, actually backed up a step.

"Now see what you've done," Kilraven admonished his brother, Jon. "You've corrupted him."

"I've traded with that damned bank half my life, and they won't let me float a loan for a third of what I've got tied up in certificates of deposit in their own damned vault!" Jason raged. "When this is over I'll close every damned account I've got there!"

"I don't blame you," Jon told him. "But don't sweat it. We can manage this with counterfeit money. I'll send for it right now. All we need is the few minutes it takes for the kidnappers to scoop up the ransom money. We can trace them to their hideout and close in. They won't even have time to know it's counterfeit." He picked up his own cell phone and started punching in numbers.

Jason relaxed, just a little. Kilraven's announcement that the incursion to rescue Gracie had met with unforeseen obstacles didn't help his mood. In the intervening time the kidnappers had finally given them a figure and a promise of Gracie's return. He was trying to get the money together, only to be refused. He went to pick up his cell phone, checked to make sure it was still working and started to put it in his pocket. The theme song from a summer action movie blockbuster blared out in the silence. Jason opened the phone immediately.

"What?" he asked.

"Uh, Mr. Pendleton?" came a hesitant voice on the line. "This is Mark Peters? I'm the loan officer at your bank…"

"What the hell do you want now?" Jason snapped.

"Please, sir, I didn't realize who you were," the man stammered frantically. "The president of the bank, Mr. Lammers, had me call you right back. He said to tell you that the bank will loan you as much as you need to ransom Miss Marsh."

Jason took a steadying breath. "It's about time," he replied curtly.

"Sorry about all that, sir. If you tell me how much you need, I'll have the money ready when you get here. I'm new, sir. I didn't know who you were."

You'll damned sure know next time, won't you? Jason thought angrily, but he didn't say it.

"The FBI has the situation under control," Jason returned coldly. "Thank you for your offer, but it's unnecessary now. Goodbye."

"But, sir…!"

He closed the flip phone with a snap. He wasn't placated. John Lammers was going to have a hell of a time trying to keep his accounts, under the circumstances.

Jon Blackhawk walked back into the room. "Money's on the way," he told Jason. "It will be here in ten minutes."

"They said they'd phone at six with the drop information," Jason reminded him. He ran an angry hand through his hair. "You sure find out who your friends are when you're in a situation like this," he said, still fuming over the bank's initial refusal. "I helped John Lammers get customers for that bank when he set it up here. I actually moved money from another bank to help him out." He sighed, calming down. "But it's Gracie I'm worried about. At least we'll have something to show the kidnappers."

"It will work," Jon Blackhawk told him gently. "I promise you it will."

A booming hard rock tune exploded onto the brief silence and Kilraven opened his own phone, calling, "Sorry!" to the others as he headed out of the room to take the call.

"I never would have figured him for a hard rock fan," Jason pointed out.

Jon only chuckled.

The counterfeit money, obtained from a property room at the local police department with a judge's order, arrived on time. While Jon was taking delivery, Kilraven caught Jason's attention and jerked his head toward the kitchen.

When Jason joined him there, he closed the door. Kilraven's face was grim. "They're moving into the village right now," he said. "It took time to get the cooperation of the Mexican authorities, but your brother-in-law, Ramirez, apparently is related to the president there. He got things on track. We should know something in less time than it will take for your ransom call to come through."

Jason didn't speak. His expression did it for him. He looked five years older. He felt fifty. Please, God, he prayed silently, let her survive it. Let her live.

THERE WASN'T ANY ICE in the pueblo. Gracie bathed her bruises with a wet cloth Angel's worried mother had brought her. The young woman was so empathetic that she made Gracie feel as if she were part of a family. Machado, too, was concerned. He'd had his men take the body of the man who'd attacked Gracie back to Fuentes with a message. He didn't say what the message was.

She didn't ask. She was just relieved to have been rescued. It had been a traumatic evening altogether.

"I wish I'd bitten him harder," she muttered to herself, although she was sad that the man had lost his life for the attack on her. She would have liked to see him locked up. But it was possible, considering his violent past, that he would have killed her if Machado hadn't shot him. She only learned later that the man had been in prison, serving time for a pled-down murder charge. It wasn't the only one he'd committed, either, she was told. He'd killed at least two women, one of them his own sister.

Cold chills ran down her spine at the thought of how close she'd come to death, or something almost as bad.

Machado chuckled suddenly. "You have spirit," he murmured. "Josita saw what you did while she was waiting for Angel to fetch me. She said you bit the *pendejo* very hard."

She grimaced, remembering. "I'll probably die of blood poisoning," she mused.

He laughed. "No, I don't think so. You were very brave. You fought back, when you must have known it might cost you your life."

"At the time, it seemed the right thing to do," she replied, and was thinking that in the space of a few days in a terrible situation, her life had turned right around.

The vapid, scatty Gracie that her acquaintances knew had become someone quite different. She wasn't sure she recognized herself in this strong, brave woman who flirted with certain death.

"They will sing songs about you around the campfire after tonight," Machado told her with a gleaming smile.

"It was almost a death song," she said wanly.

"Yes, perhaps, but still…"

He was interrupted by a sudden explosion just on the outskirts of the pueblo. Machado jumped to his feet, pulling his pistol. He yelled to his men and sent a flurry of orders at them in Spanish.

"Stay here, stay down," he ordered Gracie and Josita. "It may be some of Fuentes's men getting revenge for the death of their man."

He turned and ran toward the rising flame of the explosion.

"Where's Angel?" Gracie asked frantically.

"There." Josita pointed toward the back of the adobe house. "Inside. No worry," she added in her broken English and tried to smile.

Gracie let out a relieved sigh. But she was more nervous now. What if the men were after her, blaming her for the man's death? She was responsible for it, even if she didn't shoot him. What would they do if they caught her? Would she be executed?

While she was running through nightmare scenarios in her mind, she heard a sound just behind her. She turned her head, just a fraction, just in time to see a tall, powerful-looking man in black with a mask over his face and an automatic weapon in his hand leap toward her.

"WHY DOESN'T HE CALL?" Jason muttered, glaring at the phones. "It's ten minutes past his own deadline!"

"Sometimes they play with the families of victims like his," Jon Blackhawk said quietly, trying to reassure him. "It's cruel, but it can be part of the game plan."

"I know a game I'd like to play with them," Jason said under his breath. With each passing day, he faced the prospect of losing Gracie forever. The past few days had been hell on earth. If he thought about it too long, he'd go mad.

Kilraven looked at his watch. "Back in a minute," he told the others. "I have to call one of the guys at the office who's covering for me."

"And which office would that be?" Jon teased, because he knew his older brother was only playing a part as a Jacobsville cop. He was a card-carrying fed, working undercover there.

"Never you mind," Kilraven mused. He left the room.

Jason stared at the phone, willing it to ring. But time dragged on, endlessly.

"IT'S ALL RIGHT," a familiar voice said as the man in black caught Gracie by the shoulder.

She couldn't see the face, but she knew that deep voice. It was Grange, Jason's foreman! "What are you doing here?" she shrieked.

"I'm not here," he replied drily. "You have to remember that."

"You're not here," she repeated, still gasping for breath after the scare he'd given her.

"Dead right." He motioned to another man, also in black, wearing a mask. "Stay with her until we make sure the diversion is keeping everybody else occupied at the other end of the camp. Don't make any noise."

"I'll be as quiet as a church mouse," the man beside her assured him.

"Wait," Gracie said urgently, catching at his arm. "There's a man here. He saved me from being…assaulted. He's protected me. You must try to see that he isn't hurt."

He drew an angry breath. "Gracie…"

"Please!"

"What does he look like?" the man asked irritably.

"You can't miss him—he'll be the tallest man in the camp. He looks a little like the opera star, Plácido Domingo, but much younger."

"That'll be easy to see in the dark," Grange said.

She glared at him. "Just do what you can."

"All right." He jerked his head at the other man, who nodded. Grange took off running toward a sudden burst of gunfire.

Gracie held her breath. So much violence. She wondered if she'd ever forget. And that kind man, the General, who'd helped her. What if they killed him trying to save her? Because she knew without a doubt that Jason had sent these men in after her. He couldn't be too angry…

She glanced at the taciturn man beside her. His face was covered, too. "Did Jason send you?" she asked.

"Yes."

She frowned. "Do I know you?"

He chuckled. "No," he replied. "And it wouldn't matter anyway, because I'm not here."

She smothered a laugh. "I get it. You and the rest of those guys are here on the QT while somebody with a government agency is sitting beside a telephone waiting for a ransom demand."

"Got it," he said easily. "They say your stepbrother is catching things on fire with his language."

"He can do that." She felt warmer. But then she remembered Kittie and his defense of her, and tears pricked her eyes. Kittie would be there at the house, waiting, with all Jason's nice new young staff. She couldn't set foot in that house, not after the way she'd left it. What a good thing she had Barbara's house to go to, and her job waiting when she returned. She wouldn't have to depend on Jason's charity. And somehow she'd pay him back for this rescue. If it took her forever.

A shadowy figure moved out of the darkness and suddenly rushed toward them, raising an automatic. The tall man beside her wheeled and let fly with a K-Bar. It hit the man dead center in the chest. The gun fell out of his hand and he crumpled to the ground with an odd hoarse cry. He didn't move.

"I'm sorry you had to see that," he said quietly. "Obviously one of the Fuentes bunch sent him to make sure you didn't leave here alive."

"Yes. Thanks," she added huskily. She could have told him that she'd seen two men killed in her life already, and that her nerves were numb from the latest. But she didn't.

He went to retrieve his knife, raising his head to listen. There were frantic yells far away, but nothing near them. Gracie hoped that Machado wouldn't be hurt. She owed him so much.

They waited in a tense silence until Grange came back, moving stealthily, with two other men in camo carrying automatic weapons. They had a man with them. Machado!

"This guy knows a way to get you out," Grange told Gracie in a low voice, indicating the newcomer.

"*Sí*," the General replied before Gracie could spill the

beans. "I work for *El General,*" he said, looking at Gracie. "I don't like him much. I will help you get the *señorita* out."

"We couldn't find your benefactor," Grange told her, "but we don't think he was one of the men we took out."

"Thanks," she said, trying not to give it away. Machado obviously didn't want to share his identity with the cavalry here. Only then did she notice that he was wearing a baseball cap and a windbreaker and stooping a little to disguise his height.

"They're looking for the source of the fireworks over there," Grange indicated a flame that was shooting up against the blackness of night. "They haven't even seen us, and they can't. We need to get you out of here right now."

"I'm ready when you are," she said nervously.

Machado gave her a quiet look and nodded. She nodded back.

He led them off into the darkness. Minutes later, she and the men piled into a truck and roared away. Machado stood on the running board on the side of the ancient vehicle, giving directions. They drove to a pontoon bridge, where Machado got off.

"Buena suerte, señorita," he told her with a flash of white teeth. "I will remember you," he added in a soft, deep tone.

"And I, you. Thank you," she said.

"We will meet again one day," he said softly. "Go quickly! *¡Amigos, adios!*" And he disappeared into the darkness.

"Gun it!" Grange called to the driver.

They shot across the river onto the shores of the Texas side of the border. There wasn't a soul in sight anywhere as they turned onto a main road and started toward San

Antonio. About a mile down the road, they stopped beside a big burgundy SUV. Grange and his masked companion got out, along with Gracie.

The men pulled off their masks and moved off the road. Two minutes later, they were back, dressed in jeans and shirts and boots and cowboy hats, minus the camo and weapons.

"Keep moving," Grange called to the other men, who were now likewise divested of commando wear and gear. "I'll see you both later. Thanks!"

They waved and took off. Gracie didn't see their faces.

"I'm free," she said, suddenly realizing it. "I'm free!"

"Damned straight," Grange said with a grin. "We'll drive you into San Antonio to the hospital. It's closer than Jacobsville."

"The hospital," she protested. "But…"

"You need to be looked at," Grange told her quietly. "Who roughed you up?"

"One of the Fuentes bunch," she said. "The man who helped me shot him dead while he was trying to assault me."

"Good for him," Grange said through his teeth.

"I'm sorry we didn't get to meet your protector," Grange said.

She laughed softly. "But you did."

"We did?" Grange frowned.

"Sure. He was the man who showed you how to get me out of the camp!" she told them.

There were muffled curses, which she pretended not to hear. "Somebody should phone Jason," she said quietly after a minute.

Grange stopped the car and handed her his own cell phone. "Get your story straight before you call him," he said firmly. "The drug dealers let you off on the side of the road. You don't know why. A kindly stranger picked you up and is driving you to the Hal Marshal Medical Center in San Antonio, got that?" he asked before she could punch in the number. "The kindly stranger won't stick around to be thanked, either. You'll be there in—" he checked his watch "—ten minutes. But tell him fifteen, so he doesn't kill himself getting to the facility."

"I will. Thanks, Grange," she said gently. "You, too," she told the other man, who was tall and dark-haired. "I'll never be able to thank you enough."

"Thank Eb Scott," Grange replied. "It was his operation. I just took point."

"Yes, but you guys took the risk."

Grange chuckled. "Call Jason. I imagine he's chewing nails by now."

The phone rang and a deep voice answered. "Pendleton," he said gruffly.

"Jason?"

"Gracie! Where are you? Have they hurt you…?"

He sounded frantic. She clutched the phone closer. "I'm okay. They just turned me loose on the side of the road. This nice old man picked me up in his truck and he's driving me to the Marshall Medical Center. We should be there in about fifteen minutes."

"I'll be right there."

The phone went dead.

"Do you mind if I call my stepsister, too?" she asked Grange.

"Go for it. I'm up to my ears in leftover minutes."

"Thanks."

After her emotional phone conversation with Glory, she handed Grange the phone. "You'd better step on it," she advised. "Glory and Rodrigo are practically next door to the hospital at the ballet, and are en route as we speak. But even though Jason has farther to go, he has a new Jag, and he needs a pilot's license to fly it."

"Yes, I know." Grange stepped hard on the accelerator.

Gracie locked her fingers together nervously. She wondered if he'd bring Kittie with him.

"THEY LET HER GO!" Jason called to Jon and Kilraven. "She's on her way to Marshall Memorial. I'm going over there!"

"You're not driving," Kilraven said at once, stepping in front of him. "You'll wreck the car. I'm driving."

"They didn't ask for ransom?" Jon Blackhawk asked, aghast.

"She'll explain when we get there. You coming?" Jason asked him.

"Do ducks fly? Hammock, pack up the equipment and lock up when you leave. I'll hitch a ride with my brother. You go with Hammock," Jon told his other colleague. "I'll phone you later."

The three men hit the front porch at a dead run and didn't stop until they reached Kilraven's car. They piled in, Jason in the front and Jon in back.

Kilraven left tire tracks getting down the driveway. He pulled out into traffic without braking and flashing blue lights suddenly spun into action behind them.

"Oh, hell!" Jason burst out.

"Not to worry." Kilraven chuckled. He picked up the mike, keyed it and called dispatch to find out who was behind him. Given the officer's badge number, he changed frequencies on his radio and talked to the prowler in pursuit. "I've got a pregnant lady here and we're trying to get to Marshall Memorial," he told the officer with a straight face. "I'm Jacobsville PD, off-duty. Can you give us a courtesy fifty-nine with all flags flying?"

"You'd better name it after me," came the drawled reply. "Okay, I'm coming around you. Follow me!"

"You bet! Thanks!"

The patrol car sped past them, lights still running. Traffic was light at that time of night, so there wasn't much to contend with.

Jason glanced at Kilraven. "I want to see you explain this if he sees us get out of the car," he said.

"I'll think up something. Hold on!"

Jason took time to phone Glory and Rodrigo, who were already on their way to the hospital from the ballet. Gracie had phoned her, Glory said. They promised to meet him at the hospital. He also called Barbara and asked her to relay the news to Mrs. Harcourt and Dilly. He wished he knew where John was, but he probably wouldn't be aware of the kidnapping in the first place.

Kilralven roared into the emergency room parking lot, tooting at the officer who'd escorted them as he swung into a parking space.

Three men exited the vehicle and ran up the ramp.

"What the hell!" the officer yelled after them.

"Come on in here and I'll explain everything!" Kilraven yelled back. "We're feds on a kidnapping case! The victim is in here!"

A car door opened and closed, but they were still running.

Bureaucracy took over with a vengeance at the emergency room desk, manned by a bored matronly lady with a humorless face. Jason figured he'd end up in jail for causing a riot, but he was going through that lady if he had to in order to get to Gracie.

As it happened, that wasn't necessary. Jon and Kilraven had their ID out before they got to the desk. All they had to do was flash it and give a cursory explanation to be admitted to the authorized area, along with Jason. The clerk checked on Gracie and told the men which cubicle she was in. Her family doctor was with her, she added.

Jason led the way down the hall to the treatment rooms. Dr. Harrison was there, sure enough, watching for them. Glory and Rodrigo were standing just inside a cubicle.

"Gracie's in here," Bob Harrison said, pausing to shake Jason's hand. "She's a little roughed up, but…"

Jason was already past him. Gracie was sitting on a treatment table, her skin bruised, her clothing torn, her silky blond hair dirty and standing out all over. She looked beautiful to the haggard man facing her. He moved forward abruptly and caught her hard into his arms, burying his face in her neck. He held on as if he was terrified he might lose her. His powerful body shuddered and his teeth clenched. He was too choked up with relief to even speak.

Behind Gracie, Glory and Rodrigo saw his expression and exchanged odd glances. That wasn't the expression of a man grateful that his stepsister was going to be all right. It was that of a man passionately involved with a woman who was his whole world. They felt almost like voyeurs, just watching him.

Gracie clung to Jason, shivering. She was safe. This was the only place in the world that she'd ever felt really safe, in Jason's strong arms. If only she was a whole woman. If only she could offer him a woman's passion and be held like this forever. But he was engaged. His fiancée hated her. She'd thrown her out of the house and she could never go back again.

As the memory came back full force of the past few weeks when Kittie was around, she began to pull back from Jason, her eyes downcast so that he couldn't see what was in them.

He had to force himself to let go. And then he noticed what he hadn't registered before. Someone had assaulted her. He let out a word that had the women in the room flushing.

9

"Jason!" Gracie exclaimed, shocked.

"Who did that to you?" he asked furiously. "I'll hunt him down and kill him if it's the last thing I ever do in my life!"

She'd never seen him so enraged. "He's dead," she said at once. "I had a protector in the camp, Jason," she added quietly. "He kept Fuentes's men from harming me. He shot the man who...who tried to hurt me."

"The bastard attacked you!" he raged.

"Yes," she said huskily. "I bit off part of his face, first," she added with a smile.

His eyes sparkled. "You what?"

"I bit him," she said, laughing softly.

"My God," Jason said gruffly. Gracie had never fought anyone in the twelve years he'd known her.

"When he grabbed me, I used some self-defense that Marquez had taught me. I dug my thumbs into his rib cage and then cupped my hands and slammed them over his ears. I ran and I thought I could get away, but he caught me and wrestled me down. I thought I was done for, but the woman I stayed with sent her son to find the General and he shot the man dead." She swallowed hard. "I owe him a lot. I hope the Fuentes bunch won't kill him for helping me escape and losing the ransom."

"What General?" Jon Blackhawk asked, scowling.

"Emilio Machado," she replied. "He…"

"Machado? My God!" Jon whipped out his cell phone. "You can't leave until I get back," he added, walking out of the room while he punched in numbers.

"Machado!" Kilraven exclaimed. "So that's where he went!"

"You know him?" Gracie asked, confused.

"Know him? Hell, everybody in Justice knows him!" Kilraven replied. "He was the best friend we had in South America until this nasty little group of anarchists overthrew his government. We were afraid he'd been killed. Nobody knew where he was."

She felt lightheaded. "He's not a bad guy?"

"The reverse," Kilraven replied. "We want to help put him back in power, but the political climate isn't conducive to international meddling right now. What's he doing with the Fuentes bunch? He hates drug lords!"

"He's trying to get enough money to regain his power," she replied.

"And he helped you escape?"

She nodded, shifting to a more comfortable position. "Boy, that hurts."

Jason moved closer again, bending to put his lips gently against her bruised shoulder. "Help any?" he asked softly, his black eyes smiling into hers.

She caught her breath at his expression, and the delight that being close to him always produced. She looked at his mouth helplessly.

"Could I get the four of you to leave for a moment while I examine my patient?" Bob Harrison asked, chuckling. "You aren't supposed to be in here, you know."

"We feds bluffed the staff," Kilraven murmured with a grin. "It was the only way we could get in. We were worried."

"Yes, I understand, but I need…" The doctor's cell phone rang. He answered it, shooing Glory, Rodrigo and Kilraven out in front of him.

Jason stayed behind. "I thought I'd go mad," he whispered. He bent and grazed his mouth tenderly over Gracie's. "God, I was scared!" He kissed her harder, groaning when she stiffened and gasped.

He jerked back, his eyes blazing, his face ruddy with frustrated passion. "Sorry," he ground out, averting his gaze. "I've been out of my mind with fear. Couldn't help it."

"It's…it's all right," she stammered.

He looked back into her eyes, frowning. She didn't look as if he'd frightened her. Or disgusted her. He was remembering the ordeal she'd been through. He felt guilty for touching her like that, even gently.

His fingers smoothed over her bruised skin and he winced, as if it hurt him to see it.

Fascinated, her fingers went up to cover his. She looked into his black eyes and felt as if part of her was melting onto the examination table.

"I thought they might kill you," he said hoarsely. "And I remembered the fight over Mumbles and how I'd taken Kittie's side against you." He closed his eyes. "Hell on earth, Gracie."

Her fingers tightened around his. "I'm all right," she said. "I just look bad."

He brought her fingers to his mouth and kissed them hungrily. "You look beautiful to me."

Her whole body tingled from the contact. She studied him with shy delight in her face, a flush that was revealing and flattering.

Jason lifted his head and searched her soft eyes. His gaze fell to her mouth. Slowly, so that he didn't frighten her, he bent and touched his lips delicately to hers, brushing them tenderly. She didn't withdraw. He caught her upper lip in both of his and slid his tongue just under the silky skin, teasing it. Her breath stopped in her throat and she made an odd little gasping sound.

He drew away again, studying her. She wasn't trying to get away. In fact, she looked as if she wanted him to do it again.

He framed her face in his big, warm hands and bent again. His mouth smoothed her lips apart and moved between them in a slow, delicate, sensual tasting that made her stiffen, but not with fear.

When he lifted his mouth, hers followed it. She'd forgotten Kittie, the argument, everything. All she knew was that kissing Jason was delicious. Her arms slid hesitantly up around his neck, coaxing him back to her. This time the kiss was neither tender nor brief. It was a conflagration, like tossing matches into dry wood. It was so sensuous that she even forgot her aches and pains.

But after a minute, he pulled back from her, breathing roughly. His eyes were smoldering. There was a question in them.

"The last time, when you landed the car in the ditch, you pushed me away and ran!" he whispered, confused.

"You scared me," she whispered back. "You put your mouth on my...on my..." She cleared her throat. "I remembered my mother. He…my father…bit her there. She came out of the bedroom night after night with her gown soaked in blood!"

"What?" he exclaimed, shocked.

"She had scars," she managed to say. "She said…that men were only gentle until they got you behind a locked door, and then they were animals. She warned me. She said men liked to hurt women, that it was the only way they got pleasure out of it."

His eyes darkened even more. "Not me," he whispered. "Not ever!"

Her eyes softened as they searched his. "Really?"

His heart ran away. Those eyes were saying something incredible to him.

Suddenly they dropped, as reality came back full force. "Did Kittie come with you?" she asked coldly.

"Kittie?" He caught his breath. "Kittie… No! Hell, no! She's in New York. I broke the engagement and kicked her out of the house the minute I knew what she'd done to you and the others!"

"You're not engaged to her anymore?" she asked breathlessly.

"No," he said huskily.

"But you loved her," she began.

"Never!"

"I don't understand," she said, wide-eyed.

He bent and brushed his mouth over hers again, lingering this time. "We'll talk at the house," he whispered. "When you've been examined, I'll take you home."

She bit her lower lip. "But I don't live there anymore," she said. "I live with Barbara in Jacobsville. I have a job now, and a car…"

"What?!"

She wanted to explain, but Dr. Harrison walked in and shooed a protesting, cursing Jason out of the cubicle. After he examined her and gave her something for pain, the feds were back and she was too tranquillized to talk anymore. She told Jason that she was going to ride to Jacobsville with Glory and Rodrigo.

"I'll come down and see you tomorrow," he said doggedly.

She nodded.

"I'm coming down, too," Jon Blackhawk added. "You have to talk to me about Machado. There are plans in the works that you're becoming critical to. All right?"

"All right," she agreed.

Glory and Rodrigo stabilized her as she walked out of the cubicle. Jason watched her go with bridled rage. He felt as if the whole world was conspiring to keep him away from Gracie.

Jason walked out past the policeman who'd escorted them to the hospital. He'd been talking to Kilraven and he had an amused look on his face.

"Was it a boy or a girl?" he asked Jason.

Jason turned toward him with the frustration of the whole miserable time in his black eyes. The policeman held up both hands and walked away, laughing to himself.

GRACIE SLEPT UNTIL THE next afternoon in Barbara's guest room, where she'd been staying since she left the mansion in San Antonio. When she woke up, Jason was sitting on the side of her bed, wearing working clothes. He'd been out with his men, too, she could tell. His batwing chaps were dusty and his blue-checked Western-cut shirt and Stetson were stained with sweat.

"How do you feel?" he asked gently.

She managed a smile, but winced at the pain. "Bruised and battered," she said. She looked at him with knowing eyes. "Just like you. It can't be working cattle. Roundup was two months ago."

"We're shipping out more culls," he said. "We had a bumper crop of hay and corn, despite the flooding, so we can feed out our own yearlings, but we're getting rid of the older females who aren't pregnant."

She grimaced. "It isn't nice to eat cows who don't have calves."

He laughed softly and took off his hat, tossing it onto a nearby chair. "I don't run beef cattle," he reminded her.

"Then where are you shipping them?"

"To ranchers who do run beef cattle," he replied wickedly.

She laughed softly.

His black eyes went over her like hands, bold on her body in the soft flannel gown that clung lovingly to her breasts.

She flushed and tugged at the cover.

He averted his gaze to the floor. "We've never talked about intimate things together," he said after a minute. "I had no idea that your mother had been treated that way. Odd, that she'd marry my father," he added, glancing at Gracie. "He went through women like tissue paper. He only married the ones who refused to sleep with him."

She toyed with the coverlet. This was painful territory. She didn't want to tell him too much. "She'd been abused for so many years, I guess she was overwhelmed when your father was kind and gentle with her. Maybe she thought she could sleep with him, if she tried, and then in the end, she couldn't..." She stopped when she saw his face.

He scowled. "Gracie, what do you know that you haven't told me?"

She could have cursed her own lack of restraint. But perhaps that wasn't so very bad. She could tell him that. She bit her lower lip. "She said that he'd been kind to her and she really wanted to please him, but she couldn't… she just couldn't do it with him. He was furious. He was going to divorce her. She was afraid for me. We had no family except each other." She closed her eyes. "Everybody else thought it was an accident, but I knew better. She aimed for that tree, Jason. She couldn't live with what she was."

He let out the breath he'd been holding. "Did he know, about her first marriage?"

"She didn't want anybody to know," she said slowly. "Especially him." She lowered her eyes.

"What a hell of a way to begin a marriage."

"With lies," she agreed sadly. "You don't know what it was like," she said hesitantly. "Even when I was little, I could hear her crying, late at night. She never let me see what he did to her until I was almost fourteen. I was up late watching a movie when she came out of the bedroom. It scared me to death. Her whole gown was soaked in blood." She shuddered. "I made her let me treat the cuts. He did it with his teeth. He had to hurt her to…get anything out of it, she said. It had been that way since they married, but much, much worse after he started, well, started drinking."

He didn't know what to say. He was shocked. Speechless.

She avoided his eyes. "She had deep scars all over her chest. She said all men were like that, they couldn't get any satisfaction unless they hurt women. She said I could never trust any man, no matter how gentle he seemed, that my father had been gentle too, at first. But once they were married, and she was pregnant, it was too late. He kept her by threatening to take me away from her. She had no education, nothing except a pretty face. She believed he could do it. She stayed for me." She trembled. "I've been terrified of sex all my life, Jason. It's why I've stayed single. Every time I think about it, I see her..." She let her voice trail off.

He hadn't expected what he was hearing. It had never occurred to him that any man could be that brutal with a woman. He'd heard stories about other men, but this was out of his experience. No wonder she ran from him. He hadn't been particularly gentle with her that night, either. His passion had burst its bonds. He must have seemed threatening.

"God, I'm sorry," he said huskily. "I had no idea. None at all."

She bunched up the cover in her fingers. "We didn't talk about things like that. I couldn't find a way to tell you. Then there was Kittie..."

"Yes. There was Kittie." He felt two inches high. He'd used Kittie to wound her. It was a sickening thought, that he'd added to her emotional scars.

A soft meow caught his attention. Old Mumbles jumped up onto the bed and came to him, rubbing against his arm. He smoothed his hand over the old cat's enormous head. "Hi, Mumbles." He glanced at Gracie. "I told Mrs. Harcourt to tell you that we'd keep him if I had to build him a damned house of his own. Did she tell you?"

She shook her head. "We had other things to worry about by then."

"What other things?" he asked, suspicious. "How did Kittie get all of you out of the house without a fight? You can't have thought I'd allow it?"

She lowered her eyes to Mumbles, who came and sat on her chest, still purring. "I didn't know how you felt. You took her side against all of us. She said you felt that I was taking advantage of you by letting you support me, when I wasn't even family. I hadn't ever thought of it from your point of view, but I had to, after that. She was right, Jason. You don't owe me a thing."

He let out a barrage of bad words that cut her off. He got to his feet, running an angry hand through his hair, stuck his hands in the pockets of his jeans and stared blindly out the window.

"Don't," she said worriedly. "I can support myself. I have a job. I'm standing on my own two feet for the first time in my life. It isn't a punishment, Jason. I'm... learning that I have abilities I never guessed I had. I can do more than hostess parties and give teas," she added bitterly.

He winced. "I said that, didn't I? That, and a lot more." His tall frame seemed to stoop. "It seems like a hundred years since we went to that sale barn."

"Yes," she agreed. It had been like another life, considering what had happened between then and now.

"You pushed me away," he said after a minute. "Savaged my pride. Made me ashamed of myself. I went off to New York and got drunk at a party. I woke up in bed with Kittie."

She closed her eyes on a wave of nausea and pain. He'd slept with that redheaded spider. He'd slept with her!

"Damn you!" she sobbed angrily.

He whirled. If that wasn't jealousy, he didn't know anything about women. He moved back to the bed and looked down at her, fascinated.

"You slept with her!"

He drew in a long breath. It might have been to his advantage to let her think that, but she'd been through so much already. He couldn't hurt her any more than he already had.

"I wasn't sure if I had or not," he confessed quietly. "I knew I was too far gone to have thought about precautions. So if it had happened, there might have been a child." He averted his eyes. It was mortifying, that admission. "I had to keep her around until I was sure. She used it. We could get engaged, she said, just in case. I was hurting and ashamed of what had happened with you. I didn't have much to look forward to." He shrugged. "I gave in. Later, I found out that she'd had a couple of dozen men in the same time frame she'd supposedly slept with me. I put the pressure on and she confessed that nothing had happened."

Gracie relaxed, visibly.

"By then, everybody knew we were engaged and I was in such a black mood and so overwhelmed with business worries that I just let it go on. I didn't care much about anything anymore." He met her wounded eyes. "I met her in London and she asked if she could stay in the house and just make a few little adjustments to the décor." He laughed hollowly. "I had no idea what she was capable of until I walked in unexpectedly and saw her idea of adjustments." He flinched. "Your room looked like a bordello. All your clothes were gone, even the gown I brought you from Paris…" He looked as if that hurt most of all.

"John and I hid my few bits of furniture and some clothes and Christmas decorations in the attic," she confessed. "I doubt if Kittie wanted to risk dust and bugs by looking up there for all of it."

He smiled. "Good for John. At least not everything was destroyed."

She searched his black eyes. "You were engaged to her for months."

He knew what she was hinting at. He sat back down beside her, leaning across her prone body with a big hand beside her head on the snowy-white pillowcase. "I couldn't."

"Excuse me?"

"I couldn't have sex with her," he said bluntly. "That was the biggest source of friction. She saw a bottomless checkbook with everything she wanted in it. All she had to do was get me into bed again and claim she was pregnant. But it backfired. By that time, I knew her all too well. She didn't love me. She didn't even want me. She wanted what I had."

"I could have told you that the first time I saw her," she said bitterly.

He studied her closed expression. "She hated you. She hated every member of the staff. She wanted to shut off access to anybody who might become a threat." He laughed shortly.

"She overplayed her hand when she wanted Mumbles out of the house. That was the last straw…and upsetting Mrs. Harcourt at her birthday party hadn't helped," he added.

"Poor Mrs. Harcourt," she said quietly. "She's been through so much."

"I don't understand why she left," he said. "She knew I'd never let Kittie fire her."

Gracie moved her head on the pillow. "She talked to Kittie alone. Up until then, she said she was staying until you told her to leave. She was white in the face and just scared to death." She hesitated. "Do you think she has some dark secret that Kittie knows about in her past?"

His free hand touched her silky hair, spread it over the white pillow. It looked like pale sunlight in winter. "I wouldn't think so. She came to live with my parents just before I was born. She's been more of a mother to me than my own was. I lost my mother when I was small. Mrs. Harcourt was the one who kissed the cuts and cuddled me when I was afraid of the dark." His face hardened. "I was outraged when I knew Kittie had fired her."

"Barbara gave her a job. Dilly, too."

"Well, they've both been rehired," he said darkly. "They're already up in San Antonio overseeing the re-modeling. I hired a firm to put everything back the way it was, including your room." He added the last hopefully.

She drew in a soft breath. "I'm not coming back, Jason."

He started to argue. She reached up and put her fingers gently over his firm lips. Incredibly, the light touch seemed to fascinate him.

"I have an opportunity to stand on my own two feet, to show that I can make a living, pay rent, be independent. I've had everything I wanted since I was fourteen. Now I want to see what I can do on my own."

He caught her fingers in his hand and kissed the tips tenderly. "Something I've never done," he said quietly. "My father was wealthy. He inherited a lot, and my mother's people were also well-to-do. I've never had to make my own way." He sounded bitter.

"But you have," she protested. "Jason, when you bought that ranch in Comanche Wells, it was a broken-down, bankrupt little piece of scrub land with a few mangy cattle on it! You've built it into one of the most well-known seed bull enterprises in the state! You didn't inherit that, you earned it."

He was surprised by her vehemence. "I hadn't thought of it that way."

"If your father hadn't left you anything, you'd still be rich. You have a good business head on your shoulders."

"Courtesy of an expensive college education."

"You have to have the talent."

He smiled. His black eyes lingered over her bruises and he grimaced. "I could have spared you this," he said heavily. "If I hadn't been so wrapped up in saving a business, I'd have been home, you never would have been abducted."

"My mother always used to say that things happened for a reason," she said, trying to soothe him. He looked tormented. "I've had a cushy life. You spoiled me. You spoiled Glory, too, but especially me. I've never had to work for anything."

"You worked hard at that history degree," he countered then frowned. "You had to have tutors for every subject. You didn't have a social life, except for your male… friend, the whole time. I'd forgotten that."

She hesitated. She really wanted to tell him everything. But she was still a little afraid of his reaction.

"You don't trust me, Gracie," he said. "You're keeping things back."

She moved restlessly on the sheet. "You said it yourself. We've never really talked to each other, beyond everyday things."

His fingers went to her cheek and brushed lightly over it. "Barbara said I didn't know you at all, that I never wanted to. She was wrong." His eyes began to glitter. "I want to know everything about you."

Her heart jumped. His expression wasn't really threatening, but it held elements of a fierce passion. She'd felt it more than once, especially the day before when he'd plowed through people getting to her in the hospital.

Her fingers curled around his. "You might not like what you find out."

So there was more. His eyes narrowed. "Tell me."

She hesitated. Perhaps it wouldn't matter. But perhaps it would. How would he react to the whole truth? In the back of her mind, she recalled Kittie's threat to make it all public. But Kittie was out of the picture now. She wouldn't have any real reason to throw Gracie to the media wolves. Or would she? If Jason found out that way, would he ever forgive her for hiding it all these years?

"You're procrastinating," he accused. "At least tell me why you had to have tutors, when your mind is sharp as a whip."

That might not hurt so much. "I had a…a head injury just before my mother and I came to live with you."

His breath caught in his throat. "A head injury?"

She nodded.

"How did you get it?"

She drew in a long breath and went for broke. "I was late getting home from the library because my friend's mother's car had engine trouble. We had to walk to a service station and I got a ride home from the mechanic." Her eyes closed. It was a bad memory. "My father was waiting at the door. He said all women were sluts, like my mother, just asking for whatever they got from men. He said he'd make me sorry I'd behaved that way."

Jason didn't say a word. He waited, tense, holding her fingers tight.

"He picked me up and threw me headfirst into a wall, Jason," she said quietly.

10

JASON CURSED VIOLENTLY. In that instant, a lot of things became crystal clear in his mind, above everything why Gracie didn't like to be picked up.

He smoothed back her soft hair, his eyes reflecting the pain he felt at the admission. "I wish I'd known you then," he said softly. "I'd have wiped the floor with your father!"

She knew he meant it. He'd always been protective with her, always gentle. She wondered why she'd ever thought he might hurt her, even in intimacy.

"I guess we really do carry our childhoods around with us all our lives," she said reflectively. "My mother drilled it into me that I could never trust a man intimately. I know she was only trying to protect me, to spare me from what she went through. But she warped me. I guess the glitch in my brain didn't help much, either."

"That's why you have so many falls," he guessed.

She nodded. "It messed up some of my motor functions. Not to a crippling degree, and there has been some improvement over the years. But I'll never be completely normal. I have to work harder than most people to learn new things."

"It doesn't matter," he said gruffly. His hand smoothed down to her mouth and his thumb teased across it. "You're perfect to me just the way you are."

She was hesitant. "I thought it would change things if you knew," she said.

His black eyes met her light ones. "Would it matter to you, if you found out some dark secret from my past?" he teased.

She laughed. "You don't have any dark secrets, Jason."

"That's what you think," he murmured. "Answer the question."

"No. Nothing would change."

"Exactly." He waited for her to get the point.

She was still undecided. "Maybe there are worse things," she began.

"Maybe you should tell me, and get it all out in the open," he replied. "I told you it wouldn't change anything. It won't."

She sighed. "All right. But give me a little time, Jason. I'm pretty overwhelmed right now."

"Yes. And it was my fault," he added.

She hated the anguish in his lean, handsome face. She reached up and tugged at his head, pulling it down to her. "Stop that," she whispered. "You didn't know I was going to get kidnapped. You didn't have a thing to do with it."

He was trying to listen, but his eyes were fixed on her soft mouth. He looked as if he were starving to death.

She liked that. She enjoyed the intensity of his eyes on her mouth. She tugged and parted her lips just as his opened over them. It was like flying, she thought with pure delight. He wasn't fighting her. He was, if anything, trying to manage a little restraint. He didn't know, but that wasn't necessary. Not at all. She slid her arms around him and pulled hard.

His lean body crushed down over hers before he could brace himself. "Gracie," he groaned.

She wasn't listening. He wasn't fighting very hard, either. She raised up, positioning her mouth slowly against his so that she increased the pressure and the intimacy of the light, warm kiss. She coaxed him into recklessness. She moaned, because the feelings she was experiencing were new and hot and delicious.

"For God's sake…!" He opened his mouth over hers and thrust his tongue deep into her soft, warm mouth.

She gasped, but already the heat was washing over her, as well. She felt his lean hand at her breast, claiming it hungrily, caressing it in his palm. He moved half onto the bed beside her and his arms slid under her, grinding her soft breasts up against his broad chest. Even through two layers of fabric, the contact was electric, arousing.

"You little fool," he murmured against her mouth as his hand drew back and started working buttons out of buttonholes. "What if I can't stop…?"

By then, his bare hand was cupping her breast under her gown and she lifted completely off the bed, shivering with the delight of the contact.

"It's so good," she whispered.

"I know something better," he bit off against her lips.

While she was trying to figure that out, his mouth slid down her throat, under the gown and right onto her soft, bare breast. She tensed at first, but he wasn't hurting her. His lips smoothed over the silky, warm skin, exploring, savoring. His tongue curled around the nipple and made it go suddenly hard and sensitive.

She gasped, arching up to increase the pressure. She heard a soft, deep laugh, and then he positioned her and his mouth swallowed her up whole. He drew her inside the dark, sensual warmth with a slow, seductive suction that made her go up like a Chinese rocket.

Exploding, mindless with pleasure, her nails bit into his shoulders and she moaned, a high-pitched aching kind of sound that aroused him even more. When her body went rigid and started shuddering, he lost all semblance of control and suckled her hard enough to leave a crimson stain, a love mark, that wouldn't fade for days.

When he lifted his head, she was stunned, panicked, with tears of shame running down her cheeks.

It was hard not to feel conceited. He knew without asking that she'd never felt anything like it in her life. It was like a tiny climax, a release of the tension he'd built in her with his mouth. She shivered and flushed. He kissed away the tears, his lips warm and tender and patient.

"Nobody ever said…it felt like that," she managed shakily.

"You can't describe it with words," he whispered sensually. His mouth brushed lightly over hers. "I made you climax. Your breasts are incredibly sensitive."

She was lost for words. She didn't know what to say, how to feel. Her shy, worried eyes met his. He was smiling, but it wasn't a pompous sort of smile. It was full of lazy affection. That, and pride.

He looked down at her small, firm breast and traced around it with a long forefinger. "I left marks. I'm sorry. I lost my head a little."

She looked where he was touching. There was a crimson mark from his mouth there. "It didn't hurt."

"It isn't supposed to hurt," he replied quietly. "It's supposed to make you explode."

She flushed.

He smiled. "Now you know."

She reached up and touched his mouth with her fingers. She was fascinated by him. He was looking at her breasts and she was letting him, enjoying his eyes on her, his hands on her. "Jason," she whispered, "does sex feel like this?"

His breathing changed as he met her wide, curious eyes.

The tension in the room was suddenly so thick it was oppressing. He looked down at her body and swallowed hard. He could pull the rest of that gown away. He could throw off his clothes. He could go into her, hard and deep, and push her into the mattress with the weight of his body while he had her. She would let him. Her eyes were giving away all sorts of secrets. She'd cried out when he'd suckled her. She was noisy. She would cry out endlessly as he pleasured her... But the house was empty. Nobody would hear them.

He ached to have her. It was a pain that never eased. He would be gentle with her. He would give her a memory of him that would never fade, that would make her totally, completely his own. It was wrong, he knew. She was religious. She would regret it. But he was so far gone now that he couldn't think past relief. Even as he told himself he had to stop, his hands were going to the gown, to push it down her body...

The sudden insistent jangle of the doorbell burst like an explosion into the raging heat of the bedroom.

Jason's hands stilled on the nightgown that was already down around Gracie's rounded hips. They looked at each other in disbelief.

The doorbell sounded again.

Jason groaned. His body was clenched in agony. He forced himself to drag his eyes from Gracie's firm, hard breasts and get up from the bed. Turning away, he struggled to regain his control, to make his body release the anguished tension that whipped through him.

Gracie fumbled her gown back on. She was shaking. It had almost gone too far. She'd coaxed Jason into indiscretion and now it was going to haunt them both. She got out of bed, shouldering into a robe, grimacing as her bruised muscles and her sensitized breast protested.

"I'll get it," she whispered without looking at him.

She went down the hall barefooted. At the front door, she looked out through the peephole. It was FBI Special Agent Jon Blackhawk, in a vested suit, his ponytail as dignified as his lean, handsome face.

She opened the door. "Agent Blackhawk," she greeted.

He frowned. She looked very flushed. "Are you okay?" he asked worriedly. "I needed to ask you some questions about Machado, but you don't look well. I could come back…"

"No need," she said. "Honest." She opened the door and led him into the living room. "Would you like something to drink?"

"I'll make coffee," Jason Pendleton said from the doorway. He looked a little flushed, too. He was dressed in working clothes, amusing Blackhawk, who'd only ever seen him in dignified city clothes. He looked like a different man.

Blackhawk wasn't blind to the fact that he'd interrupted something between the two of them, but he'd learned to pretend. It helped him with his job. "I'd love a cup. I missed mine this morning."

"Coming right up. Gracie?" Jason asked in a different tone.

She smiled at him. "Yes, please."

He smiled back and turned away to the kitchen.

JON BLACKHAWK WAS THOROUGH in his questioning. He wanted to know everything Gracie had seen in the camp, right down to the number of men and how they were clothed.

"There were a lot of military men down there," she told him. "They were wearing uniforms. The General didn't like the Fuentes bunch. He said he allowed them in the vicinity, but he hated drug lords. It was one of Fuentes's men who attacked me," she added tightly.

"Someday that bunch will fall, just like Manuel Lopez's organization did," Jon assured her.

"Yes, and somebody will step in to fill his shoes," Jason added. He was sitting across from them in an armchair, looking very much at home. He stared at Gracie when she wasn't looking, filling his eyes with her flushed beauty.

"Life goes on," Jon agreed. He looked at his notes. "Did the General mention any plans to retake his government?"

She shook her head. "He only said he was going to get it back. It's why he's kidnapping people." She grimaced. "I expect he's kicking himself about now after losing my ransom."

"My brother helped that along," Jon said irritably. "He was involved with a snatch and grab, assisted by persons in Jacobsville who will remain anonymous, apparently."

"Kilraven was afraid Gracie might be killed while we

were negotiating," Jason said quietly. "So was I, frankly. If you need someone to blame, I'm your man. I wouldn't risk her. Not for anything." He looked at Gracie with eyes that could have started fires.

She beamed. "I knew you had to be behind it when they came in."

"They?" Jon asked.

"Grr…great balls of fire, is that the time?" she exclaimed, having just caught herself from mentioning the name of her rescuer. "I have to meet Barbara for lunch!"

"In your condition?" Jason exclaimed. "Are you out of your mind?"

Even as she spoke, a car pulled into the driveway. Barbara's car.

"Oh, hell," Jason muttered under his breath.

Gracie blushed.

Jon bit back a laugh. He had a good idea of what was going on. He didn't say so, of course. He was a gentleman.

He got two more questions out before Barbara walked in with bags of food from the restaurant. She stopped in the doorway and stared. There was Gracie in a nightgown and robe, her hair tousled, her face flushed. There was Jason, looking out of sorts and frustrated. And there was FBI Special Agent Blackhawk, obviously amused by it all. He stood up as she entered. So did Jason. Old-World manners, Barbara thought with indulgent amusement.

"I brought lunch," she told Gracie. She glanced at the men. "Maybe I should go back for more."

"Maybe you shouldn't," Jason said. "I've got cattle to move. I just stopped by to see how Gracie was doing."

"I was getting intel," Jon added. "I think I've got enough for now, but I'll phone you, if I may, if I think of anything else."

"Of course," Gracie said.

"Thanks. See you," he told Jason.

Barbara carried the food into the kitchen. Jason helped Gracie up from the sofa, his eyes soft and possessive.

"I'll see you later," he said softly. He brushed back the disheveled hair from her face. "In a couple of days, wouldn't you like to come over and supervise?"

"Supervise what?" she asked.

"Next Thursday is Thanksgiving. We need to put up Christmas trees and decorations," he murmured, staring at her lips. "I'll get the men to help. We'll bring Dilly and Mrs. Harcourt down from San Antonio and let them start decorating here."

She felt the joy drain out of her. "I don't want to this year," she said without looking at him. "Maybe Kittie was right. You've never liked having the place swimming in decorations, anyway. It's just a big fuss, that's all. Mrs. Harcourt can put up a tree for you at the ranch."

His heart sank. He could see the reason she'd lost her enthusiasm for the holiday. He felt guilty all over again. "Gracie, you love decorating for the holidays."

She met his eyes and winced. "I can't. Not this year. I can't, Jason."

He drew in a ragged breath. "Okay. I won't push it. You're coming over for Thanksgiving dinner, though, right?"

She hesitated.

His face hardened. He wondered if what had happened in her bedroom had influenced her hesitation. Was she feeling guilty? Had he made her feel ashamed of what had happened? She'd wanted him, he knew she had. What was wrong?

"Gracie, about what happened…" he began.

Blushing, she turned away. It was embarrassing, the way she'd practically thrown herself at him. The wild abandon wasn't like her, and she was confused and a little afraid of what had almost happened. She needed time to sort out her feelings. "I have to help Barbara in the kitchen. Goodbye, Jason."

She walked out, just like that.

He held in the bad language until he was back in his truck, speeding away from the house. He'd never been so frustrated. Something in Gracie's past was holding them apart, making her hesitant, spoiling things. He didn't know what terrible secret she was hiding from him. He'd never pushed her for answers. But what he'd already learned made him certain that there was more. Much more. He wanted answers, by God, and he was going to get them!

"JASON'S IN A SNIT," Barbara commented as Jason left skid marks on her cement driveway going out into the road.

"He's just in a hurry," Gracie replied warily. "He's not used to the ranch trucks."

"He's frustrated."

"Barbara!"

"Both of you were flushed and disheveled," she returned with a grin. "Just what was going on here while I was working?"

"Barbara!"

"It's about time, is all I have to say," the older woman mused.

"What do you mean?" Gracie asked as she joined her friend at the table, where Barbara was filling glasses with iced tea.

"I mean, Jason smolders every time he looks at you. Don't tell me you haven't noticed?"

Gracie's heart jumped. "Really?"

"Wasn't he inviting you to decorate the house?" she asked.

Gracie picked at her sandwich. "Yes. Kittie made fun of it. She said nobody put up decorations like that anymore, and that I went overboard. Jason had already been saying it for years."

"And you're going to let that stop you?" her friend asked, aghast. "Gracie, you always did have a style of your own. You should do what you like, without wondering what other people think. I loved your decorations. The neighbors used to drive by the house every holiday season—they looked forward to seeing what new color scheme you came up with." Her eyes lit up. "It was like a gift you gave to the whole community. I expect it was like that in San Antonio, at the mansion, as well."

She knew it was. But the memory of Kittie still hurt, even more now that she knew Jason had almost made a mistake that could have forced him to marry the terrible woman. Gracie would have lost him forever.

"Kittie is history," Barbara said firmly. "She only wanted what Jason had. She didn't love him."

"He was attracted to her," Gracie said quietly.

"Was he? Or was she a consolation prize for what he really wanted?"

"I don't know."

"You should go over for Thanksgiving," Barbara said firmly.

But Gracie wasn't sure she wanted to. She loved Jason with all her heart, and she'd wanted him desperately earlier in the day. But even heavy petting wasn't sex. She didn't know if she could give him what he wanted. She was afraid to find out. If she refused him a second time, he might really go off the deep end. He might go back to Kittie in desperation. It might end all her dreams. She had to have time to think about what to do.

IT WAS WORRYING THAT Jason didn't phone her or come by again. Gracie got out of bed the next day. School was closed for the Thanksgiving holidays, but she helped Barbara at the café, against the older woman's wishes. Jason didn't contact her. She thought of calling him, but she was still too embarrassed about the way they'd parted.

Mrs. Harcourt phoned her Thanksgiving night, at two in the morning. Gracie answered the phone half-asleep.

"Hello?"

"Miss Gracie? It's Eve Harcourt."

"Yes, Mrs. Harcourt. Happy Thanksgiving! I'm sorry I didn't call…"

"Oh, that's all right, we all know what you've been through." She hesitated. "Miss Gracie, do you think you could go down to Shea's Roadhouse if I have one of the boys drive over and get you?"

She sat up in bed and blinked. "Mrs. Harcourt, why would I want to go to the roadhouse at two in the morning?" she asked, still drowsy.

"You see, Mr. Jason got this package yesterday, special express. He took it into his office last night and closed the door. I don't know what was in it, but he stayed out all day today. He didn't even come in for Thanksgiving dinner. I thought he might be with you until the phone just rang and it was that bouncer, Tiny, from the roadhouse."

Gracie sat straight up in bed. "Tiny? Why would he call you?"

"He says Mr. Jason has treed the bar, Miss Gracie," she continued worriedly. "He put Tiny over a table when he tried to get him to leave. Now he's got one of the Hart boys' ranch hands trapped in a bathroom and is threatening to tear the door off if he doesn't come out. I swear, I can't remember the last time Mr. Jason took a drink!"

"I can," Gracie muttered, remembering what he'd told her about how he ended up in bed with Kittie. She wondered what had set him off this time. "I'll get dressed. Send one of the boys over. I'll bring Jason home."

"You were the only one who could ever handle him when he got drunk," the older woman said. "I hated to call you, but he wouldn't let anybody else near him."

"I know that. It's okay."

"Thank you, Miss Gracie," she said, and hung up.

She was afraid of men who drank, but this was only the second time Jason had ever gone overboard with liquor. That other time he'd gotten drunk was after his father died and he hadn't threatened her in any way when she'd interfered. In fact, he'd been incredibly easy to handle when she'd taken the liquor away from him. He did anything she told him to and followed her like a lamb. It was one more reason she'd never had to be afraid of him. Having lived with a father who drank to excess and was violent, it would have devastated her to find Jason like him. But he wasn't.

TIM, ONE OF THE RANCH hands, drove Gracie over to the bar. "You want me to come in with you?" he asked.

"Come and stand on the porch, Tim," she said. "I'll need you to help me get him to the truck. It would probably be better if you don't come in."

He looked relieved. "Boss is dangerous in a temper," he remarked.

She smiled. "Yes. But not to me."

She walked into the bar. Jason wasn't staggering, but he did look like a rattlesnake looking for a place to bite. He was cursing at a closed door in the back of the bar. Most of the patrons had long since gone home. It was just Jason and whatever poor soul he had trapped in the bathroom.

Tiny came to meet her, limping. "Sorry I had to call for help, Miss Gracie, but I'm just getting over surgery again," he apologized. "Mr. Pendleton there gets unreasonable when he drinks, and he's already swung at me once. I don't want to call the law unless I have to. He's a good man."

"I'll handle it. Thanks for calling me, Tiny. You know we'll pay for any damages."

"Of course I do."

She walked past him. Jason was still cursing.

"Jason," she called softly.

The change in him was immediate and amazing. He turned, blinked and then seemed to relax all at once. "Hello, Gracie," he said in a breathless rush. He managed a wan smile. "I'm a little drunk."

"I noticed." She took him by the hand. "It's time to go home now."

"Okay."

She led him out of the bar to Tiny's astonished amusement. He didn't even offer any resistance. Behind her, she heard a door open.

"Is he gone?" a cowboy asked plaintively.

Jason stopped, whirled. "You…!"

"Home, Jason!" Gracie said firmly, jerking on his hand.

He glared at the cowboy, who was frozen in place. Then he dragged in a rough sigh and turned away, letting Gracie lead him off the porch and to the truck, where Tim was waiting with the passenger door open.

"He made fun of my damned hat," Jason muttered as he climbed up into the seat. "I was going to feed it to him, but he ran into the bathroom and locked the door. Damned coward!"

Gracie got in beside him, motioning Tim to get the truck going.

"I don't want to go home," Jason said suddenly.

"Well, you're going anyway," Gracie replied. She'd fastened her seat belt, but she couldn't find his. He was sitting on it. She sat back and hoped the police wouldn't notice. It was against the law not to buckle up.

"Mrs. Harcourt was all upset," Gracie said. "She said you didn't even have any Thanksgiving dinner."

"No point," he muttered. "You weren't there. It isn't Thanksgiving without you."

Her heart ached at the comment. She felt guilty.

"I hate whiskey," he murmured as they approached the ranch.

"You're going to hate the hangover you have in the morning, too," she assured him. "Right up to the porch, Tim, then you go back to bed. Thanks," she added.

"You're welcome, Miss Gracie."

Between them, they got Jason on his feet and headed into the house. Mrs. Harcourt was waiting there in her housecoat, her dark eyes full of concern.

"Is he all right?" she asked worriedly.

He glanced at her. "I'm just drunk, Mrs. Harcourt," he told her. "Not drunk enough, though."

"Come on," Gracie said, aiming him down the hall toward his room. "Mrs. Harcourt, you go on back to bed. I'll get him into his room."

"Thank you, Miss Gracie." She hesitated. "But I'll need to run you back to Barbara's house."

"I'm not leaving," she said firmly. "I can sleep in the guest room. No use upsetting the household again."

"I'll make you a nice breakfast," the older woman said with a smile. "Thank you for saving him."

"Nothing's going to save him from me," Gracie muttered. She propelled Jason along with her and guided him into his room, closing the door behind them. She wanted, more than anything, to know what had set him off.

She eased him down onto the king-size bed and bent to pull off his boots. He sprawled on the patchwork quilt, knocking off his hat. She tossed it onto his big dresser and sat down beside him. He was wearing jeans and a chambray shirt, very comfortable clothes, but not dressy. Apparently he'd gone from the ranch to the bar.

"What in the world is wrong with you?" she asked. "You almost never drink."

His eyes opened and looked up into hers. "I hired a private detective."

Her heart stopped. "Why, Jason?"

He ran a hand through his disheveled hair. "To tell me what you wouldn't. To tell me about your childhood, and the truth about your family."

11

GRACIE'S HEART STOPPED. She knew every drop of blood drained out of her face at the statement. "Oh," she said weakly.

He grimaced. "I knew you'd take it like that. I had to know. I had to know, Gracie!"

She averted her face. She fought tears. "I thought I could keep it hidden forever, that you'd never find out." Her eyes closed tight. "I'm so ashamed!"

"Ashamed of what, baby?" he asked softly. "Come here to me!" He pulled her down into his arms and wrapped her up tight, fighting the effects of the liquor as he tried to marshal his thoughts. What he'd learned had been a terrific shock. "Why were you afraid to tell me?"

"We were so poor," she whispered. "We had nothing. Mama didn't want your father to find out. He was such a snob, Jason. He would never have come near her if he'd known. She pretended that we came from a wealthy background and made up stories so he wouldn't try to find out anything about us."

"Your father held a gun to your head and threatened to kill you," he bit off. "A SWAT officer who was there said he would have done it, that he wasn't bluffing. The sniper had to take him out. But the trauma—to have your father killed when he was standing behind you." He groaned. "If I'd known, I'd have had you in therapy! And not only for that. Your poor mother!"

"We were all messed up, I guess," she agreed, shivering. "I thought…I thought it might change things, between us, if you knew my real background. It's so sordid. Kittie overheard me talking to Mrs. Harcourt and threatened to tell you if I didn't get out of your life." She felt his tall body shudder. "I was so afraid…"

"It wouldn't have mattered. It doesn't matter now." His arms tightened. "You're safe, Gracie. Nobody will ever hurt you again, not as long as there's a breath in my body!"

She relaxed with a little shiver and let him take her weight. She curled up into his body and held on for dear life.

He laughed oddly.

"What is it?" she whispered.

"I've got you in my bed in the middle of the night, vulnerable and soft, and I can't get hard enough to do anything about it."

"Wh…what?"

He laughed breathily. "Drunk men can't perform."

She lifted her head and looked down into his amused black eyes. "They can't?"

"It's all that saved me from Kittie," he mused, tugging on a lock of pale blond hair. "But I don't want to be saved from you."

She propped her hands on the pillow behind his head and studied his relaxed face. "You don't?"

He tugged harder. "You could take my clothes off," he suggested. "We could see if it helped."

She flushed. "No."

"Spoilsport." He drew in a long breath. "Sleep with me, then. It's a big bed. It's freezing in here. I might catch cold."

"It's not that cold."

"Yes, it is." He moved, tugging at a colorful afghan that Mrs. Harcourt had made. The only light in the room was from the security light outside, barely enough for them to see each other. He rolled Gracie over next to him and covered them both with the afghan.

"Mrs. Harcourt will be outraged."

"No, she won't," he murmured. "She knows about drunk men, I guarantee it."

"You won't be drunk in the morning," she protested, but not very strongly.

"In the morning," he whispered at her ear, "you might not mind."

She stiffened just a little, but he knew her well enough to understand why. He lifted his head and looked into her eyes.

"You think sex outside marriage is a sin," he whispered. "I know that. I frightened you at Barbara's because I lost control. I promise I won't do it again. I'll never force you or coerce you."

Her body relaxed. "I don't want to be this way," she bit off.

He curled her close and wrapped her up tight in his arms. "There's nothing wrong with the way you are," he said quietly. "Go to sleep, angel. I'll keep you safe."

It was very late. Mrs. Harcourt wasn't judgmental.

Besides, they both had all their clothes on, she rationalized. She moved closer to Jason, closed her eyes and, finally, slept.

JASON WATCHED HER SLEEP. Daylight was coming through the windows. Gracie had been in his arms all night. She hadn't tried to leave. It was a dream come true, to see her face on his pillow, her hair spread over it like a pale gold curtain. He looked down at her firm breasts under the T-shirt she was wearing and he ached to pull it off, along with her bra, and make a banquet of that soft, warm skin. But he knew things about her now that he hadn't known before. He had to take his time, go slow, coax her into intimacy. For the first time, he had a little hope for the future. Gracie wanted him. She might not know it yet, or understand it, but she felt it. He smiled with joy.

There were footsteps outside in the hall. The door opened, just a slit, and Mrs. Harcourt peered in.

He put his finger to his lips, and indicated the soft little body next to his in the bed. He smiled.

She smiled back. "Breakfast in ten minutes," she whispered.

He nodded.

Mrs. Harcourt closed the door. She was positively radiant.

Gracie heard him chuckle and her eyes opened. She looked up at him in the soft light, fascinated by the play of emotions on his face. Her eyes went from him to the bed and back again.

His fingers traced a pattern over her breasts. "Mrs. Harcourt just came to say breakfast will be ready in ten minutes." His hand went slowly under the hem of the

T-shirt. "Do you think we can find something to do for eight minutes?" he murmured wickedly.

She caught his wrist and then slowly let it go.

He grinned. His fingers went around her to the fastening that held her bra in place. His hand went under it and teased around under her arm and then right onto her soft breast.

He bent to her mouth. "I love touching you like this," he murmured as he kissed her very softly.

Her nails bit into him, but she didn't protest. When he looked into her eyes, he found them rapt with pleasure and curiosity.

"Everything has changed," she whispered.

"Yes." His eyes were growing darker. He shifted and smoothed the fabric out of his way, so that he could see what he was touching. "Everything."

As he spoke, he bent his head and she felt his warm mouth on her breasts, exploring, teasing, possessing her. The sheer pleasure of it arched her body. He heard her soft gasp as he increased the pressure and the insistence of his lips. One lean hand slid under her. The other unfastened his shirt buttons all the way down. He pulled her hips into his and ground her bare breasts into his hair-roughened chest.

He had to cover her mouth with his to smother the excited little cry that burst from her lips as passion surged in her untried body. She shivered, grasping at him, pulling him. He rolled over onto her, nudging her legs out of the way so that he was resting blatantly in the fork of her body, letting her feel the power and heat of his arousal. He shuddered as his hips moved rhythmically against her.

She opened her legs for him, clawing his back as the pleasure mushroomed into levels she'd never expected.

"Breakfast!" Mrs. Harcourt called from the hall.

Jason jerked away from Gracie. "We'll be right there!" he called back, hoping his voice didn't sound as ragged to Mrs. Harcourt as it did to him.

"Okay!" Her footsteps died away down the hall.

Gracie gaped at him, wide-eyed.

His eyes fell to her taut breasts and down, to where their two bodies were still pressed hard together at the hips. He had to fight to breathe.

"I want to go into you, hard and deep," he whispered roughly. "I want you to feel me against you, inside your body."

She trembled, barely breathing. She'd never dreamed men spoke this way to women. Her face colored, but not from embarrassment. She was picturing that lean, fit body driving into hers. She moaned.

"You'd let me," he bit off.

She swallowed. "Yes."

He hesitated. He was hurting. Badly.

"Don't let it get cold!" Mrs. Harcourt called again.

His eyes closed and he bit off a curse. His powerful body vibrated with frustrated need.

Gracie felt that anguish in her very bones. She eased away from him. Her lips touched his face, eyelids, nose and cheeks. "It's all right," she whispered. "It's all right."

He loved that tenderness. He sank back onto the bed and let her have her way with him, let her kiss him and calm him. His dark eyes opened into hers, soft and quiet.

"Are you okay?" she asked gently. "I read that it hurts men, when they get like this. I didn't know what else to do."

"Nice instincts," he responded, still breathless. "It worked."

She smiled. Her eyes were full of wonder as they searched his. "I never understood until now. What it's like, I mean."

"It gets worse," he said, staring pointedly at her bare breasts. "Much worse…"

"Oh!" She sat up, flustered, and righted her clothing. "Sorry. I didn't realize…"

He sat up, too. "It wasn't a complaint."

He pulled her to her feet, amazed at the difference in her. He smoothed her hair.

"It will show," Gracie said worriedly.

"I don't care," he replied. He took her hand in his. "Let's have something to eat."

They watched each other between bites. Mrs. Harcourt laughed to herself. They were so transparent. It made her feel good to see the growing affection between them. It was, she thought, about time.

AFTER BREAKFAST, THEY WALKED out to the corral to watch a man work a filly on a leading rein.

"We could have Thanksgiving dinner today," he mused, smiling down at her. "Mrs. Harcourt saved it."

Her heart jumped. "I'd like that."

He turned, pulling her gently against his tall body. "Then we could decorate a Christmas tree."

She bit her lower lip, uncertain.

He moved his hands on her waist. "I know why it means so much to you," he said after a minute. "The detective was quite thorough. Your father was an atheist. He wouldn't let you have a tree or any sort of decorations or even go to church."

She nodded. "It was lonely during the holidays."

"From now on," he vowed, "we'll celebrate them

together, even if I have to put you on a plane to meet me overseas for it. I promise."

Her soft eyes smiled up into his. He was talking about a future. A shared future.

"And we'll go slow," he added quietly. "I'm rushing things. I don't mean to. I'm starving to death for you," he confessed. "But I can control that. I have to. I want to get to know you, Gracie."

"We've lived together for twelve years," she laughed.

"Not like this," he said, his voice deep with feeling. "Not ever like this." He bent to her soft mouth and touched it with his lips.

"Jason, someone might see," she protested weakly.

His face was somber. "They'll have to get used to it eventually," he replied.

He was making promises without saying a single word. She looked up at him with her heart in her eyes. "Yes. They'll have to get used to it."

His pulse ran wild. He bent and kissed her tenderly, holding her lightly in his arms. When she tried to move closer, he stepped back.

"No," he said softly. "This clouds everything. I want you. I'm sure you know it. But we have to go forward one step at a time. Okay?"

She beamed. "Okay."

THE NEXT TWO WEEKS were magic. Gracie and Jason rode together on the ranch, went to a sale, attended a rendition of *The Nutcracker* at the ballet in San Antonio. In between, Gracie gave a lecture to a third-grade class and even had the teacher listening raptly while she gave a watered-down version of events at the Alamo. Then the college called, desperate for someone to fill in for the adjunct history professor who was teaching night classes—he'd been in an automobile accident and couldn't come back in time to finish up the course. She only had to manage the class for four sessions, until the end of the semester, the first week of December. He'd left his lesson plan and lecture notes.

She went into the class nervous and uncertain of herself. But once she realized how mature these adult students were, how interested they were in the subject, she relaxed and warmed to them. She followed the injured teacher's lesson plan, which involved the history of Texas, but she added her own tidbits about the Mexican Revolution spilling over into the United States, and the conflict at the Alamo. The class was two hours long, but it went over a half hour. Gracie was on cloud nine when she drove her junky car back to Barbara's.

She'd had to fight Jason about replacing it. He wanted to give her a classy Jaguar convertible, and she wanted to pay her own way. He was irritated that she was being so independent. But he respected her, just the same. He didn't push.

It was hard, keeping themselves at arm's length, considering the growing passion that threatened to burst its bonds. Jason wanted her. It was so evident that she was amazed she hadn't noticed it before. Barbara had hinted that she'd seen it for the past two years. That would be about the time Jason started refusing to dance with her at parties. Perhaps, she reasoned, he was uncertain of his restraint if he got that close to her, and he hadn't wanted her to know how physical his affection for her had become.

THE IDEA OF DECORATING for Christmas still left a bitter taste in her mouth, but she was coaxed into it by Mrs.

Harcourt and Jason. She spent the afternoon before her class working on it. While she was putting the last touches on the big tree in the living room of the ranch house, with Jason sipping coffee in his big armchair and watching her, his cell phone rang. He pulled it out of his pocket, checked the caller ID and abruptly turned it off, tossing it onto the table beside his chair.

Gracie glanced at him curiously.

"I'm not in the mood to talk," he said without explaining.

She only smiled, going back to the last of the decorations.

A minute later, the hall phone rang. And rang. And rang again.

Gracie frowned at Jason with open curiosity. "Aren't you going to answer it?"

Jason sighed irritably and started to get up.

"I'll get it!" Mrs. Harcourt called.

He sat back down, but Gracie noted that he looked uncomfortable. She wondered why.

A minute later, Mrs. Harcourt came into the room. She gave Gracie a wary look before she handed the cordless phone to Jason.

"It's Miss Sartain again," she said dully.

Jason muttered something, glanced uneasily at Gracie and answered it.

"Yes, I know. I cut it off," he said after a minute. His jaw was taut, his expression resentful. "No, I haven't changed my mind," he said. There was a hesitation, during which his face hardened. "I know all about her background," he said abruptly, glancing at a puzzled Gracie. There was another pause. His black eyes began to glitter. "If you want to talk to the tabloids, be my guest. I don't have any secrets I'd mind sharing. That's right.

I'm not interested in getting back together with you, Kittie. You can call every damned day, but you'll get the same result. Fine. Do your worst."

He hung up and motioned to a worried Mrs. Harcourt.

"If she calls again, hang up. Don't even talk to her," he told her firmly.

Mrs. Harcourt nodded, but her face was very pale. Obviously she'd heard Jason's side of the conversation.

He stared at Gracie, who was openly watching, her expression full of uncertainty. "Has she called you before today?" she asked.

He hesitated.

She moved closer. "Has she?"

"A few times," he confessed reluctantly. "You have to understand how her mind works," he returned. "She thinks she can get me back if she's persistent enough, but it hasn't worked. Now she's thinking of blackmailing me. I spiked her guns when I said I knew about your past, but she's hinting that she knows another secret I'd pay to hush up." He laughed coldly. "Fat chance."

Gracie wasn't sure that Kittie was bluffing. Mrs. Harcourt was hiding something, but she had no idea what.

"Why are you talking to her at all?" Gracie asked.

His eyebrows arched. "Excuse me?" he asked in a faintly arrogant tone.

Her teeth caught her lower lip. "Well, she was very pretty," she said, "and you were engaged to her for several months, Jason…"

"Engaged isn't married," he interrupted curtly. "My father tried it three times with little success," he added, his eyes dark and quiet. "Even he and my mother didn't get along all that well. You know how long your mother and Glory's lasted. I've never seen a good marriage."

Gracie was even more uncomfortable now. He wasn't bothering to conceal his contempt for marriage. What if he just wanted her, and thought he could coax her into bed and keep her that way without marrying her? It wasn't the first time she'd entertained that miserable thought, and it wouldn't go away.

He was affectionate and seemed to enjoy her company, but he hadn't even hinted at a shared future for them lately. Worse, she was frustrated by the new feelings he aroused in her and irritable because the tension between them had almost reached flashpoint in the past few days. Now he wouldn't even touch her. It was as if he was toying with her, playing some sensual game. Even now, his expression was one of faint amusement. Was he getting even for the time when she hadn't wanted him, and he'd ended up with Kittie?

He noticed her expression and his darkened. "Now what's wrong?" he asked, with a bite in his deep voice.

"Are you sure you really wanted to break that engagement?" she persisted. "Or did you just feel guilty that I got kidnapped?"

His black eyes kindled. She wasn't the only one who was frustrated, except that his condition had lasted a lot longer. He was burning up to have her, and every time he got one step closer, she found a reason to take two steps back. His temper, always close to the surface, was threatening to erupt.

He got to his feet. "Maybe I do feel guilty," he replied, eyes narrowing. "You wouldn't have been on the road at night in the first place if you hadn't moved out when it looked as if Kittie might move in. You never liked Kittie."

She was shocked at the words, and the faint aggression behind them. She moved away from the tree with the last decoration, a new glass one, in her hand and glared at him.

"How do you give a rattlesnake half a chance, offer it first bite? She made Mrs. Harcourt and Dilly feel like idiots. She harped on John's age. She wanted me out of the way because I might interfere with her plans for your money."

He cocked his head and stared down at her. He was getting madder by the minute. "And that's my only draw for a woman, Gracie, my money?"

She stood very still. They were getting into dangerous areas here. The day had started with such promise. Now it was heading down a dark chasm. "Jason, I never said that."

"Do you know what Kittie said about you?" he drawled icily. "She said that the reason you never married was because you knew I wouldn't support you and some other man. She said you stayed single deliberately, so that you'd have a nice, cushy life."

Her face went several shades lighter. So that was how Kittie had kept him away from Gracie, by planting giant doubts in his mind.

"You know why I'm single."

"Do I?" he asked. "I know the reason you gave me. But you aren't that afraid of me, Gracie," he added in an insinuating tone. "In fact, I've been the one who's drawn back, every time."

Her face went red. It was true, but he was distorting it. She loved him. That was why she had no restraint with him. Now he seemed to think that she was the one playing games.

"I'm still rich, Gracie," he said bluntly. "And you're a working girl. Aren't you?"

That did it. She threw the decoration on the floor and heard it break with a feeling of recklessness. "Yes, I am," she snapped. "I'm a working girl with my own life, and you can thank your stars that I'm independent, can't you? Now you'll never have to ask yourself if I hung around you because you were rich, because this is the last time I'm setting foot in this house!"

She grabbed her purse and jacket and headed right out the front door.

"Where the hell do you think you're going?" he demanded from right behind her.

"I'm going to work!" she raged. "My class at the community college starts in two hours. I'll hang around the canteen and drink coffee! Anything beats sitting here and eavesdropping on your conversations with your fiancée!"

Jason felt like chewing nails. His fists balled beside his narrow hips. "I told you, I broke the engagement!"

"Did you tell Kittie?" she challenged sarcastically.

"Damn it!"

"That's right, start cussing," she muttered. "That will certainly help!"

She jerked open the door of her old car and got in behind the steering wheel. Jason stood there glowering, his jaw clenched so tight that it was visible even in the car. She started the engine and black smoke poured out the tailpipe. She wanted to groan. It only emphasized the difference in their financial status now.

"All right, go teach your damned course and see if I care!" he yelled after her.

"I was planning to!"

She put the car in gear and groaned again when the engine backfired as she pulled out of the driveway. The sorry old piece of junk would probably quit at the road and she'd have to walk back, sink her pride and beg for a ride into town. But she was going to start toward Jacobsville, even if she never made it there.

She felt like crying, but she wasn't giving in to the urge. She was convinced that Jason had no intention of asking her to marry him, now or ever. He wanted somebody in his bed, but not for keeps. His opinion of marriage was crystal clear.

Did he still want Kittie? If he didn't, why did he answer her phone calls? And he'd tried not to, when Mrs. Harcourt finally answered the hall phone and almost forced it into his hands. Was he trying to hide the fact that Kittie phoned him?

She was too confused to think straight. Her life had been going beautifully. Jason was attentive and affection-ate, and it had been like old times, going places with him. Well, not like old times. Not when he kissed her so hungrily and looked as if he were starving to have her.

But that wasn't the sort of hunger you built a marriage on. It was a flash fire sort of hunger that was soon satis-fied. It didn't last.

Gracie wanted a home and children. She'd just started to think of having that with Jason, and he'd encouraged her to. But Kittie's phone call had destroyed that illusion with a bang. Now here was Jason cursing and Gracie rushing back to Jacobsville with her pride stuck in her throat. Her dreams of a rosy future had just crashed and burned.

She took the dirt road turnoff that led down the back way to Jacobsville and was just crossing the old wooden bridge when the stupid car stopped, sputtered and died, right there in the right-hand lane on the narrow bridge. She hit the steering wheel with the heel of her hand and used some of Jason's best bad words. This just wasn't her day!

12

GRACIE WAS RESIGNED to walking back to the ranch to ask for help when a red pickup truck came rushing toward her.

She stepped out in front of her car and waved. The driver skidded to a halt just beside her.

"Miss Gracie, is that you?" Bobby Hawkins, one of Jacobsville's volunteer firemen, asked. "What in the world are you doing in that piece of junk?" He indicated the car.

"It may not look like much, Bobby, but it's mine. Could you give me a ride to the community college? I'll be late to teach my class and it will take forever for Turkey Sanders to get out here and tow this car in to be worked on. I can't even call him. I forgot my cell phone this morning."

Bobby grimaced. "I guess I can do that. I have to get to the bank before it closes to make a deposit, and then by the hardware store to pick up something. I've got a training class, but if you don't mind waiting while I get my business out of the way, I'll be glad to drop you off before I go to the fire station."

"I don't mind at all, Bobby," she said.

"Climb in, then," he said with a grin.

"You're a lifesaver!"

She jumped in beside him and they set off toward town. His banking business took him several minutes longer than he'd anticipated, and then the fire chief called and asked him to stop by the office supply company and pick up some pencils.

Finally through, he was on his way to drop off Gracie when a rescue call came in. He answered it, frowning in Gracie's direction.

"They've got someone in the water off the River Bridge," he said. "I have to go, I'm the only diver we've got on call. Tell you what, I'll have one of the boys at the scene bring you back to town. Somebody's life may be on the line…"

"Say no more," she said. "Go!"

He was already out of town at the strip mall. He wheeled the truck, gunned the engine and shot back down the road. It took a minute for Gracie to realize that they were headed for the same bridge her car was stuck on.

Several men were gathered on the bridge. The police were there, along with the emergency services people, a fire truck and a couple of private cars. One was Jason's red Jaguar convertible. Gracie ground her teeth together. What in the world was Jason doing out here?

"Did you see anybody on the bridge when your car quit?" Bobby asked Gracie.

"No, nobody. I wonder who fell in?"

"We'll know soon, I hope."

He pulled up as close as he could get to where Gracie's car was sitting. They both got out. Gracie peered through the crowd toward the river.

"For God's sake, could you hurry?" Jason's voice came urgently.

Jason? She pushed through the men to stand beside him, looking down at the river. "Who fell in?" she asked worriedly.

He stopped and stared down at her. "Gracie?" He caught her against him and held on hard, shuddering. "I thought you were in the river!" he groaned.

She was still trying to sort things out in her mind. "In the river?"

"Your car was sitting here, abandoned."

How had he known her car was here? Had he followed her, hoping to make up?

"You said she jumped in the river!" Assistant Chief Palmer accused, pausing beside them. "You were sure!"

Jason let Gracie go reluctantly. He winced. "Well, we'd had an argument, sort of. I got worried and followed her, and found her car sitting here abandoned!" he said defensively.

"Abandoned and with the keys gone!" Gracie muttered, pulling them out of her pocket to shake them under his nose. "Who takes out the car keys before they jump in the river?" she cried indignantly.

Jason's lips made a thin line. He was embarrassed and hating it.

Palmer grimaced. He'd been a police officer until he'd switched jobs and become a fireman. From his old job, he had a good idea about what was going on. "Listen, no harm done," he said calmly. "It's always better to be safe than sorry."

"Of course it is," Gracie replied. "Thanks." She smiled at him.

He smiled back. "Okay, guys, let's wrap it up and get back to the station."

Bobby Hawkins let out a whistle. "Good thing, I

wasn't anxious to dive into that cold water," he said sheepishly, "although I'd have done it. We can go now, Miss Gracie, I'll drop you at the college."

"I'll drop her off," Jason said firmly. "We can call Turkey Sanders on the way and have him tow the car."

Bobby stood, indecisive.

"Thanks, Bobby, but I'll let Jason drive me," she said. "I've been enough trouble."

"No trouble at all," Bobby replied. "Honest."

Jason took Gracie's arm, opened the door of the Jaguar and put her in beside him.

"Nice wheels," Bobby said with a whistle.

Jason chuckled. "It belongs to me and the bank, Bobby," he told the other man. "I don't know anybody who can lay down a cash payment for one of these."

"Still, it must be nice." Bobby sighed. He grinned on the way to his truck.

"Yes, it must." Gracie sighed, also, glancing at the sad old car she owned, sitting there in a heap on the bridge.

"You can come home and have a new Jaguar any time you want one," Jason said gruffly.

She glanced at him. "Jason, I'm not playing at being independent. It's important to me to see if I can make it by myself."

"Of course you can," he said as he pulled back onto the road and waved as he went around the rescue people. "You're no dummy."

She flushed with pleasure. "You said I was."

"I never."

"You said I was good at giving teas," she muttered.

"You're good at anything you do," he said simply. "Especially in emergencies."

She smiled reluctantly. "Okay."

He glanced at her as he drove. "I don't want Kittie. I never did."

She flushed. She glanced at the fields where plows had turned under the dead summer crops. "I was jealous," she said through her teeth.

He chuckled softly.

She turned her attention back to him, amazed at the change her statement had provoked.

His eyes met hers for an instant.

She shrugged. "I'm frustrated, too," she confessed.

"You aren't the only one."

"It was your idea, all this abstinence."

"First times are rough on women, or so I've heard," he said evenly. "If I lose it, you aren't going to enjoy the result. I'm trying to cool things off, just a little."

"With what end in mind?" she asked finally.

He frowned. "What do you mean?"

She shifted. "I mean, what do you see for us in the future? Am I going to be a notch on the bedpost…"

"For God's sake!" He pulled onto the side of the road and gaped at her. "Is that what you really think I want from you? No, don't prevaricate," he added when she tried to find a reply. "I want to know. You think I'm so shallow that my ultimate aim is to get you into bed?"

She shrugged. She had, just briefly. But that expression was unmistakable. She tried to backpedal. "I didn't know. This is all new to me. You stayed engaged to Kittie for a long time…"

"I didn't think I had anything else left," he said flatly. "I burned up inside every time I looked at you, and all you did was back away. I'd given up. I didn't care whether I was engaged or not. I was dead inside."

Her eyes grew softer as she looked at him, saw through the frustration to the need in him. She drew in a slow breath. "I want children."

His black eyes kindled. "So do I."

She began to relax.

"We get along well," he said. "Most of the time, anyway. We know the worst and the best of each other. Physically, we're dynamite together. Children would fall naturally into that."

"We'd live together…"

"We'd get married, Gracie," he said flatly.

The change in her was remarkable. "You never said…"

"You never asked!"

She began to realize just how much damage she'd done to their fragile relationship out of misplaced jealousy. She turned her purse in her hands.

"We've still got a long way to go, haven't we?" he asked absently. He pulled back onto the road. "What are you teaching at the community college?"

"History," she said. "The regular adjunct teacher was in a wreck. I'm filling in for him. I start teaching full-time when spring semester starts."

He frowned as he drove. "Full-time?"

"This class meets three nights a week," she said.

"You don't have a teaching certificate, do you?"

"If you're teaching adults, you don't have to have one. You don't have to have a master's degree, either."

He sighed. "Oh."

"I've never had to depend on myself," she tried to explain. "Until all this came up, I never thought past the next day, the next charity, the next party." She searched for the right words. "I don't want to take over a corporation or climb Mount Everest. I just want to do something that matters in the world." She laughed self-consciously. "It sounds corny, doesn't it?"

"Not really. We all want to feel that what we do is worthwhile." He glanced at her and smiled. "Even a rancher likes to know that his policies help the environment, provide for wildlife habitat, leave the world a little better than he found it."

He did understand. It made things easier.

"My father hated the ranch. He couldn't understand why I wanted to go out and dig postholes and help brand cattle. He felt it was beneath the dignity of our station in life, for me to do manual labor." He shook his head. "He really was a snob."

"That's what Mrs. Harcourt said."

He laughed. "She'd know. He wouldn't let her sit at the table and eat with us. He said servants belonged in the kitchen." He lifted an eyebrow. "I remember when that changed."

She laughed. She and Glory had gone into the kitchen with their plates and sat down to eat with Mrs. Harcourt, leaving an amused Jason and a shocked Myron Pendleton at the formal dinner table.

After a minute, Jason had followed them into the kitchen, informing his father that if he felt inclined to play upstairs, downstairs, then Jason and the girls would eat with the help. Shamed and embarrassed, Myron had invited Mrs. Harcourt to eat with them, and the custom had remained. Now, Dilly and John also had dinner at the table with the family, along with Mrs. Harcourt.

He frowned suddenly. "I haven't been able to find John," he said quietly. "It worries me."

"Can't you get that private detective to track him down?"

He scowled, remembering that he'd pried into Gracie's life without telling her. "I wasn't sure I should."

"He's probably afraid Kittie has something on him that she's threatened to reveal, and he's hiding," she said quietly. "She threatened Mrs. Harcourt. I don't know with what."

"Your own past, probably," he said easily. "Mrs. Harcourt is very fond of you."

She smiled. "Yes. I'm fond of her, too."

"We'll find John sooner or later. We'd better." He sighed. "I'm not driving myself to the airport, and I don't like hiring a car out of San Antonio to come after me. But I'm not leaving this—" he indicated the fast car "—in any parking lot. I left it in a well-guarded covered lot when I went to Europe."

She laughed. He loved his cars, especially this one.

"I'm eccentric," he said defensively.

"If you were poor, they'd lock you up. It's only called being eccentric when you're rich."

"You could come home and be rich, too."

She shook her head. "Not yet."

He sighed. "Okay."

She was standing up to him more these days than she ever had before. It felt good; not only to defend her position, but to have him so easygoing about it. He was the exact opposite of her father.

"Why can't you live with me and be independent, too?" he asked suddenly.

Her eyebrows arched. "That's a contradiction in terms."

"I don't like having you alone at night," he said. "You had a traumatic experience in Mexico. I'll bet you still have nightmares about it."

"I've had a lot of traumatic experiences, and I do have nightmares, but I'm a grown woman. I can cope."

"You could go see Dr. Hemmings," he murmured.

The doctor was a psychologist. Gracie and Glory had both gone to see him regularly in high school on Jason's insistence. He knew about Glory's background. He hadn't known about Gracie's, but he'd felt that Dr. Hemmings would help her cope with the loss of her mother.

She toyed with her purse as they drove into Jacobsville, across the railroad tracks in the center of town. "I like him. I could always talk to him about things that frightened me. I might do that, later," she said vaguely. She wasn't going to ask Jason to pay for the visits and she couldn't afford them.

"You and your pride," he said with resignation. "I don't want you to be scarred mentally any more than you already are about sex."

She jumped at the sound of the word and he flinched. "Sorry," he said.

"I'm not that messed up," she replied. "Besides, it's not so scary when I think about doing it with yo…" She clamped down hard on the word.

But he knew what she was going to say. He smiled at her. "Now that's my idea of diplomacy," he murmured.

"Baloney. Your idea of diplomacy is a cannon." She cleared her throat. "But I won't do it with you until we're married."

He chuckled. "Okay. No, really," he assured her when he pulled up into the parking lot of the college, which was already almost full. "I like cold showers and hard exercise. My muscles are getting bigger."

She burst out laughing. He was outrageous.

"What time do I pick you up?" he asked.

"About nine-thirty," she said. "I'm on the second floor, room 106. We usually leave the doors open because we're the only class meeting in that section. You can come in even if I'm not through."

"I'll come early," he said easily, studying her with warm eyes. "I'd like to hear you lecture."

She flushed with pleasure. "I'm still feeling my way along."

"One of my hands has a sister who teaches at the elementary school," he said. "She told him that the class you lectured is still talking about the Alamo. Some of them had their parents drive them over to take the tour. They said the kids even impressed the tour guides."

She laughed. "I love my subject."

"And you're good with kids." His eyes held a quiet pride in her that was flattering. "You can do anything you want to, Gracie. All that was lacking was self-confidence. You're getting that, too." He shrugged. "I like it when you stand up to me and defend your position."

"Thanks."

"Go teach your class." He glanced out the window. Heavy clouds were rolling in. "It's been unseasonably warm today," he commented. "I hope we're not in for a storm. I'm getting another lot of culls ready to ship. We'll have hell keeping them penned up if it starts lightning."

"Don't get trampled," she said.

He grinned. "I won't."

He got out, went around the car and opened her door for her. It was Old-World courtesy that always made her feel good. She smiled at him, waved and walked up toward the main hall of the quad.

IT WAS JUST NINE-THIRTY when she was finishing up that she noted Jason easing into the room at the back. He was still in working clothes, damp and stained, and he looked tired. He leaned against the wall, crossed his arms and listened attentively. Her heart jumped with pleasure at just the sight of him, even disheveled and worn as he was.

She was talking about the modern Texas Rangers now, having covered their turbulent and awe-inspiring history already.

"They still have to know how to rope and ride a horse," she said, "because their investigations may take them out into the brush. They also work on cases internationally. If you're interested in learning more about them, they have a Web site at the Texas Rangers Hall of Fame where they go into more detail than I have time for about their history and investigative methods." She paused. "Are there any questions?"

"Yes, are they still an all-male force?" a woman student asked.

Gracie laughed. "They are not. They have female officers, as well as male ones."

"Why? You thinking of joining up, Jane?" one of the male students teased.

She laughed. "Why not? I think I'd look good in a white hat."

"If that's all, we're done for tonight. I'll see you all day after tomorrow, same time."

"Thanks, teach," one of the young men in the back murmured. He gathered his books and gave Jason a long look. "Man, you ought to sign up for some classes and get yourself an easier job," he said with genuine sympathy. "Working cattle is no way to make money!"

Jason pursed his lips. "You could be right."

"He is," another male student echoed. "Besides, the way science is progressing, in a few years they'll be able to grow a steak in a petrie dish."

"God forbid," Jason groaned.

Gracie joined them at the back of the room with her briefcase and purse. "God forbid what?" she asked Jason.

"Growing steaks in a petrie dish."

She made a face. She looked at the young man. "Hall, isn't it?" she asked with twinkling eyes. "Dr. Carlson says you're his star student in microbiology. Planning to raise cattle in his lab, are you?"

He laughed self-consciously. "Actually I was thinking more on the order of heart cells," he told her. "They don't regenerate, but you can grow them in an agar, even print the cells with a modified ink-jet printer…!" He gained strength, warming to his subject.

"Barbarian," the other young man muttered, glaring at him. "What sort of sick mind would want to subject an innocent printer to that sort of abuse?"

Jason burst out laughing.

"You need to get him to join our class," the young man told Gracie. "A degree could get you a much better paying job than working cattle in the rain!"

"He could be right," Gracie told Jason, tongue-in-cheek.

His eyes twinkled as they shared a private, silent joke. "Could be. You ready?"

She nodded. She turned out the lights and pulled the door closed before she walked out at Jason's side.

"Hard night?" she asked him.

He nodded. "One clap of thunder and the cows stampeded. We had two fences down and livestock all over the state highway." He shook his head. "One of Cash Grier's officers threatened to cite me for grazing my cattle on state grass."

The students were gathered around the sporty XK convertible that Jason was driving, the new one that was radiant red. It almost glowed in the misty rain under the streetlights.

"It's a beaut, isn't it?" one of Gracie's students enthused. "I'll bet it flies! Wonder who owns it?"

"Nobody who works here—that's for sure," the young man who'd teased Jason about his job said with a sigh. "One of our professors said that an old law on the books could land the whole teaching staff in jail because it refers to anyone with less than five dollars in his pocket as a vagrant." He glanced up. "Hi, Miss Marsh! Isn't this a neat ride?"

"It is," Jason agreed as he opened the door and helped an amused Gracie inside. "The bank and I bought it together."

The boy's cheekbones flushed. "It's yours?"

Jason shrugged. "I do work on the ranch," he told him with a grin. "But I own the ranch, too. I have some of the finest Santa Gertrudis bulls in Texas."

The boy whistled. "Do you eat them?"

Jason glared at him. "Would you eat a Rodin sculpture?"

The boy chuckled. "Not really."

"Same thing. Art is art. See you."

He got in under the wheel, started the engine, made sure Gracie had her belt on and roared out of the parking lot.

JUST AS HE PULLED ONTO the state highway, the skies opened again and heavy rain pelted the windshield.

"Damn," he muttered, glancing at Gracie, who wasn't wearing a raincoat. "I don't even have an umbrella in here. I thought the rain had stopped."

"Not to worry, I won't melt," she teased, her soft eyes twinkling at him.

He laughed. "I guess not. We've got mud puddles in

the yard, but I can carry you over them." He glanced at her. "Did you have anything to eat?"

She shook her head. "Wasn't time. Besides, the cafeteria had long since closed for the day."

"I guess we can manage an omelet and some toast by ourselves," he sighed. "Dilly's gone to the movies with her mother. It's her night off. Mrs. Harcourt had to drive up to San Antonio to supervise some last-minute detailing at the house, so she won't be back tonight, either."

"I can cook," Gracie said.

"So can I. We'll share chores."

It felt so natural to be with him at the ranch house. It seemed like a long time since they'd been so comfortable together. Despite the earlier argument, they were friends again.

He parked close to the back door, but the whole yard was a mud puddle from the frenzied running of the cattle that had gotten loose earlier.

"We're going to get soaked, I guess," he said heavily as he turned off the engine and got out of the car.

Gracie stepped out into a mud puddle, tripped over her own feet and went flying facedown into the slick mud.

She let out a curse she'd heard Jason use. He burst out laughing, so overwhelmed by the picture she made, dripping mud and using range language that he couldn't even try to be sympathetic.

She picked up a handful of mud and threw it at his shirt. "There," she muttered as it hit, "now we match!"

He wasn't even angry. He just shook his head. "Okay, but you can forget about being carried inside," he said. "Neither of us has to worry about getting wet or muddy anymore," he added with a rueful glance at his red-spotted shirt.

"Sorry," she muttered. "You shouldn't have laughed."

"I couldn't help it," he replied as they walked up onto the porch. "You ought to see yourself!"

"No, thanks." She hesitated. "This mud is two inches thick on my shoes and your boots."

"Better take them off and leave them out here, I guess," he agreed, bending to pull hers off before he sat down in a cane-bottomed chair and shucked his boots. "Mrs. Harcourt will kill us both tomorrow if she has to get red mud off the rugs and the linoleum."

"I wouldn't even blame her."

They walked inside, careful to keep off the pretty wool rugs and made their way down the hall to the bedrooms.

"Ouch," Gracie murmured as her legs in their sodden slacks rubbed together and hurt. "I must have cut my leg on something."

"Go have a shower. I'll have one, too, and then I'll check the cut," he said.

She started to say that she could do it, but he looked worried. She just smiled. "Okay."

He sighed as he stared at her. "Well, you even look good dressed in red mud," he murmured.

She laughed.

He winked at her and turned into his own room, closing the door behind him.

13

IT HAD NEVER FELT SO GOOD to step under a spray of warm water, Gracie thought as she washed her chilled body and her long hair and wrapped herself in one of the big, soft Turkish towels hanging on the rack by the shower stall. She glanced down at her leg and grimaced as she saw a long scratch on the inside of her thigh just above her left knee. It wouldn't need stitches, probably, but it was fairly deep.

She picked up her stained slacks and noted a cut on the pants leg. There must have been a piece of metal or glass on the ground under her when she fell.

There was a perfunctory knock at the door and Jason walked in, wearing a pair of black silk pajama bottoms and nothing more. Gracie stared transfixed at the perfection of his muscular, tanned, hair-roughened chest. She remembered how it felt against her bare breasts. The thought excited her, and she became flushed.

He lifted an eyebrow. "Don't start drooling over me," he said. "It isn't nice to take advantage of a man who's only trying to help you."

"What sort of help did you have in mind?" she asked with a wicked grin.

He tapped her nose with his finger. "Stop that. Let's see the cut."

She propped her leg on the tub and pulled the towel that swallowed her aside just enough to display the cut. "I must have fallen on something," she said.

"Something sharp," he agreed, frowning. "When did you have a tetanus booster last?"

"This year," she said easily.

"Good girl." He looked in the medicine cabinet for elastic bandages and antibiotic cream. "I think you can do without stitches."

"I thought so, too. I don't really feel up to a trip to the emergency room. It's been a long day."

"I know."

He applied the cream and a wide square bandage, his fingers deft and sure on her soft skin. She tingled all over at his touch.

He glanced up at her with an amused smile. "Don't let me see how much this excites you," he cautioned. "Anything could happen."

"Really? Anything?"

He stood up and reached for the hair dryer. "Brave words."

He turned the dryer on and his fingers sifted through her blond hair as he blew it dry. She moved closer, liking the feel of his body next to her with so much bare skin on display. She felt positively wanton. She wasn't really afraid of him. She wondered why she ever had been. It seemed perfectly natural to be standing almost in his arms in a towel.

He finished drying her hair and turned off the blower, unplugging it as he laid it back on the vanity table.

She looked up into his black eyes with fascination. She'd known him for so long, but sometimes he was like a stranger. Especially like this. Their relationship had undergone a radical transformation in past weeks.

He took a handful of her soft, pale blond hair and his eyes narrowed as his gaze fell to the swell of her breasts over the drooping towel. His jaw clenched. "You're very pretty without your clothes."

"Am I?" She sounded breathless. The tension in the room grew explosive.

"Pretty. Desirable. Irresistible…" He bent and his mouth brushed lazily over hers, only to slide warmly down her throat and onto the soft skin of her breasts. He hesitated as he drew his lips against them, waiting for her reaction. He lifted his head, just briefly, to look into her eyes.

When she didn't try to back away, he felt a jolt of pure sensuality that ran through him like electricity. He bent again. His hands moved the towel a little lower, out of the way, and his mouth opened on soft, warm, faintly scented skin.

It wasn't scary at all, when his lips moved tenderly like that on her bare skin. She forgot to be afraid and shivered with delight. Her arms went around him, her short nails digging into his long, muscular back hungrily while his mouth explored her taut breasts. She was barely aware that the towel had fallen away from her breasts. She didn't even care. His mouth had opened right over her nipple and was pulling it inside, exploring it in a dark sensuality that made her tremble with need and just a little fear.

He felt her stiffen and lifted his head. His black eyes searched hers. "There's nothing to be afraid of," he said quietly. "I won't do anything you don't want me to do."

"I know." She traced a pattern in the thick hair over his breastbone. It felt right, standing here with him like this, in such intimacy. She ached all over. The sensations he made her feel were intoxicating. She felt so weak that her legs could hardly support her. "It isn't scary at all," she whispered. "I…I like it."

His big hand covered her small one on his chest. His breathing was noticeably labored.

She could feel the tension in him. She looked up into his glittering black eyes with curiosity and fascination.

He hadn't slept with Kittie. He'd said that, and he'd never lied to her. She knew that he'd kept to himself for a long time, not even dating anyone. If he'd felt this attraction to Gracie as strongly as she felt it for him, it must have been a very long time since he'd fed that gnawing hunger she could see in his eyes. It made him vulnerable, which, oddly, lessened her fear of him. But her past, and her scruples, had erected a barrier that she couldn't get through.

"God, I want you!" he murmured roughly.

"I know. I really want to," she whispered. "But…"

He nodded. "But." He searched her worried eyes and then smiled gently as he bent to kiss her with exquisite tenderness. And it might have been possible to draw back, just then. But as he held her closer, the towel fell to the floor, so that her nude body was suddenly pressing right against the firm muscles of his chest and stomach in an intimacy they hadn't really shared until now. He groaned in anguish.

Gracie felt a shudder run right through his powerful body as it echoed in hers. The feel of him against her was like a drug, she couldn't get enough of it. The touch of flesh against flesh made her knees tremble. She felt herself swelling in odd places, kindling exquisite little stabs of pleasure that grew with each brush of his chest against hers.

Impulsively she lifted against him so that they were standing in a blatant pose that let her feel the immediate response of his body to her closeness. She gasped under his insistent mouth as she registered the powerful capability of it. The thin silk of his pajama trousers was no barrier at all. And when his pajamas fell to the floor, the intimacy was suddenly a narcotic that made her incapable of resistance.

She held on tight, letting his mouth burrow into hers with passion and urgency. The heated exchange was only enhanced when she felt him against her where silk had separated them only seconds before. He throbbed with desire for her, and she ached to satisfy the blatant need.

Her hands ran up and down the muscles of his back as he caught her thighs and pulled her up into even greater intimacy. She whimpered against the warm penetration of his mouth, shivered as his hands slid lower and touched her in a new way. She started to protest, but his touch was suddenly so arousing that she only whimpered again instead and lifted higher to encourage him not to stop.

She hadn't expected the urgency that overwhelmed her as his hands explored her body, the aching need that blotted out reason. She dragged her breasts against his hard chest with exquisite abandon, her nails digging into him as she pleaded for an end to the tension that threatened to rip her apart.

"Gracie…" he protested, but the word morphed into a groan as he lowered her to the floor over the damp towel that had covered her.

His mouth took the place of his hands, exploring,

arousing, tasting her in a hundred ways as they lay in a tangle. All she heard was the rough sigh of his breath against her yielded body, barely audible above the racing whip of her own heartbeat.

She should stop him, she told herself firmly, but his mouth was on the inside of her soft thighs and his thumb had moved up to search against a sensitive area that quickly lifted her off the floor in a shivering little taste of fulfillment that sobbed out of her tight throat. Her long legs moved apart to ease his way. She bit into the shoulder that moved over her, tasting it with her tongue as he levered his powerful body down between her legs and slowly, exquisitely, penetrated her.

She sobbed helplessly as one lean hand slid under her hips and tilted them as he pushed down.

He lifted his head. He was shuddering with the force of his heartbeats. His eyes captured hers as he moved, his face rigid as he felt the barrier.

"I'm sorry," he whispered in a groan of torment. "I can't stop!"

"It's all right. I love you," she whispered back, shivering under him. "I love you…so much, Jason."

The words ripped the last of his control away. Anguished joy replaced the guilt in his black eyes. He set his teeth and thrust down, hard. He felt the faint resistance that quickly gave way to his ardor.

Gracie gasped at the stab of white-hot fire that tore through her as he mastered her body, but she didn't try to push him away. She swallowed hard, while he hesitated.

"It's all right," she whispered. She lifted up to him, her eyes holding his. "Don't stop."

His big hands slid under her head as he bent to kiss the

quick tears from her eyes as he moved slowly, deliberately, against her and heard a little cry of shocked pleasure.

"Did you expect it to keep hurting?" he asked tenderly. "I know how to satisfy you, Gracie. I know how to give you ecstasy. I won't stop until you've taken the last breath of satisfaction from my body…"

His mouth eased down over hers and his tongue teased at the underside of her lip, tracing it in a slow rhythm that matched the exquisite, slow thrust of his body as he found the place and the tempo that made her nails dig into his back, made her hips arch up and push against his.

"Slow down," he urged in the tense silence. "Slow down, honey. We aren't in a hurry."

"Yes…we are!" she moaned.

He laughed tenderly, his lips brushing over her flushed face, tasting tears as he began to shift over her. The new position made her cry out.

He lifted his head and watched her as he moved, saw the agony of pleasure that was growing in her, building like a symphony. Her eyes were glazed with wonder and passion, her lips parted as she struggled to find the place that would end the excruciating tension that was pulling her muscles tight as steel cords.

He moved again, feeling her body clench and shudder around him. "Yes," he whispered as he shifted one last time and began to drive down into her, savoring her hoarse little pleas, feeling the exquisite contractions that took his own restraint away in a maelstrom of building joy. "Yes! Feel me, Gracie. Feel me…going into you!"

The words excited her beyond measure. His hips arched into hers fiercely. She felt the tension snap in a hot rush of pleasure, heard her voice cry out in a sound she didn't even recognize as the glorious sensations reached flashpoint and carried her over some flowing hot lava. She shivered as the waves grew even higher. She was vaguely aware of the sound of Jason's voice in her ears as he pressed his mouth heatedly against her breast for seconds before he arched and groaned and began to convulse above her. She clung to him, her eyes wide-open with shocked wonder as she saw his face. It was so intimate, she thought wildly. So intimate!

His eyes opened, black and glazed, and pierced right into hers as they shuddered together in one final burst of pleasure. He groaned and the tension went out of him as he collapsed in a damp, exhausted heap on her relaxed body.

She held him to her, gloried in the weight of his powerful body as she felt the soft, stabbing echoes of pleasure with the helpless movement of his hips. It had been like a volcanic eruption, she thought. She'd never dreamed that such sensations existed. She'd never loved Jason more.

She should have stopped him, she thought then, as shame and guilt began to replace the silvery delight of the pleasure they'd shared. She bit her lip and fought tears. But they rained hotly down her cheeks, onto his, which was lying close against her own.

He felt them and lifted his head, propping himself on his elbows as he studied her stricken expression.

"I told you first times were rough," he said softly. "I'm sorry I had to hurt you." He kissed away the tears. "It was bad."

"It wasn't," she argued quietly. Her arms slid around his neck and her face buried itself in his strong, damp throat. "Bad, I mean. It was incredible! But that just makes me feel guiltier. I couldn't even ask you to stop!"

He kissed her closed eyelids. "Could you do this with someone else?" he asked.

"Heavens, no!"

He lifted his head. He was smiling. It was the most tender, affectionate smile he'd ever given her. "Neither could I. We aren't permissive people. As it is, we've only jumped the gun by a few hours," he added. "We'll grab a few hours of sleep. Then we're going to fly to San Antonio, followed by a trip to the Jacobs County probate judge's office."

"We are? Why?" she asked in a daze.

"To San Antonio for rings and a dress," he said lazily, kissing the tip of her nose. "We'll collect Mrs. Harcourt and Dilly on the way. We're getting married tomorrow."

"Married?" she echoed, still stunned.

He gave her a glowering look. "Married. You had your way with me. Don't think you're going to walk away and gossip about me to any woman you meet. I'm not that sort of man."

Her eyes widened. He looked sane. "Ooookay," she said, humoring him.

"After all," he added, gazing down at her pert breasts below him, "I could be pregnant."

She started to laugh, but then the thought began to flower in her own mind as she stared up into his eyes. "Pregnant."

The smile faded. He touched her soft mouth with his fingertip. "Pregnant." He drew in a long, slow breath. "Gracie, you really could be pregnant. With my baby." His black eyes glittered with pure possession.

A noticeable shiver ran through her body. She looked radiant. "I would love that!" she whispered huskily.

He nodded solemnly. "So would I." He pulled away from her and got to his feet, pulling her up beside him. He smiled at her shy glances as he went to turn the shower on. "Which is why we're wasting no time. No modern arrangements for us. We're going the traditional route."

She followed him under the warm spray and hugged him with a long, soulful sigh. "This isn't traditional."

"Actually it is, if you remember your history," he teased as he reached for washcloths and soap. "The intent to marry was all that was required for couples to indulge each other like this, even during the sixteenth century. It was called handfasting, I believe."

She laughed, because he was right. "I believe I have the history degree in this family," she pointed out.

He bent and kissed her nose. "I believe you do." He touched her cheek lightly. His eyes were full of dreams. "I should have asked, instead of telling. Will you marry me, Gracie?"

"Of course," she replied softly.

Smiling, he moved closer and began soaping her soft skin with the cloth.

SHE'D HAD SOME IDEA that they might sleep separately, but he wouldn't hear of it. He tucked her up into his arms in her bed and held her close all night. He couldn't bear to be separated from her even by a wall, he said with such sincerity that her heart raced.

The next morning, he came to wake her up with a steaming cup of fresh coffee. He was already dressed. He sat down beside her and kissed her tenderly.

"Wake up and get dressed. I've got breakfast ready. We'll leave as soon as we eat."

"I have to do something about the mess in the bathroom," she said and then flushed as she recalled what had happened in there.

"I put the lot in the washing machine," he said quietly. He touched her tousled hair gently. "Gracie, I didn't mean for it to happen like that," he said apologetically.

He looked torn. She reached up and traced his high cheekbone. "I know. Neither did I." She smiled shyly. "I didn't realize how…intense…things could get."

He laughed shortly. "Especially for a man who's abstained for the better part of two years."

She caught her breath at what he was admitting.

He shrugged. "I wasn't able to want anyone else."

For all that time, she was thinking. And while he was standing back, hoping for her to see him as a man, she'd been pretending everything was normal and trying not to translate her love for him into something physical out of fear.

"I kept backing away," she said slowly, "because I didn't think I was capable of giving you what you would have wanted. I was tied up in the past, scared to death of anything physical. I was afraid to even experiment. My poor mother," she added sadly. "I don't think she had any idea what she was supposed to feel."

"No wonder," he replied. "I'm sorry about that."

"So am I." She searched his black eyes. "I never dreamed it would feel like that," she murmured.

"It would never feel like that with any other man," he assured her quickly. "You'd break out in purple spots if you even let another man kiss you. And God forbid, if you did anything more, you'd grow an extra arm in the middle of your forehead." He put his hand over his heart. "I swear," he added, all with a straight face.

She burst out laughing and reached up to draw him down into her arms, hugging him with fierce delight.

He laughed, too. "You just remember that," he told her.

"I will." She searched his eyes. "As if I could ever let another man touch me!"

He drew away, winked at her and got to his feet. "Come on. Get a move on. I want to rush you to the altar before any competition shows up."

"There isn't any competition," she told him firmly. "There never has been. Not since the day I first saw you."

His high cheekbones went a little dusky, and he laughed.

She looked at him adoringly. "I'll never leave you, Jason."

His jaw tautened. "And I'll never leave you. The light went out of the world when I knew you'd been kidnapped. If I'd lost you…" His lips made a thin line. He turned away, still reluctant to admit to the feelings that were racking him. "We'd better get going."

"Okay." She smiled, but he didn't turn around again. She watched him walk away. He wanted her. But it was more than physical. She knew that with her whole heart, even though he hadn't put it into words. He would. She was certain of it. And she was going to marry him. For the first time in her life, she felt like a whole woman.

THEY DROVE TO SAN ANTONIO, to the mansion. Mrs. Harcourt met them at the door. She was so thrilled with their news that she burst into tears and hugged them both, murmuring inaudibly the whole time.

Jason left them in the hall and went off to his study to get something out of the safe, he said.

Mrs. Harcourt dried her eyes and smiled, but she was worried. She drew Gracie into the kitchen and closed the door.

"I have to tell you before he comes back," she said quickly. "Kittie called here. She said she's going to give the story to the tabloids because Jason won't go back to her. She said she'd make him a laughingstock."

"It's all right," Gracie assured her. "Jason knows about my past. She'll never be able to—"

"Not yours," Mrs. Harcourt interrupted, anguished. "Mine!"

"Yours?" Gracie hesitated, frowning. "But you don't have a past."

The older woman closed her eyes. "If you only knew. I've never spoken of it to a soul. We signed papers. I swore I'd carry the secret to my grave."

"What secret?"

The older woman drew in a deep breath. "Mrs. Pendleton was barren. She couldn't have a child. My husband was a good man, but I married him because my parents wanted me to, not because I loved him. I did love Myron, with all my heart. He hired me to work for him after my husband died, and we had an affair while his wife was in Bermuda one summer. I hated sneaking around. I felt so guilty. I was sure she knew…"

Gracie felt the blood drain out of her face. Mrs. Harcourt had jet-black eyes. Just like Jason…

Mrs. Harcourt wiped her eyes. "I got pregnant and Myron had to tell her. She wasn't even upset. She said the baby would still be a Pendleton. She arranged for us to go to Europe together, just me and her. She told everyone she was pregnant, and I was going to take care of her because she had to rest on account of her delicate health. When Jason was born, we came back home and they announced his birth in all the papers. Nobody knew. When she died, I thought maybe Myron would marry me."

She shook her head, continuing her sad tale. "He said

he couldn't marry someone like me. I wasn't his social equal. From that day, I never slept with him again, although he kept trying to lure me back. He married your mother and when she died, he married Glory's mother. But he warned me that if I ever spoke of Jason's real parentage, he'd have me put in prison on some trumped up charge. I believed him," she added grimly. "He wasn't above it."

"Jason never knew?" Gracie exclaimed.

"No. But he'll find out now," she said miserably. "It will hurt him. And not only that his father hid it from him. The tabloids will love it. Millionaire makes his mother pretend to be his housekeeper because he's ashamed of her." She smiled wanly. "What a headline."

Gracie was astonished. Her mind went blank. She heard Jason's footsteps in the hall. "Don't tell him," she told Mrs. Harcourt firmly. "We'll think of something."

"What?" she asked, distraught.

"We'll talk later," Gracie said quickly.

"What are you doing in the kitchen?" Jason asked the women. "We have to get to Neiman Marcus to buy wedding clothes. I forgot to drive by and get Dilly on the way," he added with a rueful grin at Gracie. "I must have had my mind on something else at the time. Anyway, I phoned Grange. He's going to bring Dilly up to meet us at the department store, then I'll drive us all home."

"Wedding clothes?" Mrs. Harcourt stammered.

"Yes," he said. "You and Dilly and Grange are our witnesses. I wish we could find John," he added sadly. "He's as much a part of the family as we are."

Mrs. Harcourt looked torn. She hesitated. "I know where he is," she confessed. "But he made me promise not to say."

"Why?" he burst out.

She grimaced. "John was in prison for being the wheel man in a bank robbery up in Dallas about thirty years ago," she said. "Your father didn't do a background check on him, so nobody knew. Miss Kittie found out and swore she'd tell if he didn't leave. She had something on all of us," she added darkly. "God knows how she found out."

"One of her friends has a detective agency," he replied coolly. "So that's why he left. Did he really think it would matter to me? John is family!"

Mrs. Harcourt watched him quietly. There was a deep pride in her expression that she fought to conceal. Gracie had seen it before and not understood it. Now she did.

"Where is he?" Jason demanded.

"He's living at the men's mission downtown," she said. "Let's go."

He was out the door in a flash, leaving them to follow.

AT THE MISSION, he left the women in the car and went in alone to find John. He was directed to a second-floor bedroom. The old man was sitting up on his bed, reading his Bible. He started when Jason walked in and stumbled to his feet.

"Mr. Jason, you shouldn't be here!" he exclaimed.

Jason looked around. "Neither should you," he shot back.

The old man looked wounded, tired, absolutely devoid of hope. "Mrs. Harcourt swore she wouldn't tell you," he said. "What are you doing here?"

Jason put a firm hand on the older man's shoulder. "Getting my family back," he said quietly. "Your past doesn't matter to me. You belong with us. Come home."

John fought the moisture in his eyes. Jason had been like the son he'd never had. It had almost killed him, having to leave. He'd been so afraid of Kittie's threats.

"Oh, stop that," Jason muttered when he saw the glitter in John's eyes. "You'll have me doing it, too. What will people think?"

John swallowed hard.

"I don't care what you've done in the past," he said shortly. "You've done your time. I can't do without you. You're the best chauffeur in Texas."

"Thanks," he bit off, still choked up.

"Pack your bag," he said, smiling. "We're on our way to get married."

"You and me?" John exclaimed with a faint attempt at humor.

Jason glared at him. "Gracie and me," he corrected.

The old man's face lit up. "You're marrying Miss Gracie?"

"Yes. When I get the family together," he added. "Will you pack? We're in a hurry."

"Pack. Yes, sir. Yes, sir!" It was the best news he'd had in weeks!

Jason stood by the door, swallowing a lump in his own throat as he watched the old fellow put his pitiful few belongings into a rickety old suitcase. He was ashamed of so many things Kittie had done behind his back, things he'd been too wrapped up in himself to notice. At least he was finally getting things back to normal.

John was enthusiastically welcomed by the two women, who were oddly quiet when Jason got in behind the wheel and started out into the street.

"Why the solemn faces?" Jason teased Gracie. "Weddings are happy occasions."

"The happiest of my life," Gracie agreed and her eyes warmed as they met Jason's. She was carrying another secret now, one much more dangerous than her own that she'd hidden for so long. This one had the power to destroy her fragile relationship with Jason. The question was, did she dare keep Mrs. Harcourt's secret in light of Kittie's threat?

14

THE SHOPPING SPREE was so enjoyable that Gracie was able to put aside her worries for the time it took to find a suitable dress for herself and outfits for Mrs. Harcourt and Dilly, as well as a suit for old John.

"I don't know about us standing up with you, Mr. Jason," Dilly worried as she was handed several garments to try on. "Miss Kittie said I was dumpy…"

"I'm not marrying Miss Kittie," Jason told her firmly. "You and Mrs. Harcourt and John are part of our family. We're not getting married without you."

"Exactly," Gracie said, arms folded stubbornly.

Dilly bit back tears. "Okay, then."

She went off to try on her dresses. Mrs. Harcourt came out wearing a nice navy suit with a soft pink blouse. "What do you think?" she asked worriedly.

Jason put his arms around her. "I think you look like a wonderful substitute mother-of-the-groom," he said tenderly and bent to kiss her cheek.

Mrs. Harcourt bawled. Gracie drew out a tissue and handed it to her.

"You have to wait and cry at the wedding," she said firmly.

The older woman laughed. "I know. Sorry. Just rehearsing."

She went back into the fitting room.

Jason drew Gracie off to an unoccupied corner of the women's clothing department and handed her a gray jewelry box.

She opened it and caught her breath. When she'd taken art classes in college, she'd drawn a set of wedding bands that she dreamed of using one day if she was ever able to work up the courage to get married. There was a square emerald solitaire and a matching band. There was a man's band, plain but with the same engraved motif as the woman's wedding band.

"I drew these," Gracie faltered.

Jason took out the engagement ring and slid it solemnly onto her finger. He kissed it with breathless tenderness. "I had them made up years ago," he said huskily as he met her eyes. "I knew that it would be you or nobody."

If she hadn't run from him that rainy night, she was thinking, all the anguish in between would have been spared. The thought lay in her expression.

"Don't," he whispered softly, and bent to kiss her. "We can't look back. Only ahead."

She drew in a soft breath. "Only ahead," she agreed. She smiled up at him. "You're going to wear a ring?"

He chuckled. "Oh, yes."

She grinned. "Okay."

Grange appeared from an adjoining department with a bag over his shoulder. He glared at Jason. "I'd just got around to buying some new jeans and shirts, and I'd got tickets to the ballet. I hate ballet," he added, "but I would have gone for her." He pointed at Gracie. "Then you have to go and get engaged to her and mess up all my plans," he muttered. "I even washed my truck!"

They both burst out laughing. So did Grange, who was fond of Gracie, but not anywhere near in love with her. She knew it, even if Jason hadn't seemed to.

"Hard luck," Jason said smugly. "You're too late now."

Grange shook his head. "At least I get to come to the wedding," he said. He jiggled the bag over his shoulder. "I bought a suit, too."

"Good idea. If you ever get married, you won't even have to go shopping."

Grange just grinned.

THERE WAS A BRIEF but poignant ceremony in the probate judge's office, in the thick of a library of law books and county records. The judge herself, Alexandra Mills, was the sister of one of Jason's cowboys.

"I'd like to say I'm surprised to see you two here, but I won't lie," she confessed. "The gossips have gone wild around here lately." She glanced from Gracie in her pretty white suit with its accompanying veiled pillbox hat, to the witnesses and then to Jason in his neat blue pin-striped suit. "Nice of you to bring witnesses."

"I didn't," Jason said complacently. "I brought our family."

Alexandra looked from one of his companions to the other, noting tears in several eyes. "Of course," she agreed warmly. Jason Pendleton might be a millionaire, but nobody could call him a snob.

She read the marriage ceremony from the Bible, and

watched them exchange rings and vows, after which
Jason was allowed to kiss his tearful bride. He lifted the
brief veil and smiled at Gracie with his whole heart. He
kissed her very softly and then hugged her warmly.

Congratulations were offered and accepted, after
which relevant papers were signed, and they all walked
out of the office into flashing cameras.

"It's okay," Jason comforted his companions, who
were looking for places to hide. "It's just Billy Thornton
from the local paper and Jack Harrison, our resident photographer. I asked them to come. Get back here and
smile," he added firmly, getting everybody into a group.
He put his arm around Gracie, holding a bouquet of
bronzed chrysanthemums. "Shoot away," he told the photographers, and he smiled.

JASON HIRED A LEARJET to take them down to Cancún for
a three-day honeymoon, complete with bodyguards just
in case General Machado tried to nab one of them again.
He checked them into an expensive hotel on the strand
of beach that was home to some of the ritziest accommo-
dations south of the border.

The room overlooked the Gulf of Mexico. It was late
evening and a full moon hung overhead, silvering the waves
as they crashed in white foam onto the sugar-white beach.

"Tired?" Jason asked as he drew her into his arms.

She shook her head. "Happy."

"Me, too."

He bent and kissed her very softly. "Sore?" he whispered meaningfully.

She met his eyes and shook her head again, very slowly.

"In that case," he said, smiling as he met her lips
with his own.

IT WAS THE WAY HE'D wanted it to be during their first exploration of each other. He treated her as the virgin she'd been, drawing out each soft caress until he made her moan and plead for more. He kissed her from the tip of her head to the tip of her toes, his lips finding her in exquisite ways with skill and mastery that took her breath away. She jumped from plateau to plateau, shivering with the newness of pleasure, delighting in the feel of his skin against hers and the warmth of his mouth on her breasts as he made their tips hard and sensitive before his tongue sensitized them even more.

She had thought their first time had given her the greatest pleasure possible, but she learned in the long night that she'd only grazed the surface of ecstasy. Jason was over her, then under her, then beside her as his hands explored her yielding body. The mutual tension built to such a flashpoint that she dragged him down against her and almost forcibly joined her body to his in a tempest of physical delight that made her sob with escalating pleasure.

Each long, slow thrust was an agony of patience that brought her to some precipice of anguish that she could hardly bear.

"You're torturing me," she wailed, pushing her hips up to meet his.

"I'm getting you ready," he corrected breathlessly, as he stilled her thrashing hips and pushed down with long, measured thrusts.

"Ready?" she pleaded.

"Ready," he whispered. "Hold on tight, sweetheart. We're going right over a cliff..."

He increased the rhythm so suddenly that she was left hanging in midair. She felt him swelling even more as he pushed harder, his body buffeting hers noisily against the white sheets in the filtered moonlight.

She cried out and her nails bit into his hips.

"That's it," he groaned at her ear. "Hold me. Feel me driving into you. Feel me…exploding…inside you!"

"Jason!" She shuddered and arched up, the pleasure growing so unbearable that she sobbed and sobbed, rigid as a board under the fierce rhythm of his hips. "Harder, Jason, harder, harder…!"

"Oh…God!"

He arched and stiffened, and then suddenly convulsed with a groan so harsh that he sounded as if he'd been wounded.

Gracie held on for dear life, her body so attuned to his that she shot up into the heat with him, arching into the sleek curve of his body so that they seemed no longer two people, but one, melted together like molten iron.

She opened her eyes just at the last and saw his face clenched, his eyes closed, his mouth a thin line as he endured the agony of climax. Her own body was just past that exquisite burst of tension, echoing with little stabs of delight as he moved helplessly inside her.

One last shudder and his eyes opened, right into hers. Incredibly, the sight of her, watching him, brought another explosion of pleasure that shook him over her. He looked down at her swollen breasts, her flat belly pressed so tightly to his, and he trembled, closing his eyes so that he could feel the tight, hot press of her all around him as he spent himself.

Finally his body unclenched and he relaxed, flowing down over her.

"We're going to kill each other, eventually," she whispered shakily.

"I noticed that."

She moved experimentally, enjoying the little echoes of pleasure that shivered in her. "Gosh! It just keeps going," she cried.

"Yes." He shifted his lean hips and lifted his head to watch her, grinning as her face expressed the pleasure he was giving her.

"Conceited," she managed.

He shook his head. "Incredibly talented."

She laughed. "Yes."

He rolled over onto his back and drew her over him, his eyes dark and warm. "And just think, this is supposed to get better with practice."

"I'll die," she lamented, moving closer.

"Yes, honey, but what a way to go," he whispered at her ear, and laughed with her.

"BUT YOU HAVE TO have a proper wedding," Glory fussed when Jason and Gracie got home. She was still upset because they'd waited two days to call her and tell her about the ceremony.

"We did," Jason said reasonably. "One without fanfare and cameras."

"You could at least have a reception in San Antonio," she continued doggedly.

Gracie and Jason looked at each other with resignation. "I guess we could," Gracie said. She hugged her stepsister. "We meant to call you, honestly. But we just forgot about everything."

Jason grinned sheepishly. "It was a pretty intense honeymoon."

Glory gave in, laughing. "I can't say I was even surprised," she pointed out. "The two of you were pretty obvious, even months ago."

"We were?" they echoed.

Glory just shook her head. "I'm meeting Rodrigo for lunch, but you have to go with us to the charity dinner in San Antonio Friday night. All the old crowd is going to be there, and they can't wait to congratulate both of you."

Jason smiled at Gracie. "We really have to go," he agreed. "We do have friends."

Gracie nodded. She'd forgotten her socializing since her move to Jacobsville. "I was trying to get back to my roots," she explained quietly. "And prove that I could take care of myself."

"Which you did," Jason said firmly. "You can keep your job at the college. I won't say a word. You can lecture at the elementary school. But we've already proven that you can have an occasional night out without staining your working girl image," he added persuasively.

She sighed. "I guess I can." She smiled up at him tentatively. "If you won't mind when I fall down the steps occasionally or trip over my own feet."

He pulled her close, very solemnly. "I'll always be there to catch you," he said. "And it won't matter. It never did."

THEY WENT HOME RELUCTANTLY. Rodrigo and Glory met them at the San Antonio mansion with a beautiful cut crystal bowl for a wedding present, and a few recriminations. But long before they got to those, Glory just hugged Gracie with all her strength. She had to bite back tears. This was a love match if she'd ever seen one. She wondered why it had taken these two stubborn people so long to see it.

"You're going to be very happy together," she said absently.

They both smiled at her. "Of course we are," Gracie said, and there were dreams in her eyes.

The charity shindig proved to Gracie that her friendships weren't a matter of Jason's money. People were honestly happy to see her, and she had more invitations than she could ever accept. She was asked to serve on committees, and she promised to work some of them into her busy schedule. When she told her friends about her new job, they were elated to see that she was using all her talents, not just the ones she had for hostessing and planning parties. She realized finally that it was her own personality, her own self, that these people valued. She'd always assumed it was position and money. Nothing was farther from the truth.

There was only one sour note. One of Jason's business associates, a little tipsy, asked him what happened to the gorgeous redhead he was going to marry.

"Gracie happened," Jason said without batting an eye, and he pulled Gracie close and kissed the tip of her nose.

The tipsy man smiled self-consciously at the people frowning at him, and went away.

Glory and Rodrigo took them by a Latin club for a nightcap.

"Your friend the General is trying to get enough money for a coup," Rodrigo told her. "We can't help him, much as we'd like to. Word on the street is that he's given up kidnapping because he doesn't like the way the Fuentes bunch do business. But he can't leave Mexico until he has enough to hire some good mercenaries to help him kick out his adversary."

"He was kind to me," Gracie said. "I wish we could help him."

"So do I," Rodrigo replied. "He's something of a pirate, but he's progressive and democratic in his politics and he has a soft spot for helpless people. His replacement has been sending people to secret prisons and he's starting to nationalize the government. He has friends in some very dicey places. We'd love to see him retired."

"Bad time politically to meddle in foreign affairs," Jason remarked.

Rodrigo nodded. "Very bad. Ah, well," he added, sipping his drink and smiling. "We don't always get what we want."

Jason looked down at Gracie with aching tenderness. "Sometimes we do."

"Oh, yes," Gracie agreed breathlessly.

Glory and Rodrigo laughed and lifted their glasses in a toast to the newlyweds.

JASON AND GRACIE HAD planned to spend the night at the San Antonio mansion, but when they drove up to the gate, they discovered a satellite truck and at least one local news team standing at the closed gates and trying to gain entrance.

"I'll get out and see what's going on," Jason began.

Gracie caught his arm. "Turn around and get out of here before somebody recognizes us," she said urgently. "Please, Jason."

He gave her an odd look, but he did as she asked. Fortunately they were far enough away that they only got curious looks. Nobody tried to follow them.

"They've heard about the wedding, that's all," he teased. "We should have given them an interview."

Gracie gritted her teeth. This was going to be hard. "Jason, there are things going on that you don't know about," she said gently. "And I'm afraid there may be more reporters at the ranch."

He pulled off the road into the parking lot of an all-night fast food joint and cut the engine. "Why?"

She felt sick. This was going to wound him. But she

knew that the reporters wouldn't have been there unless Kittie had made good on her threat. Some of the people she knew in San Antonio would surely have told her about Jason's marriage. She probably was out for revenge now, instead of money, and she was using Mrs. Harcourt's secret to get it. Gracie couldn't let him walk into this blind. She had to tell him the truth.

"Kittie knows something about Mrs. Harcourt."

Jason frowned. "So?"

She clutched her purse so hard that her nails made marks in the leather. "Jason, haven't you ever wondered why you don't look like your mother?"

He scowled. "I don't look like my father, either. He said I resemble my grandfather."

"Your eyes are coal-black," she began slowly, meeting them with her own.

All at once, he went rigid. He was remembering things from his childhood. Mrs. Harcourt's coddling. His father's coldness to her. Arguments that he overheard and didn't understand. But the reference to his eyes was like a body blow. He'd wondered about that, too, sometimes, thinking that Mrs. Harcourt might be a cousin or distant relation that his snobbish father hadn't wanted to claim. Now, however, he was seeing his father's elitist attitude in a totally different light.

"Mrs. Harcourt isn't just my housekeeper. She's my mother!" Even as he said it, he knew it was the truth. It had been right in front of him all these years.

"Yes," Gracie said heavily. "She was horrified that you laughed off Kittie's threats. She said it would disgrace you if it ever came out. Not to mention what it will do to her," she added sadly. "She's a churchgoing woman, you know. She had a child by a married man, out of wedlock. How do you think she's going to react when everybody knows? You aren't the only one who's going to be hurt by this."

He glared at her. "You knew."

She grimaced. "Yes…"

"You knew, and you didn't tell me?"

"She made me promise, Jason," she said quietly.

He was thinking that she never trusted him with any secret, beginning with her own past. It hurt him that she still felt that way, regardless of how close they'd become.

"Reporters will have her trapped at the house," he guessed, starting the car.

"I don't think so," Gracie said, pulling out her cell phone. "Comanche Wells is very small. Somebody would have seen the trucks coming, even if they didn't know why, and told her. She'd have a good idea why they were coming."

"What are you doing?" he asked.

"Calling her cell," she replied. It rang and rang. Finally a timid voice said hello. "Mrs. Harcourt, it's me," she said gently.

"Miss Gracie? Thank God! Miss Kittie called and said she was getting ready to break the story to the whole world," she said, sobbing. "She said newspeople are heading this way. I'm at Barbara's house. She's going to get people in Jacobsville and Comanche Wells organized. Nobody is going to speak to anybody with a camera. But I don't know how long she can hide me. Does he know? Is he mad? He hates me, doesn't he?"

"Of course he doesn't hate you," Gracie said, daring Jason to argue.

"What will we do?" Mrs. Harcourt wailed.

"We'll think of something. We'll see you when we get there. We're on our way."

"All right. Be careful," the older woman sniffed.

"We will." She hung up. "She's at Barbara's."

He didn't reply. He was furious, and growing more furious by the minute. He felt as if he'd been betrayed by everybody. His whole life was upside down. And the woman he thought would never sell him out was sitting beside him, wearing his wedding band.

Gracie felt that deep anger, even though he didn't speak. She could have knocked Kittie over a table for putting Mrs. Harcourt and Jason through this. The greedy, heartless woman shouldn't be allowed to get away with it.

"It was cruel, doing it this way," Gracie spat out.

Jason glanced at her. "Secrets are dangerous," he said bluntly.

She flushed. She knew what he meant. "All right, I'll agree that I shouldn't have kept things from you. I didn't tell you about my own past because I was so ashamed of it. But I didn't tell you about Mrs. Harcourt because I gave my word."

He swerved onto the Jacobsville road. "She's working as my damned housekeeper," he said shortly. "How is that going to play out in the press?"

"Badly, if we don't come up with a strategy before we get home," she said. "Mrs. Harcourt will be hurt more than you will."

He shifted in the seat. "I know. She was always there when nobody else was. My mother was a socialite. She spent little time around me," he said slowly. "But Mrs. Harcourt was always there to kiss the hurt places and cuddle me when I had nightmares." He closed his eyes for an instant. "She's been living on the fringes of my life since I was born, playing the part of the housekeeper, never asking for anything."

"It's the way she is. When Kittie threatened her, it was you she was most concerned about. She said the media will make you look heartless. It made her cry."

He pursed his lips, scowling. "I've got a rental property in Jacobsville, down the street from Barbara's house. It's vacant right now, and already furnished. We can move her into it. We'll have Neiman Marcus send down the right sort of clothes, in her size. I own that craft shop in Jacobsville, too. I'll phone the manager at home. We can put her name on the bill of sale as owner and put some of those beautiful afghans she's made in there for samples."

"Now you're thinking straight," Gracie said with a beaming smile.

He drew in a long breath. "It's going to be tricky."

"We can pull it off."

"We can't turn my new mother into a socialite overnight," he groaned. "She's still herself. I don't want to change her into something uncomfortable, but she can't go on being my housekeeper, under the circumstances."

"She's scared to death."

"I know. We'll handle it."

Gracie relaxed. How many times had she heard him say that, in his deep, confident voice, when her world was falling apart? He never seemed to lose control of himself.

"We'll need Barbara to help."

"She will," Gracie assured him.

They drove the rest of the way in silence.

JASON PARKED UNDER Barbara's carport and escorted Gracie inside. Mrs. Harcourt was standing in the middle of the living room with a soaked handkerchief and red eyes. She stared at Jason with anguish.

"I'm sorry," she cried. "I never meant for you to know!"

Jason stood in the doorway, unmoving, his face a mask. He didn't know what to say. The news had come as a terrible shock.

Gracie caught Barbara's sleeve and tugged her out of the room. Only two people needed to be in on that discussion, and it wasn't going to be easy for either of them.

"WHY DIDN'T YOU TELL ME years ago?" Jason asked curtly.

She dabbed at her eyes. "Myron made me sign a legal document," she choked out. "He swore that if I told, he'd frame me for an awful crime and have me put away forever. I knew he wasn't bluffing. Then, after he died…I didn't know how to tell you. I was afraid he might have left some secret papers or something to incriminate me." She bit her lip. "He was ruthless."

Jason knew that. His father hadn't made his millions without walking on other people in the process. He was hard-hearted and calculating, and his enemies never thrived. Jason had never liked that part of him. It had put a barrier between them.

"Our eyes are alike," he said, watching her with his hands in his pockets. "Funny I never noticed." He frowned. "Who did we inherit them from?"

She smiled nervously. "My father. My grandfather was a Spanish duke," she added. "He came to this country after the First World War to take over a ranch that belonged to someone in his family. He married my grandmother, who was the daughter of his cook."

"The ranch…my ranch?" he asked, fascinated.

"Yes."

He frowned. "I bought it from you."

"There wasn't much left of it," she said. "It was just about bankrupt. It made me so proud, to see what you did with it. I knew you could stand on your own two feet. You didn't need your father's name or wealth or position to make a success." Her eyes glittered. "He was sure you'd fall flat on your face. I knew you wouldn't!"

For the first time, his face relaxed. He moved a step closer. "How did you end up in this situation?"

She sat down heavily on the sofa. Her tired eyes met his. "My husband had just died and I needed a job, badly. Mr. Pendleton's housekeeper had quit—he couldn't keep any of them for long because of his temper. I just talked back to him instead of cowering. He liked it." She managed a smile. "He was a very handsome man, and he could be charming, absolutely charming. His wife went to spend the summer with her sister in Bermuda." She avoided his eyes. "I was lonely. He brought me presents, gave me flowers, made me feel like a princess. I got pregnant. He seemed to be expecting it. He smiled and said I wasn't to worry, he'd take care of everything." She shook her head. "He told her. She was very calm. She said it would be easy for us to go away together. She'd tell people she was pregnant and her health was fragile. The cover story was that I had to look after her until the baby was born. He put us on a plane. We came home after I had the baby. They assured me that they'd take care of the baby, that it would never want for anything. And I could stay on and help raise it."

"Good God!" he burst out, aghast.

"I know, it sounds insane. I was too upset to fight. I didn't want people to know how stupid I'd been." She shook her head. "Apparently your mother knew what he planned to do." She grimaced. "Your father...well, he wasn't exactly a model of the virtues."

"Yes, I know," he said coldly. "My mother knew?"

"She was barren. They were both horrified that the mansion and all their money might go to a distant relative. They wanted a child, but not an adopted one. I was so naive," she added miserably. "I had a great time overseas. I loved being pregnant. Myron flew over when I went into labor. When you were born, they were overjoyed. You were at least half a Pendleton, you see. I was just the incubator."

"It was cruel," he said heavily, dropping into an armchair across from her. "It was even worse when he died. He left you out of his will entirely. I won't tell you what he said. If only I'd known," he groaned, and his eyes were anguished as they met hers.

"I didn't mind about the will. I never expected anything. I was just happy that I got to be with you while you were growing up. I'm sorry you had to find this out," she apologized. "I know you loved your mother."

His black eyes darkened even more. "I never loved her," he returned at once. "She was as cold as ice. I remember being sick and throwing up with the flu when I was about five years old. She was horrified that I might soil her dress."

"Yes, you had measles," she recalled softly. "I sat up with you for two nights, feeding you ice chips, so you wouldn't get dehydrated."

"You were always the one who took care of me," he replied huskily. "My mother had no time for me. She was too busy being a socialite. My father wasn't much better. He was interested in making more money. Neither of them had the foggiest idea of how to be a parent."

"I did my best to make up for them," Mrs. Harcourt said.

"And you did," he said, his eyes soft as they met hers.

"I had a wonderful childhood, thanks to you." He grimaced. "You should have told me!"

She dabbed at her eyes. "I know," she said heavily. She looked at him worriedly. "Those reporters are going to make it look so bad," she moaned.

Jason lifted an eyebrow. "That's what you think. Gracie and I already have a plan."

Her eyes widened. "A plan? What is it?"

He smiled gently. "We're going to turn the tables on Kittie."

"We are?" she exclaimed, fascinated.

He chuckled. "Oh, yes. Her plan is going to backfire on her, big-time!"

15

⁓

"YOU'RE GOING TO MAKE a businesswoman out of me?" Mrs. Harcourt exclaimed. "But I'm just a plain old country woman. I'll never be able to convince anybody that I'm business material. You'll be ashamed of me, Jason. Everybody will laugh at you."

He got up from his chair and pulled her up, looking into her eyes that were so much like his. "You're my mother," he said, and the words came out raspy and with wonder. "My very own mother. I could never be ashamed of you!"

As more tears flowed down her pale cheeks. "All these years," she whispered, "I've watched you grow. I've seen the way you treated people, how you make everybody feel important and never look down on anyone because they're poor. You have so many good qualities, Jason, so many more than your father ever did." She gazed up at him. "I've been so proud of you. I wanted more than anything to tell you. But it wasn't Myron's threat that kept me quiet. It was the fear that you'd, well, be humiliated to know your mother was an ignorant, common sort of person...."

"You stop that," he said firmly. "You're the nicest person I know. You never gossip, you're always smiling, you give away what little you've got to anyone with a greater need, and you cook like an angel. You have wonderful qualities. I'm proud to be your son." His voice broke on the word. "More proud than I can tell you."

"Oh, my dear," she whispered tearfully, and suddenly pulled him into her arms, rocking him as she had when he was little and scared and hurt. So many times she'd ached to do this, to hold him and have him know that he was flesh of her flesh, blood of her blood. She'd loved him more than her own life. And now, at last, she could tell him. "My son!" she choked.

Jason couldn't answer her. His voice would have betrayed him. He held her tight and rocked her in the silence of the living room. Nobody was going to hurt her. He'd fight the world to keep her safe. She was his very own. His mother!

A long time later, he eased her out of his arms and dashed a hand across his eyes before he turned back to her.

"We've got to get moving, fast," he said. "We may not have much time."

Mrs. Harcourt beamed through her tears. "Okay! I'll do whatever you want me to do."

FIRST, THEY MOVED HER into Jason's rental house with some help from their friends. Grange was sent back to the ranch house to pile some afghans into a box and bring them to the small craft shop off the square in Jacobsville. He hadn't seen a single reporter or satellite truck yet, he told them, which was a relief. It gave them time to put their plan into operation.

Jason opened the shop with his key and he and Gracie spread the pretty crocheted pieces in the front window. Jason called the manager at home from his cell phone while they worked and gave her instructions. She was a good woman, and she liked Mrs. Harcourt, who bought all her yarn there. She agreed to tell any reporters who turned up what Jason had said.

All the shifting accomplished, they went back to Barbara's house and waited for Grange to call them. He was contacting some people he knew to try to find out where the satellite trucks had gone.

Jason and Gracie drank coffee at Barbara's kitchen table and discussed what to do next.

"It's disgraceful," Barbara muttered. "That awful woman, to do such a thing out of wounded pride!"

"Wounded wallet, more like," Gracie murmured with forced humor.

Jason glanced at her. They'd hardly spoken ten words since the nightmare began. His eyes were promising trouble when things settled down. Gracie didn't know what else she could say in her own defense. He was upset and he wasn't really listening. All his energies right now were concentrated on saving his mother from the media.

Finally, Jason's cell phone rang. It was Grange. Jason listened, his eyes widened and he burst out laughing. "Okay. Thanks. I owe you one." He hung up. He looked at the two women. "You aren't going to believe this. They don't know about Mrs. Harcourt after all. That computer game software I bought in California has just hit the shelves and it's a runaway bestseller, setting new records. The media's after me for a quote. They said my decision to fund the creators was a stroke of genius."

"Well!" Gracie exclaimed, relieved. "We went to a lot of trouble for nothing."

Jason pursed his lips. "Do you think so? I don't." He pulled out his cell phone and called the detective he used for special jobs. He outlined what he thought Kittie was planning and asked the man to check around and see if she was gossiping about her future schemes. He gave him information about Mrs. Harcourt, to Gracie's astonishment, that he wanted leaked to the tabloid media. Then he added a request to look in Kittie's own background and see what turned up. He was smiling coldly when he hung up.

"That takes the fight into the enemy's camp," Jason said. "We'll spike her guns by releasing the story before she has time to. God help her if she's hiding any dark secrets. This thing works both ways."

"That's what I would have done," Barbara commented coolly. "She's good at starting trouble. I wonder how she is at handling it?"

"We're going to find out," Jason said. "First thing in the morning, the tabloids will announce to the world that my housekeeper has just confessed to being my mother. We'll add that she was the owner of a craft shop and hadn't told me. She worked at the house just to be close to me."

"What about the rest of it?" Gracie asked worriedly.

"The rest of it will never come out," he said easily. "I've already taken steps to assure it. Never mind asking, I won't tell you. Now, suppose we go home and get some sleep? I don't know about you two, but I'm tired."

"Are you going to call Mrs. Harcourt?" Gracie asked.

"We're going to get her and take her home with us," he replied. "No need letting her brood alone."

Gracie smiled. "Good idea."

"Thanks, Barbara," Jason said, kissing her cheek. "You're the best."

Gracie hugged her, too. "I'll second that."

Barbara watched them off before she turned out her porch light.

THEY DIDN'T SPEAK ON the way to get Mrs. Harcourt. They didn't really speak when they got back to the ranch house, either. Jason left the women in the living room while he checked with Grange on any problems around the ranch.

"I thought he'd be furious," Mrs. Harcourt told Gracie. "He's taken it very well."

"I wonder," Gracie said quietly, because he was too calm. She knew him. He was brooding and still angry at her, she was certain of it.

He came back into the living room just in time to wish Mrs. Harcourt a good night's sleep. He smiled and kissed her cheek.

"Maybe we can all sleep," she agreed. "I'll make you a nice breakfast."

He chuckled. "Something to look forward to," he teased.

"Sleep well…son," she said, trying out this new word. She flushed a little when he grinned at her.

His black eyes warmed. "You, too, Mom." It came easily to him.

She lifted her cheek for him to kiss, hugged him and then laughed self-consciously as she wished them both good-night and went down the hall toward her own room.

Jason turned back to Gracie. He wasn't smiling now. "I'll sleep in the guest room," he said curtly. "We'll talk tomorrow."

"Jason…"

He ignored her. He walked down the hall, turned into the guest room and closed the door. Gracie stood staring at the empty space with quiet misery.

THE NEXT MORNING, they had a quiet breakfast after which Jason announced that he was driving up to San Antonio to the mansion to see if any satellite trucks were still guarding the entrance. If they were, he said, he had a story to tell them.

"I could go, too," Gracie began.

"You've taken several days off already," Jason said without meeting her eyes. "If you want to keep that job, you'd better get back to it."

She grimaced—he was right. Her teaching position at the college wouldn't survive another three days of begging for substitutes to fill in for her. Besides, there were only two more class periods left in the semester. "I guess so."

He finished his last sip of coffee and got to his feet. "Everything was delicious," he told his mother with a grin and bent to kiss her cheek. "I'll be home for supper."

"You be careful," Mrs. Harcourt said. "Those kidnappers are still out there."

"You could take Grange with you," Gracie added worriedly.

He glared in her general direction. "We took bodyguards to Cancún with us, and there wasn't even a hint of trouble. They've got other fish to fry now."

She sighed. "Be careful, anyway."

He made a sound deep in his throat and met her eyes for a long minute before he could tear them away. He was still hurt that she hadn't told him. "I won't be too long."

He walked out onto the porch. The women exchanged worried glances. He was headstrong and stubborn. But maybe they were concerned for no good reason.

AND MAYBE NOT. SUPPERTIME came, but no Jason. Gracie called the mansion, with Mrs. Harcourt wringing her hands next to her.

The interim housekeeper there answered the phone. "No, Miss Gracie," she said, "I haven't seen Mr. Jason at all today. Are you sure he said he was coming here?"

"Yes. What about the satellite trucks?"

"Oh, they left yesterday. Nobody's even called here. Well, except this strange man," she added slowly.

Gracie's heart jumped. "What strange man?"

"Some man with a thick Spanish accent. He said he had Mr. Jason, that he was going to stay with him for a few days and he'd be in touch about what he wanted in return. I thought he was some kook, so I didn't—"

"When did he call? How long ago?" Gracie interrupted urgently.

"Just a few minutes before you did…"

"If he calls again, you reach me on my cell phone. Here's the number, so you won't have to search for it." She gave it to the woman, waiting impatiently while she found a pen to write with. "You call me if he phones. Okay?"

"Yes, ma'am, I sure will."

"Thanks." Gracie hung up. Her face was white. "I knew it. I knew they'd keep on until they got him! It's that damned Fuentes bunch. They want him for helping Rodrigo shut them down, for paying Eb Scott's group to get him out!"

"What do we do?" Mrs. Harcourt asked miserably. "They'll kill him! Even if they get some ransom, they'll kill him!"

Gracie took her by the shoulders. "They're not killing Jason," she said. "Not while there's a breath left in my body!"

"But what can we do?"

Forcing herself to stay calm, Gracie thought feverishly about what her next move should be. Jason had a cell phone. If he'd been kidnapped, his kidnappers would have the phone. She had a direct line to them if it was still on. She wasn't involving the government or Eb Scott. She had money of her own, although she'd never touched it. She had over two hundred thousand dollars in certificates of deposit that Jason's father had left her—identical bequeaths to both her and Glory. She could use that money to ransom Jason, if only the General was still in charge down there over the border. He needed money to fund his counterrevolution and she had some. Now all she had to do was get him on the phone and have him get Jason away from the Fuentes bunch. But first she had to get through to Machado.

She picked up her cell phone and dialed Jason's number. She crossed her fingers, teeth clenched, as it rang and rang and rang. She'd almost given up when a deep voice came over the line.

"*¡Digame!*"

She could have cried with relief. She knew that voice. She would have recognized it anywhere. "General Machado!"

There was a pause. "Gracie? *¿Eres tu?*" he asked in the familiar tense.

She smiled through tears. "Yes, it's me. Do you have Jason?"

There was another pause, with muffled laughter. "*Sí.* Fuentes had him kidnapped, but I took him away from that bunch. Yes, I have him. You want your stepbrother back, huh?"

"My husband," she said gently. "He's my husband now."

"You married him? *Niña,* the man is a tiger," he groaned.

"He knocked the teeth out of two of Fuentes's men and then he crippled one of my own. He is one mean hombre!"

Gracie laughed softly. "Yes, he is. Can I have him back? I can bring you more than enough money to take back your government."

"You can? But he has the money, no?"

"I have money of my own. It sits in a bank and draws interest. You can do good things with it. Almost a quarter of a million dollars."

"*Caramba,* I could take over the world with that much!"

"I don't doubt it."

"You have not called your government?"

"I don't need to. I knew that if you had Jason, we could come to an agreement that was mutually beneficial," she added with a relieved laugh.

He chuckled. "As we can. The bank will need to be open, in order for you to get the money, no? Suppose you meet me in Mala Suerte at eleven tomorrow morning, at the Chinese restaurant, in the parking lot?"

She laughed. "The Chinese restaurant?"

"I like Chinese food," he laughed. "Besides, we will attract less attention there. You must drive something less noticeable than the big Jaguar, *sí?*"

"I'll drive one of the ranch trucks," she said easily. "Don't hurt him, okay?" she added hopefully.

"It is not him that I must worry about," he said drily, "but my own poor men. But no, I won't hurt him. See you tomorrow. *Niña,* if I see more than a truck, I drive back to Mexico, *entiendes?*"

"I understand, and you won't see more than my truck. Good night."

"Good night."

She hung up with a long sigh. "He's okay. He's busted up some of the kidnappers, but he seems to be fine," she laughed.

Mrs. Harcourt laughed, too. "That's my boy." She grimaced. "I wish I could give you the money. I hate that you have to give up your inheritance."

"I love Jason," she said simply. "I'd give up anything to get him back. It's just money. Besides, I'd never be able to get access to any of Jason's assets. You remember what happened when he tried to get a loan from his friend who was president of that San Antonio bank when I was kidnapped."

Mrs. Harcourt whistled. "Yes, I do. The very next week, he pulled every dime he had out of that bank and opened a new account with a competitor. They say the president's still crying."

"Serves him right. Mr. Reeves won't treat me that way, I guarantee it," Gracie said.

SHE WAS RIGHT. When Mr. Reeves, the president of the Jacobsville Municipal Bank, heard why she needed to cash in her CDs, he went right to work on helping her out.

"You're sure this is the way you want to do it?" he asked as they were closeted in his office while the head teller counted hundred dollar bills out and put them in the briefcase Gracie had brought from home. "Without calling in the FBI?"

"Mr. Reeves, I know one of the kidnappers personally. He's an honorable man. If he says he'll hand over Jason when he has the money, you could bet your life on it."

"If he's so honorable, why did he kidnap your husband?" the head teller, Marge, asked worriedly.

"It's complicated," Gracie told her gently. "He didn't

actually kidnap Jason, he took him away from the men who did. But it isn't to fund drug running or anything like that. He lost his country to a man who's torturing and killing innocent people. He wants to stop the terror. He can do it with the ransom money."

Marge smiled, her red hair gleaming in the light overhead. "He doesn't sound like your average kidnapper."

Gracie smiled tiredly. "He's not." She sipped the coffee Mr. Reeves had brought her. She hadn't slept.

Marge finished counting and had Mr. Reeves himself confirm her count. The papers were signed, the penalty for early withdrawal waived under the circumstances.

"You don't have to do that," Gracie said quickly, because she knew the bank president meant to pay it out of his own pocket.

"Jason is our best customer," he said firmly. "The kidnapper may be honorable, but he'll expect the full amount."

She got up and hugged the old man. "You're just the best person I know."

He hugged her back and laughed. "We're cousins, you know," he reminded her. "Family takes care of family."

"Then could you give Cousin Marge a raise?" Marge asked with a grin.

He made a face at her and they both laughed.

Gracie took the briefcase. It was heavy. "I'll let you know what happens," she told Mr. Reeves.

He nodded. "We'll say a prayer for you both."

"Thanks. I really mean that."

She walked out of the bank, nervous to be carrying so much cash, and almost walked right over Kilraven. He was wearing street clothing, not the police uniform she was used to seeing him in. She knew all too well that his brother, Jon, was an FBI agent in San Antonio. Both had been involved with her own ransom.

She stopped dead with a comical expression on her face.

"Don't bother making up stories. I know everything," he added with twinkling black eyes. "I'm in an unmarked car. I'm going to drive behind you most of the way to Mala Suerte, just in case anybody overheard the conversation you had with the General and decides to liberate the ransom money before you can hand it over."

Gracie was aghast. "How…?"

He held up a big hand. "Some secrets have to be kept. We're not going to interfere," he added quickly when he saw her concern. "We're just going to keep an eye on you, from a distance. I won't even follow you into Mala Suerte."

"But you have somebody in Mala Suerte already," she guessed.

His face went bland. "Why would we want to do that?"

"God help us if he's a fed trying to blend in a town of two hundred souls!"

He glowered at her. "He lives there," he returned.

She relaxed. "Okay."

"Let's go."

She climbed in behind the wheel of Jason's oldest ranch truck, with a battered fender where one of the cowboys had hit a fence trying to avoid an escaping young bull. She thought it would look less suspicious than a newer vehicle.

Kilraven was somewhere behind her, and she felt safer. The money was so big an amount that she despaired about having it taken from her before she could get to

Machado. She'd never be able to replace it in time to save Jason, especially if the Fuentes boys were going to get a cut of the kidnapping money. The General might have to cut them in to get Jason to Gracie.

She'd had great concerns about going such a distance alone with a king's ransom in her truck. She didn't know how Kilraven knew what was happening, but she was glad to have him nearby. If only the General didn't spot him and blow the deal!

Her hands were sweaty where they gripped the steering wheel. Her mouth felt as if she'd been chewing cotton. Jason might be angry with her, but it didn't matter. She loved him more than her own life. She'd have done anything to get him back, sacrificed anything. Her mind went racing back over the past months, to that first anguished kiss in the rain, to his engagement to Kittie, to her own kidnapping and the horror in Jason's eyes as he'd rushed to her side and gathered her up so close that she could feel his heart beating right into hers. The endless weeks in between Kittie's appearance and the long, exquisite night with Jason at the ranch, when she'd realized that her mother's words were false—that sex wasn't a nightmare of pain and injury, but a beautiful sharing of souls and bodies that approximated paradise. The joy of that first intimacy would remain with her forever.

As she drove, she recalled something else, something that made her feel warm and bursting with happiness; they'd never used any sort of protection. She could be pregnant even now with Jason's child. Her heart soared. What a glorious gift that would be, with Mrs. Harcourt to spoil her first grandchild and Jason's strong arms carrying a baby around. He'd be a wonderful father.

She heard a screech of brakes and looked in her

rearview mirror in time to see a pursuing vehicle suddenly cut off by another car. While she'd been day-dreaming about the future, somebody had been rushing up behind her—most probably not some motorist in a hurry, either. She saw Kilraven jump out of the second car and rush to the first one, jerking the door open and manhandling the driver up against his own vehicle.

She put the accelerator pedal down hard. It was only a mile to Mala Suerte. She knew she'd make it now, thanks to Kilraven's vigilance. It didn't do to think what might have happened if she'd tried to do this alone.

She drove through the small town, looking for the Chinese restaurant and found it, finally, on a side street just past the single flashing yellow light in the center of the sleepy little border town.

She pulled the truck into the parking lot with fear and hope equally mingled, looking for the General. But the parking lot held only two old cars. One of them was parked in the only reserved spot—probably the owner's—and another sat beside it, but nobody was in the car.

Her heart sank. Had the pursuing vehicle back on the highway sensed trouble and phoned ahead to alert the General? Or had the pursuing vehicle been a double-cross of some sort, an attempt to take the money without giving Jason back? What if Jason was dead?

Tears stung her eyes as she put the truck into Park and cut off the engine. If Jason was dead, she had nothing left. Her new job, her independence, nothing would make up for his loss. The world would end for her.

But while she was agonizing over a future without Jason, a beat-up old truck pulled into the parking lot and drove up beside her. She turned her head and looked straight into Jason's black eyes in the passenger seat.

"Jason!" she exclaimed, fumbling her way out of the truck. "Oh, Jason!" She jerked at his door, felt it open and she jumped up onto the running board. Throwing her arms around him, she kissed his mouth, his cheek, his eyes, everywhere she could reach, mumbling endearments while tears soaked her flushed face.

She realized at some point that his hands were bound and that he was kissing her back.

"Uh, you two know each other, eh?" came an amused drawl from the driver's seat.

She lifted her head and blank eyes met the General's. "General Machado!" she exclaimed breathlessly. "Sorry. I was just so happy to see him alive and well…" Her eyes went over Jason like hands, seeing a black eye and bruises on his face, and when she looked down past his dirty, torn shirt she saw that his knuckles were raw. "Alive, at least," she revised.

"I had a slight altercation with some of Fuentes's men," Jason said, managing a grin.

"To their discredit," the General mused. His dark eyes narrowed as he looked at Gracie with helpless delight. "Fuentes, the rat, sent one of his men to appropriate the money before you could get to me. I couldn't warn you."

"He's in a ditch a mile out of town wearing handcuffs," Gracie murmured jovially.

"Kilraven?" Jason asked with a short laugh.

She grinned. "Kilraven. He promised not to interfere, but I guess he anticipated trouble. Not from you," she added to the General.

He chuckled. "Not from me. I want very badly to get my country back. I am sorry to have to do it this way," he said solemnly. "But in all honesty, it was not my idea, this kidnapping. It was Fuentes's. I only took advantage of it by stepping in before he could act."

"I hope you blow his head off," Gracie said shortly.

"Bloodthirsty girl," the General teased.

"Fuentes deserves everything he gets! Maybe his henchman will spill his guts."

"If Kilraven interrogated me, I'd spill mine," Jason offered.

Gracie laughed. "So would I." She moved reluctantly away from Jason, dived back into the ranch pickup and pulled the briefcase out, glancing around to make sure the parking lot was secure. She pushed the briefcase into the General's hands. "Mr. Reeves, the president of the bank, counted it himself, while I watched. I can assure you that the bills are unmarked and there's no booby trap in there."

The General looked at the neat rows of bills. "Booby trap?" he asked, frowning.

"Banks sometimes put explosive containers of ink in stacks of money to thwart robbers."

"Ah. I see." He lifted one of the stacks of bills and looked at it long and hard. "Amigo," he told Jason, "I will erect a statue of you when I regain my office. And we will name a street for your lovely wife."

He pulled out a knife and cut the rawhide bonds on Jason's wrists. "I am sorry for your condition, but you know it was not my doing or my wish that you were harmed."

"I do know," Jason assured him. "I hope you succeed."

"So do certain members of your government," he chuckled. "We will see. Gracie," he added, smiling at her, "it took great courage to do what you did, coming here alone. I will not forget your part in my success when I achieve it. And I promise you on my soul that I will repay every penny of this money when I am back in power."

She flushed; she hadn't expected that. "I didn't ask you to do that," she reminded him.

"It is a point of honor." He looked at Jason. "Go home. You could use a bath, *señor,* and I am certain Gracie will enjoy patching up those cuts," he added with a wicked grin.

"So will I," Jason said, smiling. *"Buena suerte."*

"And good luck to you both, as well. *Vayan con Dios."*

"Y tu," Gracie replied, using also the familiar tense, because the man felt like family now.

He winked at her.

Jason got out of his truck, went around and slid in beside Gracie with a heavy sigh.

"You're going to let me drive?" Gracie asked, shocked. "You never let me drive."

"Honey, you rescued me all by yourself," he reminded her with soft, loving eyes. "You made a plan, looted your inheritance, drove up here mostly by yourself and got me out of Mexico without firing a single shot. Hell, they ought to employ you at the FBI. You're a wonder!"

"And I could absolutely put in a word for her with my brother," came a deep murmur from right in the cab of the truck.

"Kilraven?" Gracie exclaimed. She looked around. "Where are you?"

"Not in the truck," Kilraven replied. "I'm in your purse. So to speak."

"You bugged me!" she exclaimed.

"Had to. We had word that Fuentes had been foiled in his kidnapping attempt by your friend the General, and he was going to send men after you to intercept the ransom. We had to keep tabs on you. Safest way to do that was bug your purse. Paid off, too. I got both Fuentes's men in custody and they're spilling their little guts in exchange for immunity." He chuckled. "Merry Christmas."

Gracie and Jason exchanged amused looks. "Merry Christmas to you, too. And thanks!" she said.

He chuckled again. "No problem. I'm cutting off the receiver, by the way. Just in case you two want to park along the way and get reacquainted. I wouldn't advise it, though. Fuentes may try again."

"We'll watch for him."

"You won't need to," came the reply. "You won't see us, but we're watching you just the same. If anybody tries to stop you, they'll regret it. So long."

The line went dead and there was a minute's static, and then silence.

Gracie looked at Jason hungrily. "I was scared to death. So was your mother."

"I'm okay, thanks to you," he said, smiling ruefully. "I'm sorry I was such an idiot," he added gruffly. "It was a shock, finding out that my mother was my housekeeper. You gave your word to her and kept it. I shouldn't have expected you to break it, even for me. That loyalty is one of your best traits."

"Thanks," she said emotionally. "Shouldn't we go by the hospital and let them check you out?"

"I'm just bruised and dirty," he replied, smiling. "I want a bath and a big bed. And you in the middle of it," he added in a deep, soft tone that made her toes curl in her shoes.

"Me, too," she replied. She smiled and pushed down

on the accelerator. "I'll, uh, wash your back for you," she mused, blushing.

He threw his head back and laughed with pure joy.

16

MRS. HARCOURT WAS CRYING when they got to the house. Gracie had phoned her at once and told her that Jason had been ransomed and was okay. She'd called everybody else, including Glory and Rodrigo, who were shocked and relieved at the same time because they'd had no idea what was happening. Glory had thought about rushing over to the ranch, but she giggled when Mrs. Harcourt said tactfully that Gracie and Jason just might want a few minutes alone after the horror of the night. Glory said she'd come over for supper. Mrs. Harcourt said that would be good, because she had an announcement to make. She hung up, leaving Glory still in the dark.

The minute they walked into the house, Mrs. Harcourt threw herself into Jason's arms and hugged him tight. "We were scared to death!" she sobbed.

He hugged her close, smiling over her gray hair at Gracie. "All of us were. But I'm fine. Just a few skinned knuckles, and a bruise or two, that's all."

She pulled back. "Skinned knuckles."

He displayed them. "Some of Fuentes's men got a little too disrespectful and I gave them an attitude adjustment," he said drily.

She laughed and clutched him again.

"I need a bath," he said ruefully.

"Yes, you do," Mrs. Harcourt said. "I have to go into town and get milk and eggs and potatoes and beef steak or there'll be no lunch," she added, pulling off her apron. "I expect you're both starving. I know Miss Gracie... Gracie," she corrected when the younger woman glared at her, "must be hungry, she didn't have a bite to eat before she left for the bank."

"Remind me to put some more money in Reeves's bank," Jason told Gracie.

"I certainly will."

"I won't be too long," Mrs. Harcourt called as she went out the door with her car keys.

Jason looked down at Gracie and smiled. "In that case, hadn't we better hurry?" he asked in a low, suggestive tone.

IT WAS THE STORMIEST coming together of their relationship. He tried to make it to the bathroom to shower first, but Gracie wouldn't stop kissing him. They ended up on the patchwork coverlet, ripping off clothes in between frantic, hungry kisses.

He pushed her down and possessed her fiercely, his eyes black as diamonds as he lifted himself above her in an arch, watching her face as he joined himself intimately to her.

"Wrap your legs around mine," he whispered roughly.

She did, moaning when the change of positions brought a stab of intense pleasure.

"Yes, just like that," he said, and his hips lifted and pushed.

She gasped.

"If you could see your eyes," he breathed, flushing as the whip of pleasure made him shudder.

"If you could…see…yours," she replied, moaning again as he found the very place that started building a sweet, almost painful tension. "Yes, like that, like…that, like…that, Jason!"

Her nails dug into his lean hips as he shifted and began to drive into her with passionate urgency. He rested on his elbows, kissing her rapt face as he moved deeper and deeper into her arched, aching body.

"I'll die," she managed in a high-pitched wail as the pleasure soared toward some high, anguished goal.

"We'll both die," he whispered raggedly as he increased the rhythm.

It was so fast. So fast. One minute she was reaching, reaching, almost touching the center of ecstasy itself. The next she was convulsing with something so hot with throbbing pleasure that it was almost pain. An inhuman cry tore out of her throat as she went up like a Chinese rocket and exploded into a million flaming pieces of pure joy.

She felt him stiffen and heard him cry out even as she was shivering in the aftermath, curling up with every movement of his powerful body on hers. Echoes of satisfaction pulsated through her. She moaned yet again as his own harsh fulfillment triggered yet another wave of ecstasy in herself. She clung to him, drowning in pleasure. It was so intense that she thought she might pass out.

Feverish minutes later, she looked up into his relaxed, tender features, struggling to get her breath.

"I thought I might never see you again," she whispered.

"Yes. So did I." He bent and kissed her eyelids shut,

his body still intimately joined to hers. He moved lazily, intensifying the little shocks of pleasure. "I'm sorry I was so cold to you."

"You just made up for every single complaint I ever had," she assured him. Her soft eyes searched his. "You know, we've never really talked about taking precautions."

He grinned. "We can talk about it in a few months."

She smiled back. "We can forget about it altogether as far as I'm concerned."

He traced her eyebrows with a long forefinger. "What about your job?"

"I can be pregnant and still work," she said easily.

He smiled. "Okay."

She reached up and kissed him softly. "We should probably have a nice shower. I imagine your mother will be back with food soon."

"My mother." He drew in a long breath. "I felt so guilty. And so stupid for not even guessing. I knew the woman I called my real mother wasn't anybody's idea of the ideal parent. She never seemed to have a bond with me, and I never understood why I didn't feel anything much when she died." He winced. "My poor mother. My father was such a damned snob he wouldn't even marry her when his wife died. He thought she was beneath him socially."

"You'll make up for all that," she assured him. "And we'll give her grandchildren to spoil."

He pursed his lips and looked down their bodies to where they were joined. "Pretty soon, if we keep doing this."

"I have no plans to stop," she said softly, her eyes searching his. "My poor mother. In her whole life, she never knew what love could be. I believed her, you know. It ruined my life. Well, up until a few months ago," she conceded with a shy smile.

"I wish you'd told me everything a lot sooner," he said. "But better late than never."

"I love you so much," she whispered huskily. "More than my own life."

He drew in a long breath and touched her face tenderly. "Those words come hard to me," he confessed. "I never heard them from my father or from the woman I thought was my mother. They were two of the coldest people on earth. My father had women, but he used them. He had no respect for them."

"My mother at least did love me," she said. "And she said so, all the time. I'll say it to our children all the time, too," she added doggedly. "They'll always know they're loved."

"As I love you," he said in a deep, heavy tone, bringing her shocked eyes up to his. "With all that I am. I loved you when you were in your teens and went away to make sure I never acted on it. You were so young. Later, when I knew how deeply I loved you, I still held back, hoping you'd see me with different eyes. The night it rained and your car went into the ditch, I'd waited so long that I became desperate. I lost control and almost ruined everything," he groaned. "You looked so shocked…"

She put her fingers against his lips. "Shocked, but overwhelmed with joy," she whispered. "It was sex I was afraid of, not you, and I couldn't find the nerve to tell you. I've loved you for so long," she said, choking. "Most of my life! I loved you, but I was afraid I'd never be able to give you a woman's love, a physical love. I was going to tell you everything that next morning. But you were gone." Her eyes shadowed. "And then there was Kittie."

He buried his face in her throat. "My fault. All my fault. Wounded pride made me into a man I never was. I'm so sorry, honey. Sorry for everything."

"Not for what we just did, I hope," she whispered into his ear, moving restlessly under him until she felt his body clench and then start to swell. "Because I want to do it again." She lifted her hips and curled them into his, laughing breathlessly when he gasped, and then groaned, and then started to move helplessly on her body. "Yes, that's it," she whimpered, holding on tight. "Love me. Love me. Love me!"

"I...do," he managed to say. And then he was too busy to get another word out.

THEY WALKED HAND IN HAND into the dining room where an amused Mrs. Harcourt was putting food that she'd already reheated once. She didn't say a word. They were so much in love, so much a part of each other already that her heart lifted with joy.

She'd put a Christmas centerpiece on the table and she was using the holiday plates, too. "It's almost Christmas," she reminded them.

Jason laughed. "Almost time for presents!" he said, looking at Gracie teasingly. "I got you something lovely."

"I got you something, too," she replied, her eyes teasing.

"Tell me what it is," he said. "Come on. Tell me."

"And ruin the surprise?" she laughed. "Not likely!"

He bent and kissed the tip of her nose. "Okay. I like surprises." He glanced at his mother and smiled warmly. "Good thing, considering how many I'm getting lately!"

They all laughed.

GLORY AND RODRIGO CAME over for supper, much later, and listened to Gracie explain how she'd ransomed Jason from the General. They were astonished that it had all taken place without their knowledge.

"Listen," Glory said, "you two have got to stop letting yourselves be snatched by kidnappers," she said firmly. "Jason, you need a bodyguard. I'm not kidding," she added when he laughed. "These are dangerous times. John is a great driver, but he can't handle young toughs. I want you to think about it."

"I've got Grange," Jason reminded her. "He's done a lot of things besides being an officer in the military."

"Then let him go places with you," Glory insisted. "I mean it. You and Gracie take too many chances."

Jason glanced at his wife and smiled complacently. "I guess it's safe enough to let him tag along, since we're married."

"I'm very fond of him, jealous heart," she teased, leaning close to kiss him. "But it was never more than fondness. Okay?"

He grinned. "Okay."

Mrs. Harcourt stood behind Jason at the table and quietly told them the truth about who Jason's real mother was. There was a sudden silence. But then, Glory got up and hugged her while she cried. It was, Glory whispered in her ear, one of the nicest surprises she'd ever had, because she knew how much Mrs. Harcourt loved Jason. That feeling was very obviously mutual from Jason's dark-eyed smile. She couldn't imagine that Jason would ever be ashamed of such a good, kind, loving woman. She said so. And everyone else at the table agreed with her.

THE NEXT DAY, THE STORY of Jason's parentage hit the tabloids. Reporters gathered to ask questions, and Jason produced his radiant mother and hugged her for the benefit of the photographers. It was really a Cinderella story, someone remarked, but Jason reminded them that his mother was a businesswoman in her own right, and that her crafting abilities were formidable. He displayed one of her afghans, which was also photographed. For once, the light of the media had a sweet taste. The furor died down with the advent of a murder right there in Jacobsville, which was whispered to have ties to another murder seven years ago in San Antonio, which involved Kilraven and might have ties to still another in Oklahoma.

Days later, another tabloid carried a story about a model who had attempted to blackmail a millionaire with secrets about his past. No names were mentioned, but the story assured readers that the millionaire was already pursuing criminal charges against the woman, which would be announced soon.

One of Jason's friends in San Antonio called him after he read the story. He asked Jason if he knew that his ex-fiancée Kittie Sartain had given up her contracts in the United States and was moving to London to pursue her career. Her friends were mystified as to her reasons, but Jason's friend said he had a sneaking hunch that he could answer that question. Jason replied drily that he did, too.

CHRISTMAS WEEK WAS FULL of joy at the ranch house. The college was closed until January, when spring semester would start, and public schools were also on holiday, so Gracie had time to rack up the decorations all over the ranch. The housekeeper in San Antonio was doing the same there because Gracie and Jason always threw a bonzer New Year's Eve party there. This year would be no different.

But it was at the ranch that they spent the holidays. They opened presents on Christmas Eve, a family tradition for Mrs. Harcourt, who was beaming and full of joy as she sat on the sofa beside Glory and Rodrigo while Gracie, Jason, John and Dilly handed out packages.

Gracie gave her present to Jason with her own hands. He did likewise.

"I bought this with my own money that I earned," she said gently. "So it's not extravagant. But it's something I think you'll like."

He bent and kissed her. "I'd like a napkin if you gave it to me, honey," he said softly. "It really is the thought, you know, not the expense."

She kissed him back. "Open it."

He did. Inside was a knife, an expensive one with a bone handle and with the Texas Ranger logo on it. Jason had always been fascinated with the law enforcement organization, and he always carried a pocketknife. He turned it over in his hands, smiling. "I'll use this all the time. Thanks." He kissed her. "Now, open yours."

She did. It was a gold link necklace with a pale green stone pendant hanging from it. It was elegant and exquisite.

She looked up at Jason, frowning. "It's like peridot, but it doesn't really look…"

"Moldavite," he interrupted, smiling at her surprise. "It's moldavite, Gracie. Something from the stars, to add to your meteorite collection. But it's wearable."

"Moldavite!" She turned the stone over in her hands, holding it up to the light. It was a rare stone, meteoric in origin, and it cost a small fortune. Not that Jason couldn't afford it, but he'd found something that he knew would please her, and gone to a lot of trouble at that. She hugged him close. "Thank you! It's the first piece of moldavite I've ever owned!"

"What's moldavite?" Mrs. Harcourt asked, peering over her shoulder.

"It comes from meteors," Gracie enthused.

"I'd rather have mine," the older woman teased, holding up a beautiful soft pink housecoat with matching slippers that Jason had bought her. "It feels like a cloud."

Jason bent and kissed her cheek. "It looks motherly," he teased back.

Mrs. Harcourt hugged him. "I hope you like yours. It doesn't look motherly, but a mother who loves you made it," she teased.

"I love it," he chuckled. She'd knitted him a cover for his bed in the earth colors he liked. She'd done Gracie one, too, and been enthusiastically hugged for it. They both knew how much labor and love Mrs. Harcourt put into her knitting. Glory and Rodrigo also had afghans, and so did old John, who almost cried when Jason and Gracie gave him a color television for his room. Dilly got one, too, and hugged everybody.

"This has been a wonderful Christmas," Glory said with a sigh when she and Gracie were briefly alone. "Can you believe how far we've both come from our early lives?"

"I'd never have thought we'd end up like this," Gracie agreed. Her eyes went to Jason. They were radiant. "Especially me."

"I saw the way he looked at you years ago," her stepsister said gently. "I wanted to tell you, but I wasn't sure I should. Now I'm glad I waited."

"Me, too." She embraced Glory. "We have a family. A very big and wonderful one."

"Yes." Glory hugged her back and sighed. "I wish Rodrigo and I could have a baby. I've never really gotten over losing the first one."

Gracie looked her in the eye. "Miracles happen all the

time, Glory. Look at how I got Jason back, how he got me back from the kidnappers. What are the odds?"

"Everyday miracles," Glory mused.

"Yes. Everyday miracles. Including," she whispered, "the one I'm almost positive I'm carrying." Her hand went to her flat belly.

Glory caught her breath. Jason, glancing their way, caught his, too, when he saw the look on Gracie's face and where her hand was resting. He dropped the package he'd started to open and went to her, pulling her into his arms.

"Tell me," he said with a hungry look in his eyes.

"I'm not sure," she said softly. "It's too early to be positive. But I think…"

He wrapped her up tight and rocked her, in the sudden silence of the room.

"Merry Christmas."

"Merry Christmas to you, my sweetheart," he whispered into her ear.

"Is this a personal secret, or do the rest of us get to hear it, too?" Grange asked from behind them with a grin.

They looked up. Gracie's eyes were wet with tears. Jason was beaming.

"We might be pregnant," Gracie confessed shyly.

There was pandemonium in the living room. Mrs. Harcourt wept and hugged them, and so did old John, to the surprise of everyone present. For a long time, there was palpable joy and expectation around the huge, glittering Christmas tree.

MUCH, MUCH LATER, when the guests had gone home and Mrs. Harcourt had lugged her gifts down to her room, Jason sat in his big armchair in front of the glowing gas logs with Gracie curled up in his arms next to the Christmas tree.

He handed her a small box. "I saved this one for last," he said, smiling indulgently as she pulled off the wrapping, opened the box and stared at its contents until tears began rolling down her cheeks. It was the items she'd pawned, her mother's jewelry. She looked up at him through a mist.

"Thank you," she said huskily.

He kissed her tenderly. "Don't be mad. You can still be independent. But these are heirlooms that we'll hand down to our children, and they to their children. They belong in the family. I wanted to make sure they didn't accidentally wind up in someone else's hands."

She sighed and nestled closer. "I was worried about that, too. I'm not mad. It was a sweet thing to do."

He grinned. "I'm very sweet," he informed her. "I have nice qualities. My mother said so."

"Very nice qualities."

"Can you die of happiness?" he murmured, kissing her hair.

"I guess we'll find out together."

His arms contracted. "When will we know for sure about the baby?"

She brushed her lips against his throat, drowsy from the long day and the delight she was feeling. "In a few weeks, I think. The home pregnancy test I used was encouraging. My monthly is days late and I'm very regular."

He sighed. "We'll make beautiful babies," he murmured. "I hope some of them are blond."

"I hope some of them have black eyes, like you and your mother."

He chuckled. "We'll see what we get. I just want whatever it is to be healthy."

"Me, too."

She nuzzled her face into his throat and closed her eyes. "Jason?"

"Hmm?"

"Merry Christmas. I hope you like your present."

He lifted his head and looked down at her soft face. He smiled tenderly. "Merry Christmas, honey. I do like it. But the one I like best is the gift of love."

She hugged him. "The gift we give each other," she agreed. She peered up at him wickedly. "I've just thought of something."

"What?"

"You're the most expensive Christmas present I ever got!"

He didn't get it for a minute. Then he realized that she meant the ransom she'd paid for him, and he burst out laughing. "Was I worth it?" he teased.

She reached up and kissed him softly. "Worth every penny. Every tear. Every lonely minute."

"Life is sweet, my precious," he whispered, searching her loving eyes.

She nuzzled his face with hers. "Yes. Sweeter than honey."

He cuddled her back into his arms and sighed, closing his eyes as the flames in the gas logs danced like sugarplums. Gracie watched them across his broad chest, feeling the happiness like a flame inside her heart. Somewhere she heard Christmas carols being sung and a dog barking in the distance. Closer, she heard the strong, regular beat of Jason's heart under her ear. Christmas wasn't only in her heart. It was in her arms.

Will four courageous women follow their hearts, wherever they may lead?

Find out in these heartwarming classics from *New York Times* and *USA TODAY* bestselling author

DIANA PALMER

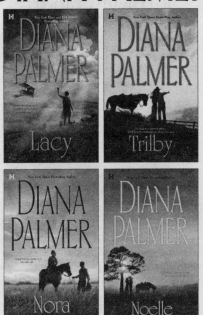

Available now wherever books are sold!

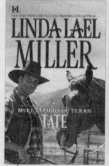 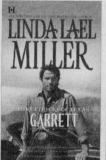 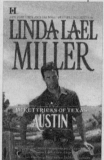

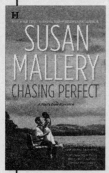
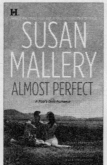

REQUEST YOUR FREE BOOKS!

2 FREE NOVELS
FROM THE ROMANCE COLLECTION
PLUS 2 FREE GIFTS!

YES! Please send me 2 FREE novels from the Romance Collection and my 2 FREE gifts (gifts are worth about $10). After receiving them, if I don't wish to receive any more books, I can return the shipping statement marked "cancel." If I don't cancel, I will receive 4 brand-new novels every month and be billed just $5.74 per book in the U.S. or $6.24 per book in Canada. That's a saving of at least 28% off the cover price. It's quite a bargain! Shipping and handling is just 50¢ per book.* I understand that accepting the 2 free books and gifts places me under no obligation to buy anything. I can always return a shipment and cancel at any time. Even if I never buy another book, the two free books and gifts are mine to keep forever.

194/394 MDN E7NZ

Name   (PLEASE PRINT)

Address   Apt. #

City   State/Prov.   Zip/Postal Code

Signature (if under 18, a parent or guardian must sign)

Mail to **The Reader Service:**
IN U.S.A.: P.O. Box 1867, Buffalo, NY 14240-1867
IN CANADA: P.O. Box 609, Fort Erie, Ontario L2A 5X3

Not valid for current subscribers to the Romance Collection
or the Romance/Suspense Collection.

Want to try two free books from another line?
Call 1-800-873-8635 or visit www.morefreebooks.com.

* Terms and prices subject to change without notice. Prices do not include applicable taxes. N.Y. residents add applicable sales tax. Canadian residents will be charged applicable provincial taxes and GST. Offer not valid in Quebec. This offer is limited to one order per household. All orders subject to approval. Credit or debit balances in a customer's account(s) may be offset by any other outstanding balance owed by or to the customer. Please allow 4 to 6 weeks for delivery. Offer available while quantities last.

Your Privacy: Harlequin Books is committed to protecting your privacy. Our Privacy Policy is available online at www.eHarlequin.com or upon request from the Reader Service. From time to time we make our lists of customers available to reputable third parties who may have a product or service of interest to you. If you would prefer we not share your name and address, please check here. ☐

Help us get it right—We strive for accurate, respectful and relevant communications. To clarify or modify your communication preferences, visit us at www.ReaderService.com/consumerschoice.

MROM10R

DIANA PALMER

77369	FEARLESS	___ $7.99 U.S.	___ $8.99 CAN.
77283	LAWMAN	___ $7.99 U.S.	___ $7.99 CAN.
77234	OUTSIDER	___ $7.99 U.S.	___ $9.50 CAN.
77536	BEFORE SUNRISE	___ $7.99 U.S.	___ $9.99 CAN.
77050	RENEGADE	___ $7.50 U.S.	___ $8.99 CAN.

(limited quantities available)

TOTAL AMOUNT	$ _____
POSTAGE & HANDLING	$ _____
($1.00 FOR 1 BOOK, 50¢ for each additional)	
APPLICABLE TAXES*	$ _____
TOTAL PAYABLE	$ _____

(check or money order—please do not send cash)

To order, complete this form and send it, along with a check or money order for the total above, payable to HQN Books, to: **In the U.S.:** 3010 Walden Avenue, P.O. Box 9077, Buffalo, NY 14269-9077; **In Canada:** P.O. Box 636, Fort Erie, Ontario, L2A 5X3.

Name: _____

Address: _____ City: _____

State/Prov.: _____ Zip/Postal Code: _____

Account Number (if applicable): _____

075 CSAS

*New York residents remit applicable sales taxes.
*Canadian residents remit applicable GST and provincial taxes.

HQN™

We *are* romance™

www.HQNBooks.com

PHDP0510BL